Felonious Jazz

a novel

BRYAN GILMER

Copyright © 2009 by Bryan Gilmer

All rights reserved.
Independently published in the United States as a Laurel Bluff Book.
bryangilmer.com

Gilmer, Bryan, 1972–
Felonious Jazz, a novel / Bryan Gilmer – 1st ed.

Printed in the United States of America

10 9 8 7 6 5 4 3 2 1

First Edition

For Kelly

One

Leonard Noblac stood in someone else's kitchen and shoved the cork back into the neck of the '82 Haut-Brión. He held the stemmed Riedel glass by its base and checked the wine's color against a white kitchen towel lit by the afternoon sun. Deep garnet.

So, all the hype was justified. The smell of leather filled the glass. The taste was earthy and beautiful; practically made you hallucinate you were in the vineyard – just like clove cigarettes always made him think of his big night at the Village Vanguard, of standing in the point of that triangular basement, the Carnegie Hall of jazz. Yeah, man, 1982 had been a good year. Maybe his last one.

These Reuss cats had stashed a full case of this stuff in a temperature-controlled cellar under the granite kitchen island. The wine ran $600 a bottle if you could find it, and you had no idea if it had been stored worth a damn. He was smart enough to taste the shit before stealing it.

The Haut-Brión was the only artistic thing in the whole house besides the 9-foot Steinway concert grand. Maybe they picked up the wine on their honeymoon, or maybe it was a present from Mommy and Daddy. Either way, it was just one more status symbol for the Reusses to show off when other zeroes came for dinner. Had to give them credit for holding the '82 until it was at its peak. But now it was time for an artist to enjoy it. Creativity fuel.

Leonard slurped the last sip with the same moan that slipped out when he saw a fine looking lady. He stuffed the glass into the empty cell of the cardboard wine case and slammed the partial bottle after it, smashing the crystal like a drummer hitting the cymbal to end a number at the set break.

The loopy golden retriever stumbled up to him, its toenails clicking against the maple floorboards. He'd jammed a Valium inside a piece of pork sausage, and – what was its name? He didn't remember what Catalina Reuss had called her – Booboo or whatever – ahh, he didn't want to know her name – had gobbled it right up. Then the sweet old dog had followed him around wagging her tail and sniffing the hand that had held the sausage while he'd hauled every TV out of the place.

Now Leonard knelt next to the animal. She was a pretty thing, with a little gray dusting her orange fur. He gently draped his arm across her back like they were on a date to the movies. The dog pressed the side of her head against his thigh, a gesture of affection that brought a tightness to his throat. But Leonard kept moving. He found the bulge of a vein on the dog's neck and shoved the needle in. The dog felt the prick and aimed questioning eyes at him.

He pushed the plunger hard to squeeze out all the liquid. Within two seconds, the heartbeat stilled. The dog twitched against him, her eyes still open, as her muscles contracted involuntarily. Then she relaxed, and her bladder and bowels spilled onto the floor.

Leonard's heart was racing, and the air in the room suddenly felt freezing. He gently laid down the dog's body and stood. He bent again and pulled out the needle. He fought to calm himself and dropped the syringe into the wine case among the necks of the bottles. Animals – all living things – got sick and eventually died. He felt a lightning strike of anger at having to give himself this talk. He pushed the feeling away. Somebody had to do the right thing, even when it was hard.

Leonard went three paces, flailing his head side to side with the anguish of it, flapping his cheeks violently against his teeth. He sniffed in a great breath as the dizziness wore off.

He reached into his pants pocket for the little plastic bottle of hand sanitizer.

Leonard flipped the lid, and the citrus scent calmed him immediately. He tipped back his head and squeezed the tangy goo into his mouth. The first drops dissolved directly into his tongue and cheeks.

The grapefruit tang spread through his sinuses as he pressed his lips together. The gel slid down his throat with a glorious burn. It took just two more mouthfuls to finish the four-ounce bottle. As he screwed off the top to fish out the last bits with his tongue, he welcomed the soft, mind-cleansing surge of ethyl alcohol.

Leonard breathed out slowly. His breath smelled pure. His mouth was clean, free of 99.9 percent of bacteria. He took another breath and got back to business.

The vino fit easily with the TVs and other crapola in the back of the minivan he'd left in the garage. He'd gotten the van in there using his black-market garage door opener. All you had to do was hit the button, and the box would transmit all the known garage-door opener radio signals, one after the other. There were only a few dozen.

Now one quick press of the button, then another after driving through the opening, and the van dipped unnoticed into the broad, curving street as the door descended again behind it.

As Leonard thought again about his album, he cheered. He plucked at the seatbelt shoulder strap with the fingers of his right hand as if it were the strings of his bass. His head felt airy, and in his mind, he heard the riff he'd written for this track.

Man, he could feel his great mood coming back now. He was grooving again. This new composition was putting the world right, was unquestionably his big break. His music was finally going to make him famous.

He was really drunk from the sanitizer now.

He put on a pair of women's sunglasses he found above the

visor and smiled at his incognito reflection in the mirror. Just another square in Squaresville, baby.

Two

Just after 4 p.m., J. Davis Swaine III parked his Audi TT Roadster along the curb in a subdivision of McMansions called Mill Run Estates.

This house's multi-gabled roofline resembled a range in the Rockies. A two-story stacked-stone portico dwarfed a man and woman in business clothes standing by Mexican-tile house numbers staked into the ground by the front steps. The woman, who had brittle-looking blonde hair, waved her mobile phone. Jeff Swaine pushed the car door open with his left ankle.

Mickey Reuss wrapped the new Mrs. Reuss against his chest with the arms of a college football player gone to seed. "That *bitch*," the woman spat into his extra-large golf shirt. "Beebee? She kills sweet, old Beebee? This is not her house any more. This is *our house*. Fuck all of this. Just get me a gun and let me go kill her right now. Give me a pistol, Mickey. Right now. Let *go*."

Mickey Reuss was a real estate developer on the board of the Raleigh Chamber and knew key state representatives. And he was a top client of the Raleigh trial firm, Cross Baker Allison, where Jeff was a staff investigator.

Mickey was an asshole. Jeff remembered photographing

Mickey's previous wife disappearing into a Hilton room on her lunch hour a year before, her skirt already unzipped, a younger man's hand under the edge of the fabric. That picture had gotten Mickey the division of property he wanted.

Jeff could smell the asphalt, damp from an earlier spring shower, as he pulled his camera bag out of the trunk.

According to Sarah Rosen, CB Allison's managing partner, Mickey's new wife had come home half an hour ago and found her golden retriever, Beatrice, dead on the kitchen floor and the house vandalized. Instead of calling the cops, she'd called her husband. And Mickey, instead of calling the cops, had called CBA. So Sarah had sent Jeff and would happily bill $150 an hour for his time.

Jeff was a tall, blond, man coming up fast on 30. People thought he looked well bred, and he *was* well educated. Yet he had grown up near Charlotte in a working-class family with parents who retained the earmarks of their impoverished South Carolina upbringing. Some part of him felt as if there were holes in the socks underneath his cherrywood Italian loafers.

He shut the driver's door of his expensive car parked in this neighborhood. People assumed he belonged here. And maybe he did, now. He started up the cobblestone walk.

The front door stood half open. Jeff had the impulse to extend his hand to Mickey Reuss, but Mickey was busy preventing a homicide. So instead Jeff made eye contact, jerked his head toward the house.

"You ain't gonna believe it," Reuss said in lieu of a greeting. "Go on in."

Jeff said to the back of the woman's head, "Don't worry, ma'am. Davis Swaine from CB Allison. We're going to take care of this."

Jeff was good at talking to people. He could slather on or completely drop the Southern accent at will. That made him a monster investigative interviewer, but he had a hell of a time choosing between lacrosse and NASCAR while flipping channels.

The woman's venom seemed to be receding now, so Mickey let her go, and she turned around to pout at Jeff. "I want you to nail that saggy sow. Put her in a jail where she never gets anything but oatmeal. Then sue her and get everything. She got all of it from us, anyway."

Now the new wife dabbed her eyes against the shoulder of her jade green blazer. She certainly wasn't saggy, but why women thought Botox and surgery made them more attractive, Jeff couldn't figure. Nor why the new wife, who had been Mickey's mistress for two years before the divorce, felt she had any moral standing. The divorce had gone Mickey's way only because he had the top trial firm in the state handling his end of it. Jeff hoped gathering ammo for class-action suits against pharmaceutical companies that shoved drugs with deadly side-effects through FDA review made up for the sleaze work he did on high-stakes divorces.

"We do have to call the Sheriff's Office," Jeff told Mickey, to get that straight from the start. "Let me do it. I'll make sure they send the right people. But let me make a quick pass first and get everything we're going to need. How'd she get in?"

"Hell if I know," Mickey said. "Nothing's busted. I got the door locks all re-keyed after she left, like y'all said, but maybe there's something she still has a key to."

"Garage door opener?"

"Shit."

Jeff nodded. "Where's the dog?"

"Kitchen."

Jeff reached into the camera bag and hefted his Nikon D2. He clicked off black plastic caps and twisted the wide-angle lens into the socket. He left his loafers on the mat, urging open the heavy front door with his elbow.

A solvent smell irritated Jeff's nose as soon he stepped in: spray paint. "White, white, white," was painted in black above a childlike drawing of a picket fence just inside the front door. Mickey's ex-wife was Hispanic, Jeff remembered.

He grabbed a photo of the scribbles and followed a marble-tiled hallway straight back to the kitchen.

The gorgeous golden retriever looked like it had sprawled out for a nap, except for the feces and urine around it. The room reeked.

Jeff blinked and turned away. He remembered his aunt Rebecca's harmless and affectionate golden. His throat tightened as he triggered the shutter for a scene-setter.

Now he made himself kneel beside the dog's body and lean in close. No wounds or strangulation marks. It looked as if she'd been poisoned, but they would need a necropsy.

He sniffed and shook his head. Jeff took three quick close-ups with the Nikon from various angles, his fingers tingling.

He stood and shook his head again. He chose his footing carefully and stepped into the dining room. There he read, "White Bread" painted on the surface of the mahogany dining table.

What he found in the next room didn't fit at all: Another message painted in foot-high letters around the perimeter of the family room, across the walls and the pictures that hung on them: "Poor kids out of sight out of mind." The sentence ended with the word "mind" painted angrily across the sofa cushions. This wasn't something an angry ex-wife would write at all. He doubted Mickey and his new wife had come into this room or seen this.

Jeff noticed a pedestal for a giant-screen television, bare with stray cables dangling across its surface. He inhaled a quick breath through his nose and widened his eyes.

It wasn't her. He was pretty sure petite little Catalina Reuss hadn't hauled the set out of here.

Jeff measured his breaths through dilated nostrils. This burglar was a pro. He had gotten in without leaving evidence of forced entry. And a bastard: Most intruders simply moved on when they came across a house with a dog, but this one had killed her. That probably meant there was some reason it had to be this house and not another. This was all a message for Mickey Reuss and his wife.

Jeff stretched his neck to the left, then to the right, hoping it would pop, but it didn't. He noticed faint, parallel tracks in the carpet and followed them back toward the kitchen as he pulled out his mobile phone to call one of CB Allison's favorite cops, Sheriff's Lt. Randy Cooperton.

CB Allison paid Cooperton and several other local law officers twenty bucks an hour to provide off-duty "security" at the CB Allison offices one night each week. They all got their checks without showing up, so they were reliable when the firm needed them.

While the desk officer tracked Cooperton down, Jeff stooped. The tire tracks continued as faint, linear diamond patterns about two inches wide smudged into the high sheen of the maple flooring. Tire marks on the kitchen floor.

"A handtruck," Jeff said out loud. The pattern led to the door to the garage. A couple of fresh-looking dings smiled from the molding. He bent down and exhaled onto the door handle, and the condensing moisture revealed no fingerprints – only marks from being wiped with a cloth. So he wrapped the knob with his shirttail, turned it and looked into the garage. Empty.

Cooperton finally came onto the line, and Jeff outlined the situation, stepping back into the kitchen so his words wouldn't echo across the concrete garage floor.

"Shit fire, son," Cooperton said. "Get your ass out of that house. They might still be inside."

"I don't think so. Y'all get on out here."

"We're coming."

Jeff took a photo that showed the tire tracks. He decided to wait for Cooperton to look upstairs. This was unlikely to have any civil legal dimension, so he had less of an excuse to traipse through the crime scene.

He stepped back onto the front steps with the Reusses. "It's not her."

The new wife looked ready to find a pistol to use on him now. "What the hell?"

"It's too slick. This is pros. Do you know the TV's missing from the living room?"

Their faces showed they didn't.

"Have you been upstairs?"

"Me neither. We'll let the deputies check up there."

They shook their heads and started to ask him questions, but now Jeff's eye locked on a tan minivan stacked with items rolling past the house. The driver was wearing oversized sunglasses. Jeff wasn't sure why it grabbed his attention. Going a little too slow. Maybe not quite expensive enough for this neighborhood. A Chrysler. He looked down for the tag number, but now the road was curving the wrong direction and he couldn't make out the digits.

Jeff interrupted the Reusses. "Turn around. That van. Is that your neighbor?"

"Nuh-uh," Mickey Reuss said, as the van signaled a right turn out of the subdivision's fake stone gateway.

Jeff shoved his feet back into his loafers, shot five quick frames from the hip – the van was small in the center of the frame, but he could blow it up digitally – stuffed the camera into the nylon bag and sprinted to his Audi. He threw the camera bag onto the passenger seat, started the engine, yanked his seatbelt across himself and nosed the little car into the next driveway to turn around.

* * *

Leonard saw the three zeros on the porch turn and follow him with their eyes as he went back past the house. He felt a shot of panic. He watched in the rear-view as J. Davis Swaine III dashed across the street to the little sports car. He couldn't believe the Reusses had found what he'd done this quickly or that they'd gotten Swaine involved so fast.

* * *

By the time Jeff squeaked to a stop at the neighborhood gateway, the van had folded into the evening wall of cars on five-lane Rocky Falls Boulevard. He'd missed his chance to read the plate. If he'd had the long lens on the Nikon, he could have zoomed in and seen it.

Jeff used the center turn lane to pass a garbage truck, then jammed the car back into the left-hand travel lane. He spotted the shape of the van about fifteen cars ahead. He worked the Audi into a two-car-length crack in the right lane and got chastised with horn bleats but drew a couple of cars closer. One more aggressive lane change, and he got close enough to see the van's plates.

Finally, he fell in directly behind the van. He'd only recited the number to himself once when he looked up to see a red-headed elementary boy and his little sister craning their necks around in the back seat to see what all the honking was about.

Now a traffic signal changed to yellow, and the mom driving the van snatched it to a stop, trapping Jeff behind her at the light. He shaded the Audi left in its lane to see around the decoy van. A quarter mile ahead, he thought he saw another tan van turning onto the I-540 on ramp.

"Fucking damn it," Jeff told the steering wheel. Asking the Sheriff's Office to look for a beige Chrysler minivan in Rocky Falls at rush hour was like telling a Rocky Falls high school principal they were looking for a white kid with acne in a Polo shirt and jeans.

Jeff reminded himself the van he'd seen pass the Reuss' house might have nothing to do with the burglary.

But it was the guy. Jeff could feel it. Fucking damn it.

* * *

An unmarked Crown Victoria rolled up to the curb at the Reusses' just as Jeff returned. Two marked cruisers already stood in the driveway, and the uniforms were talking to the couple.

As Lt. Randy Cooperton stepped out of the car, Jeff wondered whether they made Wake County deputies pass a physical fitness qualification every year, and if so, how this guy pulled it off.

Jeff saw a goose egg in Cooperton's jaw and knew he was about to shake hands with someone who had been spitting all day.

He gripped Cooperton's hand swiftly, shoving his own forward until the webbing of their thumbs met. Jeff's father had taught him the trick to protect his fingers from being crushed in a Southern Baptist handshake. Cooperton always made Jeff glad.

"Where you been?"

"Trying to run down a suspicious vehicle, but lost it in traffic," Jeff told him.

Cooperton pulled out his notebook to write down the description, but when he heard it, he just laughed. "Without a plate, most likely have better luck working the crime scene. Come on, take me inside."

Jeff nodded, and Cooperton directed a perfect stream of

brown saliva onto the pavement.

* * *

In all, the burglar or burglars had taken Mrs. Reuss' jewelry box, two DVD players, a PlayStation game console, a 60-inch plasma-screen from the family room and an under-cabinet LCD TV from the kitchen, where they'd taken the trouble to undo the four mounting screws.

So the burglars had been in the house a while. Twelve grand in property, maybe twice that much again in property damage. Still no sign of forced entry. Jeff was still thinking garage door, and Cooperton agreed.

Cooperton sucked a wad of snot deeper into his head, a sound that echoed loudly in the garage. "If they had a truck in here with the door down, they had all the damn time in the world. Two or three men could have loaded everything up in about 15 minutes."

Somehow, it was now 11 p.m. He and Cooperton raised the garage door and walked outside.

"Press is here," Cooperton muttered and nodded toward a young woman at the end of the driveway talking to Cooperton's uniform sergeant.

She looked as if she were in her late 20s like Jeff, and she held a skinny reporter's notepad. Her oversize nose marred an otherwise pretty face. Brunette hair with obviously artificial blonde streaks fell past her shoulders. She wore a floral print sundress Jeff thought he remembered from the cover of one of Ashlyn's catalogs. It showed off the tanned undulations of her shoulders and collarbones. The sergeant was giving her the longest no-comment Jeff had ever heard.

"Caroline Kramden, queen of the dipshits at the Rocky Falls bureau of the P&L," Cooperton said. The *Triangle Progress-Leader* was the big paper in the Raleigh-Durham-Chapel Hill metro area. "She's a giant pain in my giant ass."

Jeff told the Reusses he'd meet with them the next day at the Courtyard by Marriott, where they planned to spend the night.

He fired up the gray sports car and discarded the urge to

stop at a quickie mart for a pack of Camel Lights – a bad habit from prep school. Instead, he turned up a song called "Cross the Bridge," by Nickel Creek, a band that played bluegrass instruments in an innovative style. He'd seen them in concert four times, but now they were on a "hiatus." Damn shame.

He took Rocky Falls Boulevard south toward downtown Raleigh, blinking when he again recalled the body of the gorgeous dog in such an undignified pose on the kitchen floor.

He turned onto Wake Forest Road, then crossed the I-440 inner perimeter, where the neighborhoods still looked suburban, but old enough that there were trees taller than 10 feet. He parked in his usual spot at Ashlyn's complex, climbed the concrete stairs and let himself back inside. She was leaving the next morning for a six-week continuing education thing at Johns Hopkins in Baltimore. But even tonight, he'd ended up working late again, and she'd ended up going to bed before he got home.

Jeff took off his clothes. Ashlyn slept in a tight ball at the top corner of the queen-size bed. She stirred as he got underneath the patchwork quilt – she slept under it year-round no matter how cold she had to set the air conditioning.

He tried to savor the feeling of being next to her, but his thoughts returned to the still form of Beatrice – Beebee. And he remembered a woman with whom falling asleep spooned up was always like becoming part of one body with two hearts, and that led him to the realization that he merely felt pressed against Ashlyn.

After he turned onto his back, he finally fell asleep.

Three

Jeff's dream always began with the near-comic ring of the empty Coke can tipping over on top of the dresser, bouncing three quick times and then rolling across the polished wood.

Within the dream, the sleeping Jeff wakened alone in his old bedroom in Scranton to see a shadow move, then suddenly freeze. Then he gathered the comforter from the underside in soft, warm fistfuls and leapt out of bed at the figure, trapping it in the fabric, crushing it against the dresser, smelling the intruder's stale sweat, seeing nothing, wondering with startling clarity whether any of the bones he heard and felt breaking against the sharp wooden edge beneath his weight were his own – wondering whether the intruder had a weapon, expecting to feel its blade or scorching projectile.

"I will fucking shoot you, cocksucker!" dream Jeff heard himself yell, a panicked bluff, since he was armed only with the blanket.

Then the startlingly childlike yelp and whimper, the wounded figure wriggling free of the fabric, dashing through the open bedroom door, half-falling down the stairs and throwing open the front door. He stood in confusion, tumbled toward his cellphone ...

Tonight, like always, three ringing gunshots ended the dream.

He sat up panting in bed now in this real room, sweating and gasping air and scanning the shadows, knowing no one was here but his girlfriend, snoring. And yet again Jeff's brain and blood pulsed with the remembered emotions of the dream without the anesthesia of shock that had helped him survive the day it had all been real.

Four

Just after midnight, Leonard had fenced the guns and TVs and stuff through the back door of the pawnshop he'd found in Raleigh. It was easier than he'd thought; he'd never sold off stolen property before. He'd never even stolen anything before – except one package of bass guitar strings from the instrument store in the old neighborhood, 30 years ago. But man, had he been thinking about it. Especially these past few months.

Track Two was finished. He followed Rocky Falls Boulevard north over the overpass for I-540, the new west-east arc of road 13 miles north of North Carolina's capital building, and drove past a brand-new shopping center with a Bed, Bath & Beyond among a standard assortment of big-box chains. Signboards on neighboring vacant tracts stood in silhouette. Leonard couldn't read them, but they all said something similar: "Will Divide," "Build to Suit." This land along the highway retained a few archeological sites of industrial and agricultural North Carolina, but they were soon to be bulldozed.

The outer perimeter freeway and the boulevard, which had been widened from a two-lane road, were creating this new, soulless suburb, unofficially dubbed Rocky Falls. The asphalt scars cut through thousands of acres of paper-company pine forest and farmland that had fallen out of use. Now developers were jamming it full of garage doors and sod and nursery-perfect saplings.

Leonard clamped his jaw. It was time to trade in the van. He was keeping the sunglasses, though. He stuck them into his shirt pocket. He had to stop at Kroger for more of their house-brand sanitizer. It was both the cheapest and best-tasting he'd tried.

He steered the minivan into Jeb's Paint & Body, brightly lit, but with no neighbors – and deserted as usual at this hour. At the back of the lot, he was pleased to find a gray Nissan Pathfinder that hadn't been there before. No major damage he could see. Perfect.

In the month since he and his wife had separated, Leonard had been composing the perfect jazz album of burglaries.

More than a year ago, his wife – ex wife, estranged wife, whatever – the soulless bitch – had dragged him down here to the North Carolina burbs from New York City, which was where a jazzman belonged. From the first day, Leonard had hated almost everything about the generic sprawl around the McHouse where the two of them had lived.

Leonard backed the minivan into a parking spot at the body shop and turned off the ignition. The teddy bear charm was cute, he thought as he palmed the keys. He loved keychains.

He scanned the van's interior to make sure he'd cleaned everything up. Just for fun, he wiped the steering wheel and door handles with the tail of his shirt, not that anyone would check the van for prints. He plucked the white envelope from the map pocket of the driver's door, got out and locked the van with the plastic remote. Ugly piece of crapola, this van, but it had been good camouflage for his work. He was glad to be rid of it. He slammed the door with his butt and dusted off his hands as he walked toward the building.

The white envelope had some lady's name and address on it. There were instructions to replace the van's slightly dented front fender, which might have been hit by a basketball or something, the kind of thing sane people wouldn't fix. But everything had to be perfect in Rocky freakin' Falls. Leonard dropped the keys back inside, where he'd gotten them, and pressed its re-sealable flap closed.

He pulled his fishing pole from his bag: Three feet of springy wire with a disk magnet soldered onto the end. He walked to body shop's key drop, a brass mail slot next to the door. He threaded the tool through the hole. He heard three ticks and fished the wire toward him. Three envelopes were stuck to the magnet.

He read the labels but didn't see one for the Pathfinder. So he set those aside and stuck it in again. This time, a single envelope came up; bingo, the Nissan. In for scratches down the side to be "filled/re-painted." Cosmetic surgery for a car.

He opened the flap and poured the key into his hand. Damn, he was smart. Keys were usually made of brass, which meant a magnet couldn't grab them, but the people who lent him their cars were kind enough to leave their keys on steel key rings, in this case, one with a gold-tone Duke University "D."

Leonard dropped the minivan envelope back into the slot with the three rejects and headed for the Nissan. Body shops never started work on a vehicle the morning after it was dropped off.

He hit the remote to unlock the Pathfinder, tucked the envelope into the map pocket of the driver's door and started it up. Half a tank of gas, probably plenty even at the rate this beast drank it. After the quick stop at Kroger, he would go home to get his tools and catch a couple hours' sleep. Big day tomorrow.

Five

Jeff woke to the seductive smells of banana pancakes and coffee. He put on his boxers and T-shirt, ducked into the bathroom to pee, then wandered down the short hallway to the kitchen.

Ashlyn stood at her stove wearing a grocer's apron over her nightshirt. She was just five feet tall and pink-skinned, with blonde hair that flipped up naturally where it brushed her shoulders. She had a reluctant smile and an adorable nose, and people thought she was 10 years younger than 27, probably because of her meek way of speaking to people. She worked as a regional immunization consultant for the North Carolina Division of Public Health.

"Doesn't this look delicious." Jeff pressed into her narrow back, urged his hands underneath her arms and inside the apron front.

She curved her body back against him and curled her neck for an upside-down kiss. Moments like these kept him sticking around with her.

"You had another bad dream."

"I guess so. No big deal."

"You were up for 20 minutes. What was it?"

Ashlyn knew Jeff had nightmares. He had told her the story

of the break-in in Scranton. But he'd never told her how they connected, how much all of it still bothered him. "I don't even remember. Whatever it was sure enough woke me up. I just went to get a glass of water and check my e-mail before I lay back down."

Ashlyn never seemed satisfied with these explanations, but he'd snapped at her once when she'd pressed. Jeff drew in and let out a breath. She gave up too easily.

He turned away from her and poured a cup of coffee. "You want me to carry your stuff down while you finish cooking?"

"I decided I'm not going."

"That's crazy talk." But when he looked, she was smiling.

"I know. Maybe you can fit into my suitcase." A pause. "Hey, we didn't get a chance to say goodbye last night."

Then she was slipping her arms around him from behind, and then they were sitting on the same kitchen chair, her on top facing him, apron on the floor nearby, her head thrown backward.

Afterward, they drowsily ate the pancakes and showered, her first, then him. They washed the dishes, and he loaded her last couple of boxes into her lime green Volkswagen New Beetle. She cried a little and made him show her his copy of her apartment key.

He watched the cute little car turn out of the parking lot and wondered what the time apart would tell about their relationship.

He wasn't sure what he felt besides vaguely uncomfortable. He went back upstairs and packed some of his things into his hiking day pack. He'd been sleeping at Ashlyn's every night since he'd sold his condo. But he very specifically hadn't moved in with her, though she kept putting his deodorant into her cabinet and hanging his pants in one end of her closet.

He had told his mom their relationship was complicated, and she had responded, "I don't really think so, J.D. She's pretty and she's sweet, but I just don't think you love her. I think you're just passing time with her because you're lonely."

Six

The doorbell rang while Sandie Lyman was in the bathroom. She pulled her scrub pants back into place and checked herself in the mirror. The bell rang again, so she skipped washing her hands. No one would know. She went to answer the door.

She'd gotten another nurse to cover the first two hours of her shift so she'd be home to meet the piano tuner. In the 15 minutes she'd been by herself, she'd realized how much she liked having the place to herself occasionally, without the girls or Nathan around. She resolved to create time home alone at least once a month.

She could see a slight man peering through a clear section of the leaded glass in her front door. He wore a tweed, snap-brim cap and an unruly graying beard, though he didn't look any older than her, mid-40s, maybe. She was pleased he was on time.

She opened the front door and said hello. He gave her a furtive glance that avoided eye contact and shook her hand. Then, he looked past her, as if trying to locate the piano. He had his hands jammed into the pockets of his twill pants and a leather pouch slung over his shoulder. Probably 5-10, but that slump of his made him look more like 5-6.

"It's right in here," Sandie said, and led him to a walnut paneled side room they called the library, even though there were no books. "I'll run get an extension cord so you can plug in your tuner."

He mumbled something toward the carpet and shook his head. When she asked him to repeat it, he exaggerated the pronunciation and the words came out terse; his voice was startlingly high: "I don't use one. I tune by ear."

"But how do you know which pitch to start with?"

He seemed to be humming now. Socially awkward little man.

"Um, I say how do you get your starting pitch?"

"That's it – A440," he mumbled. "Four hundred forty vibrations per second. The A above middle C. It's the tone orchestras tune to."

"You have perfect pitch?"

"Active absolute pitch." The words spilled out now. "Perfect pitch just means if somebody plays a note, the person can tell you which note. But I can hum any note you name, perfectly in tune, without a reference pitch."

"Active absolute pitch. Never heard of that."

"Only about 1 in 10,000 people."

She was skeptical of this guy now, but her neighbors in Crabapple Orchard swore by Leonard Noblac. Her regular guy was in Vienna for six weeks, and the piano sounded terrible. Her neighbors were all pains in the ass; she figured this Leonard knew what he was doing if he could keep them happy.

He sat on the bench of her Kimball console and opened the lid. He snapped out the panel that concealed the tuning pegs, then struck the A key near the center of the keyboard.

"Wow. That's it."

"The piano is slightly flat. They tend to do that between tunings. But most people would consider them the same."

Sandie suppressed the urge to roll her eyes, but she guessed this was what you wanted in a piano tuner. "Will you be longer than an hour?"

He struck a series of keys to play octaves up and down the keyboard, then struck a couple of two-note harmonies. He pulled out the wood-handled wrench piano tuners always used. He didn't turn around. "It's not off much. I'd say maybe 40 minutes."

"Great. I'll be in the kitchen if you need anything."

She went to the kitchen, took a cup of blueberry yogurt from the refrigerator, poured a glass of orange juice and sat in the rocker in the sunroom. The man played keys over and over as he brought the octaves into tune, then major-fifth intervals, striking each one at three different velocities.

There was something meditative about the repetitive tones. She found herself looking forward to playing the instrument in tune.

She flipped through *Glamour*, a magazine she knew she was too old for. She gripped the little roll of fat below her navel as she looked at a Gucci ad. It made her feel worse than the wrinkle reducer makeup one on the facing page.

She skimmed three or four articles and finished lunch before the sequences of notes stopped. She heard Leonard putting the piano back together and closing the lid, so she headed to the library. Her normal piano tuner played to test his work, and she always enjoyed hearing someone besides herself.

But the guy already had his tool pouch slung over his shoulder. He was facing away from the keyboard, with her toy poodle, Sphinx, on his lap. He petted the animal more gently than most men would.

"She likes you."

He glanced up and blushed again. "She's pretty old, huh?"

"Yeah. We have a good vet."

The man looked up, and Sphinx suddenly bounded from the bench and hid underneath the armchair in the corner.

"Sorry about that," Sandie said. "She can be skittish until she gets to know you. Or maybe she thinks I'm going to stick her back into the carrier because I said 'vet.' "

He cleared his throat and stood. Maybe he'd lost a pet; the line of conversation seemed to make him uncomfortable.

"It's all set," he mumbled, patting the piano lid. "Good little instrument. Perfectly tuned and tempered now. That's one hundred fifteen."

"Aren't you going to play something?"

The guy kept his gaze down. "The piano isn't my instrument."

"How can you check your work?"

"I can hear each string when it comes into perfect tune," he said, sounding put off. "You can try it before you pay me, if you want."

That was exactly what Sandie wanted, but now that he'd made a big damn deal about it, she felt she couldn't. So she wrote a check in the amount he'd named. He spelled his name for her. N-O-B-L-A-C.

She showed him to the door, but he lingered just inside, commenting on things in the house. It made Sandie nervous. Finally, she checked her watch and made a big show of being surprised she only had 10 minutes before she had to head to work.

He finally took the hint and walked through the door, and she turned the key to lock the deadbolt behind him.

She returned to the library and sat to play Chopin's prelude in A Flat Major. The piece and her piano had never sounded so beautiful. Now the Kimball sounded like the Steadmans' expensive Kawai she always drooled over. Weird as he was, Leonard Noblac was her new piano tuner, Sandie decided. Sphinx finally ventured from under the armchair.

Seven

Jeff carried his box down the steps from Ashlyn's apartment and set it on the passenger floorboard of the Audi. While she was away, he would camp on the floor of the new place he'd just bought – an old donut factory on a sketchy edge of downtown Raleigh that he'd gotten rezoned residential and was renovating into three loft apartments. The drywall crew had supposedly put up the new interior walls, but he hadn't had time to stop in and check.

He let out a breath and again caught himself palming his shirt pocket for cigarettes that hadn't been there for 10 years as he started the Audi and looked at the dashboard clock. He'd be in the office by 9:30, which should be early enough after working all night. He hit a button to fold down the convertible top, accelerated onto Wake Forest Road and was in downtown Raleigh in a few minutes.

The open roof gave a good view of the building that held his office, the newest and tallest in the city, Wachovia Capitol Center. It wouldn't be a big deal in Atlanta or Manhattan: a 30-story blue glass tower trimmed in pink granite with a pyramid-shaped top. In Raleigh, it impressed people. Jeff had one of 84 reserved parking spaces underneath the tower's plaza. He swiped his card to raise the metal entry door and parked the car inside without bothering to raise the top.

He got onto the elevator. At the lobby level, a couple of women who worked for Merrill Lynch paused their conversation as they joined him and lit the button for their floor. He breathed their light perfume and watched the reflection of them cutting their eyes at each other in the hemispheric chrome light fixture until a regal electronic *bong* sounded at his floor.

CB Allison occupied the entire tenth floor, with more than 20 attorneys and another 30 paralegals and support staff, including Jeff. The air in the office was chilly, comfortable for people who wore wool suits year-round. The air carried the mixed scents of cinnamon air freshener and photocopier toner. A model named Jacyln smiled under heavy brass letters behind an imposing black-granite reception desk. "Good morning, Mr. Swaine."

He nodded and walked through a cluster of cubicles, stopping at the last to check with Sarah Rosen's secretary, Annie, who also took calls for him. She was on the phone, but she handed him a pink note: "Sarah wants to see you right away." Andrea Knox was black and one year out of UNC-Chapel Hill with a bachelor's in business. She wore her hair straightened and pulled back tight. She favored classic, tailored suits and simple flat shoes.

Jeff spotted a pack of Marlboro Lights in the top of her purse. He looked again to make sure it wasn't a package of chocolates or cosmetics; she seemed far too put-together to smoke. Definitely cigarettes. Odd. She hung up the phone, and Jeff refocused on the pink note.

Annie nodded toward Sarah's closed door and shook her head. It meant Sarah was not to be interrupted, no matter what her pink notes said.

Jeff unlocked the door of his own corner office. That wasn't as impressive as it sounded. The clever architect had designed the building with sawtooth sides that created 12 corner offices per floor, three at each corner. Still, he enjoyed his view of the Capitol and its leafy grounds through his two walls of windows.

He sat in his mesh desk chair and called up the Progress-Leader website. He was surprised the golden retriever story was in the intensely local "Rocky Falls Progress" section, not on the main page of the site.

The headline was: "Dog Dead after Break-in," a little too cautious, he thought. He skimmed the story. Cooperton had been mighty skimpy with details. There was his own name: "The Reuss family said they hired attorney J. Davis Swaine of the Cross Baker Allison firm to investigate and to represent them in the matter, but no one from the firm returned a call early today."

It wasn't the first time he'd been mistaken for an attorney, or that he'd known a reporter to be sloppy with details on deadline.

So much for keeping it confidential that they'd hired an expensive investigator, but that was the client's choice. The reporter Caroline had even gotten the Reusses to lend her a pre-death photo of the dog, Beebee, which the new wife must have had in her purse. But the reporter didn't have the graffiti angle. Jeff was impressed, if dismayed, that Caroline had gotten the story into the paper on such a tight deadline.

Now, the TV guys, who got most of their story ideas by reading press releases or the newspaper, would have all of it today, he was certain. He would have scanned the morning news shows if he'd known. He checked the stations' websites. Just a three-paragraph item from the Associated Press North Carolina wire, based on the Kramden piece, on WRAL.com.

Jeff checked his voice mail and, sure enough, found one from Kramden with a 12:15 a.m. time stamp. "The Reusses are referring all questions about the break-in to you. Please call me as soon as you get this."

Today, Caroline would be expected to have a fresh angle for her piece, or at least more details. He called her. They agreed to meet at her office at noon and go to lunch to "compare notes," though he figured she'd mostly pump him for information.

Annie buzzed him that Sarah was free, so Jeff walked next door.

"You sleep in?" Sarah was a little over 40, with short red hair cut blunt. She didn't bother with makeup. She was looking a little lumpy in a black suit that had once been tailored to fit. She wore a wrist brace on her right hand for carpal tunnel syndrome.

On her desk stood a photo of her infant son, but not her husband. She'd recently announced she was divorcing him. The most notorious divorce attorney in town was drinking her own Kool-Aid, and rival firms were ready to rep her ex for free, just for sport.

"Ashlyn left for the summer today, and she made me breakfast."

Sarah gave a smile that seemed to have no feeling behind it. "What's your theory about the dog?" Her accent was New York/New Jersey/Connecticut. He'd never asked exactly which.

"Waiting to hear from the necropsy, but my best guess is the thieves put the golden down as a precaution. But knowing Reuss, this whole thing could be revenge. I doubt it's his ex; might be somebody he screwed in a business deal. There's graffiti all over the walls that the newspaper doesn't know about. He left me with the sense that he wants the firm to stay involved anyway, though."

She nodded as he explained, then nodded again when he said he would talk again with the Reusses and then with the reporter.

"Yeah, do that. Do you think we can stick Mickey with at least 60 hours of time this week? You may want to put the Vaproxycin stuff down for now – we don't know if we'll ever see a dime out of that case." She was looking down at a folder on her desk, and Jeff knew these were not suggestions.

He gave a nod. "I'll keep you posted."

He ducked back into his office and signed onto his e-mail, which he hadn't yet checked. Only one subject line caught his eye: "Mr. Swaine, Thanks for Your Gift" from a PWallace@trichildmed.org.

He double-clicked it.

"As chairman of the board of directors of Triangle Children's Medical Fund, I want to thank you personally on behalf of the 182 children we've helped to get life-saving medical treatments so far this year. Generous donors like you make our mission a reality."

Jeff gave a couple thousand dollars a year to charities, but he hadn't given to these guys. Maybe there was another J.D. Swaine in the area, and the fund had them mixed up. He skimmed to the last paragraph. "As you know, Triangle Children's Medical Fund is a 501c(3) non-profit, so your gift of $8,765.43 is fully tax deductible. You will receive a formal thank-you note and receipt by postal mail, but I wanted to express our gratitude without delay."

Jeff laughed. If he were inclined to give away that much money, he'd go ahead and round it up to nine grand. He made a note in his palmtop computer to reply to the e-mail and find out what was going on.

Eight

Mickey Reuss was still at the Rocky Falls Courtyard by Marriott with New Wife, having given himself the morning off from work. Jeff met them in the lobby.

The deputies had told them that by 1 p.m. they would be able to re-occupy their house. New Wife looked at Jeff as if she was positive he would sympathize and said, "I just don't know how I'll ever feel safe inside that house alone again."

Jeff nodded and pursed his lips. He figured they'd be in a Realtor's Lexus before 5.

He made noises as if he empathized, then asked who they thought might have done it.

"I still think it was that bitch," New Wife said.

Mickey Reuss glared at her, and she stood quickly and said she was going to buy a newspaper.

"Who else could have done it?" Jeff asked Mickey Reuss when she'd gone.

"That's a long list." He mentioned several names, including two state senators, and Jeff wrote them down on his yellow legal pad.

Jeff asked how much Reuss wanted him to share with the

Progress-Leader. "One theory is that people might read the story and offer tips that'll help solve the crime. But maybe you want to keep this as quiet as you can."

"You put out however much you think will really help us. And definitely put out word that we're gonna find out who did this to us, and there will be hell to pay."

That would take some finesse, Jeff thought.

Now Reuss said, "Damn dog was a money pit anyhow."

"What?"

"Fucking thing had cancer."

"So it was dying anyway?"

"Nah. I spent about 10 grand on chemotherapy and radiation, and the damn thing was completely cured. That's the bitch of it."

* * *

Jeff drove the short distance to the Rocky Falls bureau of the *Progress-Leader*. It was in a strip center bay once occupied by a hair salon. The paper had kept the check-in counter and waiting area near the front door, and the glass shelves that had held overpriced shampoo were stacked with back issues of the *P&L*. Each desk had a huge mirror and plenty of electrical outlets four feet above the floor. Even more half-assed than small-market TV news.

Some reporter in the bureau should have a sense of humor and keep electric clippers on his desk, and maybe one of those jars of combs in blue liquid, Jeff thought. The bureau chief's desk was in back, next to the hair-washing sink, and the guy had the basin filled with tropical potted plants. He was using the sprayer to water them and telling Caroline, "You got us a jump on a pretty good story, maybe a hate crime. Readers are gonna go batshit over Beebee, poor puppy."

She gave a teacher's-pet smile. "I was psyched when she pulled out the dog's picture."

Then they saw Jeff and shut up. Caroline whispered to her boss and then walked over to Jeff. "You're early. Can you give me a couple of minutes to wrap something up before we leave?"

"Sure." She showed him to an empty chair at the desk beside hers. Today she wore a suede miniskirt and a pale blue V-neck blouse. "Feel free to use the Internet."

Jeff killed a few minutes checking stock quotes – a mostly flat day, so far, except that the former telecom high-flier he had kept buying more of had gone down yet another dime per share – then he jumped over and logged into his work e-mail.

Around the edge of the monitor, Jeff noticed Caroline slide her fingers inside the neck of her blouse to absentmindedly soothe an itch. She was sitting perpendicular to him. Now he glanced down at her smooth legs. When she glanced up to meet his gaze, he stared past her out the front windows. Jeff realized his primal brain was on the prowl again.

"Sorry," Caroline said. "Can you give me just a few more seconds? I have to return this e-mail."

"No problem."

She looked back at her screen, typed in a flurry, then clicked her mouse with authority. She stood, turned and leaned over the desk where Jeff sat, resting her palms on the desk. The pose gave Jeff such a great view down the front of her blouse that he could have positively identified the bra from a lineup of Victoria's Secret catalog photos. He hoisted his gaze. Her breath smelled like cinnamon gum, and she was smiling warmly. "Let's do lunch."

As he stood, he noticed a brass plaque on her desk that read, "The Maneater" in large letters, with her name engraved below. It said "Editor" below that. Yeah, the student newspaper at Mizzou was *The Maneater.* Funny.

She led him to her Ford Explorer. He found a spot for his feet among the photocopies and empty water bottles in the floorboard.

"Impressive to see you on the scene last night," Jeff told her.

"Dumb luck. I was working late at the bureau, organizing some notes for my next suburban-woe-of-the-moment story – whole batches of credit card bills from at least three banks got lost in the mail last month, so a bunch of people never paid on their accounts, and now they're getting late fees."

"How many bills?"

"The first two banks say about 9,000 accounts – just going by the number of customers in the two Rocky Falls ZIP codes where no one seems to have gotten a statement this month. Got a call out to the third bank; I'm having to work my way through their PR department in Nebraska."

"That's a nightmare."

"Seriously. The Postal Service doesn't think the problem's on their end. The big sacks of bills for the area just never showed up this month. But they were coming from three different states. It's too weird. Postal inspector says off the record he's afraid somebody's stolen the bills to get the account numbers for credit card fraud."

"That's got to be it."

"I know. If I get that on the record, it's a pretty good story."

Jeff gave her a shit-eating grin. "You *put* it on. Call the bank flaks back and ask them whether they're concerned that someone is stealing the bills to enable massive credit card fraud. Then at the very least, you can write, 'Bonnie Bankflak says they have no reason to believe a credit card fraud ring stole the missing bills to get the account numbers.' That's enough to put the idea out there."

She smiled at him. "You think like a reporter."

"Used to be. TV news in Scranton-Wilkes Barre, Pennsylvania, fifty-third largest TV market in the country. It was 'Nine on Your Side' with Jeff D. Swaine."

She grinned and raised her eyebrow. "You've got the looks for TV. Why'd you get out of it?"

Jeff smiled to himself. "Low pay and appalling working conditions."

She smirked. "Anyway," she said, "So last night, I'm standing up from my desk to head home when I hear the Mill Run Estates address over the scanner again. They never have said what's going on out there, so I decide to ride by. I missed the deadline for the print edition, but they got it up on the Web for me."

That explained the odd way the story had been underplayed, Jeff thought.

She steered into the parking lot of The Rocky Falls Brewery & Grille, named after the front of a car, judging from the spelling. As she withdrew the ignition key, she looked at Jeff and said, "I knew you were dressed too fancy for a sheriff's investigator last night. I was figuring maybe assistant district attorney."

He just shook his head and smiled. Another likely explanation for her referring to him as an attorney in her story.

He held the restaurant's front door for her, and they got a table right away. As soon as Jeff swallowed the first big bite of his Grillemaster's Blueburger, Caroline Kramden fixed him with a mischievous smile. "So, this is what Mickey Reuss gets when he buys a country trailer park and tells the old ladies and rednecks to get out by the first of the month so he can put up fifteen dozen McMansions."

It was a great reporter trick to hit someone with a shocking statement and gauge your reaction. The trick, if you weren't the reporter, was not to look surprised by anything.

And not to have a clueless look like this on your face if it was all news to you.

He took another bite and tried to look cagey, but they both knew that Caroline Kramden was a step ahead of him.

She stuck out her tongue at him like one of his girl cousins had always done when they were kids. But the way Caroline did it, he wondered if it made him blush.

Nine

Britney climbed out of her booster seat in the back of Mama's car. She made sure to watch her feet as they hit the hard garage floor. Her tennis shoes lit up red when she did that. Cool. She jumped a couple of times so they'd do it again.

"Britney, move, sweetie, so I can unbuckle your brother," Mama said.

Britney walked over to Daddy. He had out his jingly ball of keys. He put one in the door. As soon as it opened, she ducked under his elbow and ran into the house. Somebody had left the door to the deck open. Daddy might be real mad when he saw.

"Porcupine, I missed you!" Her kitty always ran to meet her when she came home. Mama said it was because she fed him. But nuh-uh.

Britney didn't see Porcupine yet. Sometimes Porcupine played hide-and-seek under Mama and Daddy's bed. Britney ran down the hall. It was dark. Her shoes lit up the white boards by the floor.

She had to go pee pee, but not until after she hugged Porcupine. She lifted the blanket and looked under the bed. Her nose tickled. She didn't see yellow eyes. She looked in her room, but

Porcupine wasn't in his hiding places in there, either.

Britney stood in the doorway to her room with her hands on her hips. She bet that silly cat was hiding behind Daddy's recliner in the square of sun on the carpet! In the living room ... Britney's feet went dwonk dwonk dwonk on the wooden hall. She breathed through her mouth. She ran into the living room, jumped one big time onto the hearth – flash! – jumped onto the floor – and then peeked behind Daddy's black chair. Porcupine!

"Hi kitty!"

Porcupine was asleep. Britney got on her knees and crawled toward him. She would wake him up with a sneaky hug.

Britney sniffed. Porcupine needed a bath. Britney hugged her kitty, but Porcupine didn't squirm. He didn't feel cozy-warm. Sleepyhead wouldn't wake up.

Britney petted his brown fur. He felt funny. Icky. Britney felt like crying. Maybe Porcupine was sick. Maybe he had the flew, which didn't really make people fly. It made them take naps.

"Daddy!" she hollered. She felt kind of dizzy walking down the hall to Daddy's den, the first place he always went when they had been out of town. Daddy was looking into his big metal closets, the ones she was never, ever supposed to touch. Daddy did look real mad.

"Don't come in here, baby," Daddy said. He was at the door so fast. His face looked scared now. "What's the matter, darlin'?"

"Daddy, Porcupine's real still and he won't hug me back."

Daddy grabbed Britney's hand in a nice way, not real hard like when she had to go to time out. Mama came out of Daddy's den now, too. She was sniffly and her face was wrinkly like she was crying.

Britney led Daddy and Mama to the sun square behind the chair and showed them Porcupine.

Daddy bent down and crinkled up his nose because of the funny smell. He poked Porcupine with one finger.

"Lord, Britney. Your cat died."

Mama made funny noises and started crying, hollering, almost. Britney started to cry hard too. Couldn't Daddy give Porcupine some Triaminic or take his temperature? She pressed her nose against Daddy's blue jeans, and his scratchy fingers rubbed on top of her hair. Daddy was hugging Mama at the same time.

Ten

Leonard thought it might be good to have a spare vehicle, so he decided not to give the Pathfinder back to the body shop. He drove through shopping center parking lots until he found another Pathfinder that looked to be the same year. It had a youth soccer sticker on the back window. He parked beside it and, with a little cordless screwdriver, swapped the vehicles' license plates in less than a minute. Unless that driver had her license plate number memorized and stared at her own rear bumper a lot, she'd probably never notice.

Then he drove his Pathfinder to another shopping center near his farmhouse, parked it, locked it and walked the mile home along the shoulder of Rocky Falls Boulevard to his long, gravel driveway.

From there, he drove his own Chevy station wagon to Pet HealthPlex. He loved being back in performance mode. It was a hell of a lot better than tuning pianos. Tuning pianos was one of those things he was naturally good at but hated, because he just did it for money. Like most of the shit wrong with his life, that was The Soulless Bitch's fault. Well, Soulless Bitch No. 2's.

Leonard realized with a rush of joy that the little Kimball

might be the last piano he would ever tune. He'd found his muse. He hadn't had this kind of energy in a long time. This album would finally make him known as a jazz artist, not just a technician or a musician.

Maybe he had kept the one tuning appointment just to relish that transition in his life. He'd turned down everyone else who'd called last week, telling them he was too busy. Who knew why he'd kept it? He'd gotten nervous when she'd brought up the veterinarian, but he knew he was just being paranoid.

He flipped the cap of a new 15-ounce bottle of Waterless Hand Sanitizer and squeezed a puff of citrus air into his nostrils that made him salivate. Had to go slow on this bottle; probably enough isopropyl alcohol mixed in with the ethyl in this volume of gel to stop his heart if he sucked the whole thing down at once. Hell, probably enough ethyl to give him alcohol poisoning, too – the stuff was 121 proof, one and a half times as strong as vodka. He'd just have a little bit.

He tilted back his head and filled his mouth until the gel spilled down his cheeks, then took it down in one gigantic, blazing gulp. He wiped the drips into his mouth

Then he forced his fingers to flip the cap shut and toss the bottle into the back seat, out of reach. This was enough to kill the germs. About three ounces. Should be okay; he'd had plenty of 4-ounce bottles with no problem. Same thing as six martinis.

* * *

Leonard held the mixed-breed dog and stroked its fur, feeling the bulbous tumor on the animal's head. When the dog finally stood still under the hot-white exam lights, Dr. Nagra injected the phenobarb. The animal's muscles contracted, and then it was still.

It wouldn't be a bad way to go at all, Leonard thought, head fuzzy from the gel.

A volunteer carried the carcass out on the metal tray as another part-time employee of PetHealthPlex carried in a chow with an infected broken leg. Leonard positioned a fresh tray, took the chow in his arms and petted her until she lay still for her own injection.

By 9 a.m., they had also put down four cats with feline immunodeficiency virus. All of it was pro-bono work Dr. Nagra did for a north-county animal rescue non-profit.

Dr. Nagra shook her head as the helper carried out the tray with the last cat. "Thankfully, those are the last ones today. They've been finding homes for all the healthy ones, somehow. Thank you, Corey, for your help. I know this is hard for you, too, but it helps me so much to know someone's comforting the animals so they're not frightened."

Leonard squinched up his face, but the tears came anyway. It was very hard to see the animals die, but ending their suffering was the right thing. He looked at the floor and nodded modestly.

"I know," the doctor said. "I need to get out of here. That last cat reminded me of mine."

"Do you mind if I just stay in here a minute … You know, calm down?"

"Of course." She took off her white lab coat as she shouldered through the swinging door.

Leonard gave her 30 seconds, then pulled the drawer the rest of the way open. He wiped his eyes and took six more disposable syringes and two vials of phenobarbital and slipped them into his pocket. He shut the drawer silently, then pushed through the door.

He walked between the rows of caged dogs toward the office, which set off a wave of frantic yipping. In the reception area, he set his volunteer badge on the front desk – "Corey Hart."

Marinna the receptionist was standing beside her round desk. He told her he was leaving. She was early twenties, blonde. A super nice girl. She knew what they had been doing, and now she was staring at his irritated eyes.

She stuck out her bottom lip, stood and walked to him. "I know it hurts. But we know it's what's best for them." She stretched her arms around his neck and pressed her body against him in a generous hug.

More warm tears spilled onto his cheeks. He squeezed back, letting the fingertips of his right hand come to rest on her warm, velvet neck.

He could feel her pulse.

Eleven

Jeff reclined in his desk chair, sucking on two powerful miniature peppermints and reading about Mickey Reuss and the trailer park controversy in the *Progress-Leader* online archive. It was interesting that Reuss hadn't mentioned the deal that morning when talking about potential motives for the burglary. He called him to ask about it but had to leave a voice mail.

One of his digital photos showed a clear image of the mini-van at the subdivision entrance, and the resolution was good enough to make out the tag number – a different number than the one from the van with the redheaded kid. He cropped it on his computer and e-mailed a copy to Cooperton, hoping it was something.

Then he called Caroline to try to buy an extra day before that angle made it into the paper.

"You're going to try to talk me out of my exclusive angle for tomorrow's story?"

"Let's go off the record a minute."

She let out a long breath. "Okay."

"Look, off the record, I don't want you to get off track on this story. Right now my quote to you would be that we have absolutely no reason to believe this is connected with the trailer park deal. Why not just wait a day and see if I do find some connection. Nobody else is asking about it. You still have the get, and you get our cooperation for a better story."

"And if not, you'll try to persuade me not to do a story at all, when I can do the story right now, with the no-comment from you, for tomorrow's paper, then write the one with your comment the next day."

"That works only if our comment isn't, 'It has absolutely nothing to do with the trailer park deal.'"

She was smiling. "Nah, based on your advice at lunch, that's 'Builder denies attack is retaliation for land deal.' "

"Let's go back on the record."

"Okay."

"We have absolutely no reason to believe this has anything to do with the trailer park deal."

"That's your quote?"

"Yep. Let's go back off the record." Jeff took a breath, made sure it felt right to change his tack with her, and decided to go ahead. "If you publish that story, I'll be calling your bureau chief tomorrow morning to demand a printed correction."

"What makes you think my story will have an error?"

"Not that story. Your story today. I'm a legal investigator, not an attorney, like you said."

It would seem a small mistake to most people, but Jeff knew the Progress-Leader took accuracy seriously. Editors counted printed corrections against reporters in their annual reviews, even an error as minor and understandable as saying a law firm's investigator was an attorney. Enough corrections could get a reporter fired.

"Damn you," Caroline said, in a tone that was peevish, though not entirely so. "You'd have better luck playing nice with me instead of rough."

Jeff raised his eyebrows. "Look, just wait a day; I'll look into it. If you might be right, my quote tomorrow will be something like, 'That's an excellent observation, and you're the only news outlet to connect those dots. That's our main theory of the case.'"

"Trade me something I can use *today*."

Being a good reporter was all about being an effective negotiator, and Jeff was gaining respect for Caroline Kramden, *Progress-Leader* staff writer, who also struck him as somebody he didn't want to get into a pissing match with. "Okay. Here's what you want: Beatrice the golden retriever had won a battle against cancer just before the ruthless burglar burst into her owner's home and stole her life. None of the TV guys has it. Nobody outside the investigation does."

"You're giving me that on the record?"

Jeff grinned. "No, trading you for it."

"Deal. Give me details. And get me an interview with Mrs. Reuss."

* * *

Around 4 o'clock, Cooperton called. "We got ourselves another dead pet. This 'un's a kitty cat. I just e-mailed you the news release we're fixin' to send out."

"Hold on. Let me look."

Jeff hit the "get mail" button, and the message ding-donged into his inbox. An expensive gun collection was missing, but all the televisions were still there. There was more graffiti in black spray paint: "Guns kill poor, helpless animals" in the den where the gun cabinets had been cleaned out. In black marker on the great-room wall, the intruder had printed: "The thief cometh not to steal and to kill and to destroy – I am come that they might have life, and that they might have it more abundantly."

"Sounds like our boy from the other night," Jeff said. "The text of the messages is a little stranger, though."

"Uh-huh," Cooperton said. "Right down the street, too. It's the guy that owns the framing contractor Mickey Reuss likes to use for throwin' up houses."

"No shit."

"That Bible shit is weird," Cooperton said. "I would let you come take a look, but the place is covered up with press now, and it wouldn't look too good. But I'll keep you posted on what-all we know, maybe get you in there tomorrow or sometime."

"Get any physical evidence? What do you know that isn't in

the release?"

"Naw. Just that the whole neighborhood is in a damn tizzy, and it's gonna be the whole county, soon as all this comes out."

"What about that plate number I sent you?"

"Beige Chrysler Town and Country registered to a single mom who cleans people's houses. Says her van isn't missing."

"Damn." Jeff felt foolish for having chased it, then had a thought. "Was she in Mill Run Estates yesterday afternoon?"

"Don't know. Not sure if we asked her. I'll make sure we check."

Sarah Rosen was standing in Jeff's doorway now, her arm hooked through the handle of one of those bucket-like infant seats, from which a tiny foot poked upward. "Thanks for the heads-up, lieutenant," Jeff said. "I have to run. I'll call you back."

"Hey, boss," Jeff said. He walked over and tickled Jacob's little foot and got a delighted squeal in return. "And how's my little buddy?"

His boss cooed into the bucket. "Mother had to bring Jacob to work today because of your stuffy nose, didn't she? But you're going to be nice and quiet and sleep a lot." She rolled her eyes dubiously, turned back to Jeff. "They don't want them at day care if they have the slightest fever."

Jeff hoped his adult immune system would protect him.

Sarah shivered a little, morphing, Jeff realized, from mother back to boss. "I've just learned there was another dead pet after a burglary in Rocky Falls yesterday we don't know about," she said. "It's looking like it's going to make the evening news."

Sarah lived in a new house in Rocky Falls herself. Now the firm's name had been connected with it in the newspaper.

"I was just talking to one of our favorite deputies about that," Jeff said. She moderated her stern look by a degree or two. "Probably happened the same time as Mickey's dog. It's the house three doors down, a subcontractor he works with a lot. It wasn't discovered until just now. The homeowners came back from a trip out of town early this afternoon. How'd you hear about it?"

"A guy I know through Rotary Club lives across the street," Sarah said. "His nanny started seeing the cops and TV trucks at the other house after lunchtime. Sounds like all the stations are setting up to lead the 5 o'clock news with a live shot and talk about both cases."

Without warning, Jacob started bawling full-tilt. Sarah twisted a pacifier into his mouth.

"I'll head up there," Jeff said. "Cooperton can't get me inside right away, but I'll talk to the neighbors and homeowners if I can. I'll let you know what I find."

* * *

Sarah Rosen sat at her desk and unwrapped a Chick-fil-A sandwich – which had regrettably become her standard lunch. Jacob had fallen into a restless sleep.

She tried the sitter again and finally got her this time, arranged to drop Jacob off at 5:30. She fretted that the boy could melt down screaming any second now, and that just didn't add to your aura as managing partner.

She thought about Davis Swaine heading out to get the skinny and smiled there in her office. He was an odd age. He was a handsome one, though of course he worked for her, so nothing would ever come of that. If she were seven years younger and a peer…

She knew she was a good mentor for him, and that she had his respect. She liked him better and thought he was smarter than most of the firm's attorneys, so it was hard for her not to treat him like one, or even show him favoritism over them. He moved so easily among people.

Not like her louse of a husband – the term "estranged" flashed into her head. Since Davis wasn't in the right position in her life for her to think of as the kind of man she'd like to marry next, she thought of him as the sort of man she wanted Jacob to become.

Sarah saw her old ambition in Davis Swaine, remembered how much more hopeful and less encumbered she'd felt at that age, wished she were still at that point in her life where she was rounding 30 but had never married, wished she'd had backbone enough not to rush ahead in the first halfway serious relationship she'd stumbled into after realizing her job didn't warm the bed at night. She'd swung from having impossible standards for men to impossibly lax ones.

She looked down at her Jacob, sucking on his pinky and ring fingers, dozing a little there in his carseat. At least she'd met the biological deadline for having the kid, and being a mother was the most amazing feeling. But she was soon to be divorced, a single mom. What could you do? The man had just turned out to be kind of a louse. She hoped her own genes predominated in Jacob.

She chewed the sandwich – kind of cold by now – and looked at her phone. Davis should be getting there pretty soon. And she couldn't wait to hear this one.

Twelve

The address was actually just two doors down from the Reuss home in Mill Run, not three, Jeff realized, a brick two-story with a three-car garage. TV trucks lined the curb, the stalks of their microwave transmitters stretching into the air. Three stations' reporters stood so each of their photographers could pan for a shot of both houses. Jeff remembered the discomfort of spending all day slathered in makeup.

An assistant producer looked out from one of the vans, where she sat at a bank of tiny monitors. "You from the *Progress?* Save you the trouble. Not home."

"Thanks," Jeff said, and waved. Funny to be mistaken for a reporter, and it made him realize he didn't see Caroline around. She must have come and gone already. "I'm gonna go press the doorbell just so I can tell the boss I did."

Jeff noticed a couple of the TV cameras focusing on him at the Hegwoods' front door. He pressed the doorbell button, and it reminded him of ambush interviews he had done for Nine On Your Side.

The chimes clanged. No one answered.

On his way back toward the street, he peeked through the

garage windows. A boat rested on its trailer next to a pickup truck that had vinyl lettering for a contracting company, "Ridgeline Construction." He memorized the phone number. The third slot, closest to the doorway inside, where a family sedan or SUV probably parked, was empty.

He tried knocking on the doors of a couple of neighbors, but apparently no one was home in the middle of the afternoon – except maybe the nanny of the guy Sarah knew, and if so, she wasn't answering the door. Jeff sat in his car and called the number from the side of the truck. He had the family's name from the Sheriff's Office: Dean and Cathy Hegwood. A country-sounding older woman answered at the business and asked how she could help him. He used his full Southern accent and asked to speak with Dean.

"He ain't here today, sweetie," the lady said. "They're on their way up to the lake, at his daddy's, to bury that cat this evenin'."

"That's why I was callin'," Jeff said, hoping to be mistaken for a subcontractor or something. "I just heard about that. Think I could get him on his mobile?" He composed a phone number on the spot and recited it to her.

"Lord, no, baby. That must be an old number." She gave him the real one. "He's probably got it turned off, though. If you want, I can tell him you called."

Jeff smiled to himself. "I was thinkin' of another boy's number, maybe. 'preciate it. Just tell him J.D. called and I'm thinkin' about him."

Jeff called the cell number. A woman answered, probably Cathy. She sounded like she'd been crying. Children fussed in the background.

"Miz Hegwood? I was sorry to hear 'bout your cat."

"'preciate that. Who's speakin'?"

Jeff identified himself as an investigator looking into the Mill Run Estates pet killings. The whole community felt for the family, he told her, because a lot of people knew what it was like to lose a pet. "Ms. Hegwood, are y'all still going to bury Porcupine this evenin'?"

"Sure are. We're in Raleigh picking up the body right now.

They just got done with the autopsy. We're gonna have a little funeral for him, mostly for Britney and Jason, up at their grandma and grandpa's."

"I wonder whether you'd feel all right about letting me come up there and talk to y'all. I need to speak with y'all as quick as I can."

The line was quiet for six seconds. "All right. Just don't let any of them TV reporters follow you."

Jeff felt a little strange using the techniques he'd cultivated to interview families of human murder victims to investigate a cat's demise. For today, that was his gig in Rocky Falls. He got directions to the grandparents' house, about 40 minutes northeast in Vance County. She said they'd be there by 6.

Jeff meandered to the TV gaggle to listen to their reports. They all started promptly at 5, so he knew the pets were the lead story on all three channels. From what he could hear with everyone narrating at once, they were just cribbing from the *P&L* story about the dog and sticking to the news release about the cat. When the pretty faces stopped talking, Jeff peeked into the WTVD van to watch the station's video clips on the monitor: a couple of random people from the neighborhood had told the camera they were "real frightened" and wondered, "Who would do that to somebody's pet?" Standard 2-inch-deep TV news.

* * *

Jeff followed the directions from Highway 54 to the gravel driveway with a mailbox marked "Hegwood."

The drive wound through maples, birches and poplars to a house with wrap-around screened porches on both stories. Past it and down a steep slope, he could see a dock with a canoe at the shore of the man-made lake, a valley flooded to make a drinking water reservoir. It was cool and dark back in these woods and smelled like composting leaves and pine trees, the kind of place he'd like to spend a week of vacation. He parked next to the gold Honda Accord he figured went in the empty slot in Dean and Cathy Hegwoods' garage.

Jeff could see several people on the downstairs porch near

the front door. When he was halfway up the steps, a little girl, about 4, pushed open the screen door for him.

"Thank you, sweetheart," he said. "You must be Britney."

She had been crying. Her lower lip jutted in a grief-stricken pout. She clutched a stuffed bunny tightly enough to strangle it.

"I'm very sorry about your kitty."

She nodded, wrinkled her chin and threw both arms around Jeff's left leg. He patted her head and smoothed her wispy, blonde hair as she sobbed. Now emotion welled in his throat. He gently stepped back from the girl and looked to the adults, who seemed near tears themselves watching her.

"Britney," the man who must have been Dean said, "come over here by Daddy."

The girl went to her father and hopped onto his lap, and he folded her against his chest with one huge, callused hand. Jeff followed her and shook Dean's other hand. He looked about 40, muscular, with a buzz cut and muddy brown work boots. "You must be Dean Hegwood, sir. J.D. Swaine."

Dean nodded. An older man, Dean's father, looked at Jeff and said, "I ain't too sure 'bout all this. Tell us again what you told my daughter-in-law."

Jeff explained that he was investigating the case. The old man looked dubious, but Cathy Hegwood said, "We ought to do what we can to help them catch 'em." The little boy, Jason, sat cross-legged at her feet.

Dean Hegwood said, "I done talked to four men from the sheriff's department." He pronounced it "shurfs." "Let me take a look at your badge."

Jeff gave Dean the surprised look he had practiced on dozens of people. "Oh, I don't work in law enforcement. I'm a legal investigator. I work for the Reusses, the other family down the street that lost their dog."

"That's my boss man, pretty much." Dean looked at his mother. "Mama, take the kids inside the house, please, so we can talk with J.D. here. I reckon he wants some money." Dean set Britney's feet on the floor, and Cathy patted Jason on the back to underscore her husband's directions. The grandmother took their hands and promised them a cookie.

"No, sir," Jeff said. "I'm not here after money. I just need y'all's information. Go on and call your boss, if you want to make sure I'm working for him."

When the front door shut behind them, Dean looked at Jeff and lowered his voice, and Jeff could sense he now believed him. "I 'magine me and Mickey are in the same boat, so I'll play along, and maybe you'll wind up helping us. But two things: You don't tell the kids nobody killed Porcupine. He's been sick, and they just think he went on and died. That's how it stays. We didn't even tell them nobody broke in the house, 'cause we was afraid they'd get scared. Britney come across the cat in the living room. And she seen all that writin'. Thank the Lord she's too little to read it."

Jeff nodded once.

"Two, we ain't gonna answer any bunch of questions until after their little funeral. That's why we come up here. That, and to get away from the reporters. This is important to my wife and to my kids first and foremost. So you wait around here with us if you want to, but behave. 'Cause if I see you doin' something I don't like, I'll toss your butt out of here."

"Fair enough."

Hegwood nodded. "Baby, go in and tell them they can come back out, if they want, and get me and Jeff here some iced tea, please."

She stood without a word and went to do it.

"Sheriff's Office said they stole your guns," Jeff said. "Sounded like a nice collection."

Dean's cheek twitched at the thought of it. He glanced toward his dad, the only other person on the porch now.

Dean's dad said, "They're lucky they didn't break in while Dean was there, or he would have used one or two of them guns on 'em."

Jeff shifted his weight and re-crossed his legs.

"Damn straight," Dean said, then toed a nail head sticking up from the deck board in front of his chair. "They got 'em all: a couple of ol' flintlocks, my grand-dad's single-shot .22, an Army .45, an SKS ..." Jeff knew it was a Chinese knockoff of the Russian AK47 assault rifle. "And they took my shotguns and pistols and all the rifles I hunt with. Fifteen guns in all. What the hell did that writing mean, you reckon? 'Guns kill innocent animals,' then they kill my kids' pet.'"

"That's a damn good question," Jeff said, happy for the opening. "You said Porcupine had been sick?"

"Yeah, diabetes and kidney disease and every other damn thing, seemed like. I 'magine we spent eight or nine thousand dollars on him, little bit at the time, and lately he was doin' fine. Then somebody breaks in to steal from us and does him in. Ain't that a bitch?"

So the same burglars had apparently killed two animals on the same day, three houses apart owned by two people in the subdivision construction business, and both the pets had been sick and received expensive treatments. If you figured in the graffiti, it seemed like the kind of crime someone committed to make a statement, maybe some kind of radical anti-sprawl organization. But what organization looking to gain sympathy would kill a child's pet?

Dean's father interrupted these thoughts. "They didn't even get the Bible verse right."

"They didn't?" Jeff asked.

"Daddy's a preacher," Dean said.

"Gospel of John, chapter ten, verse 10," the old man said, and closed his eyes. He had a giant wave of white hair swept back over his right ear. "'The thief cometh not, *but for* to steal, and to kill, and to destroy; *I* am come that they might have life, and that they might have it more abundantly.' See, that was Jesus talking, showin' he wasn't like the evil thief that comes to destroy. The robber left out the 'but for' and used it like the whole thing was talking about the thief, sayin' that the thief wasn't there to steal or kill or destroy. I hate when people twist the words of the Bible to their own use."

If he was like the preachers Jeff had known growing up, Jeff bet he mostly hated when other people did it. But his clarification of the scripture verse was interesting. Now that Hegwood pointed it out, Jeff remembered the "but for." John 10:10 had been a Memory Verse in Sunday School at Bellhaven Baptist Church when he was a child.

The front door opened again, and everyone re-joined them.

Jeff accepted a tall glass of tea from Cathy and finally took a seat, on the porch swing. It was good tea, as tannic as a young Napa cabernet and as sweet as a Popsicle. The group fell silent.

At five 'til six, Dean walked down to the driveway and opened the trunk of the Accord. He took out a cardboard box like the ones pet stores send new puppies home in. He looked inside, rearranged Porcupine's body, and then carried the box to the side yard. Jeff fell into the procession of mourners that spilled down the porch steps. Dean's father brought up the rear, his Bible in one hand, a long-handle shovel in the other.

The little funeral service grieved Jeff. He watched Britney and Jason peer into the top of the cardboard box. They reached down and petted Porcupine's still form again and again. They seemed to believe enough strokes might refill the cat's body with life.

Jeff remembered his grandfather lying in state at the funeral home the previous year, how Jeff had briefly thought he'd seen the dead man's chest rising and falling, an illusion caused by the slight motion of Jeff's own breath and his rapt stare.

Dean Hegwood gently pulled the children's arms from the box and lowered it into the hole.

The things the burglars were doing made some kind of sense inside their own minds, Jeff realized. Yet whoever would make children suffer like this was thoughtless or evil. And people who would do it while casting themselves in the role of Jesus were crazy – and dangerous.

As he walked back to the driveway to his car, a heavy determination tightened Jeff's forehead. This time, he wasn't just billing hours to a client who could pay them. He would find whoever this was and stop them.

Thirteen

Jeff was back in Raleigh by 8:30 p.m., exhausted from thinking about the case and making no headway. He got close to his new place. A homeless guy shuffled down the amber-lit sidewalk. Jeff stopped at an all-night corner store that sold beer with regard mainly to giantness of container and extreme concentration of alcohol, but he was able to find a civilized six-pack, a microbrew called Carolina Blonde from Charlotte.

He drove one more block to the two-story beige brick factory building he'd bought from a bankruptcy trustee for just $150,000 – including its contents – because no one else bothered to bid. The place had been built in 1939 to house Capitol Pastries, one of the few industries in Raleigh besides producing, packaging and selling legislative bullshit. The company sold donuts to Eastern North Carolina diners and groceries until Winston-Salem-based Krispy Kreme put it out of business in the late '60s. The building had stood unused for decades.

On the corner of the flat roof stood a 20-foot, porcelain-enameled donut, brown with white frosting and faded rainbow sprinkles. The Capitol Pastries name had once been superimposed in orange neon letters along the upper and lower arcs of the outsized treat. Jeff was getting a historic preservation tax credit for the four grand it would cost to restore the sign. It would be a great way to tell people how to find the house: Party under the giant neon donut.

The building was lined with tall, metal-mullioned grid windows on both levels – about 2,000 panes of glass. Jeff had hired a company to replace missing panes and clean the surviving ones. He was still waiting for the first rock from some carload of jackass kids riding through on their way home from a teen club. A jackass kid like he'd been . . .

Jeff pulled into the alley and yanked the Audi's parking brake. He pulled a padlock key from his wallet and loosed the chain looped through a set of temporary plywood doors. He'd had construction workers demolish this section of brick wall for a garage door. He drove the Audi inside, pulled the straps of the backpack with his clothes over one shoulder and threw a massive industrial switch.

Five rows of gymnasium lights in the ceiling – the ones with good bulbs – came on with a hum. He smiled and rode the freight elevator upstairs. On the top floor, he threw another big switch and lit that whole level.

The place had the clean, earthy smell of fresh drywall compound. New partition walls went halfway to the 20-foot ceiling, describing a couple of bedrooms and huge bathroom. A floor-to-ceiling wall would eventually divide both the upper story and lower story in half, making two apartments upstairs and one apartment and a shared garage downstairs. Jeff would live in this end of the upstairs, and he hoped to cover the mortgage by leasing out the other two lofts.

He envisioned stainless appliances and granite countertops and kitchen cabinets. Somehow, it all made him feel lonely. He stashed five of the six beers in the mini-fridge that now squatted in the kitchen area and plugged his cell phone charger into the same outlet.

He shucked off his business clothes and piled them in a spot where they wouldn't get covered with fine, white drywall dust. He changed into shorts and sandals from the backpack and pried the top off the Carolina Blonde.

Looking through the 50 running feet of windows across the main living area, Jeff could see the spectacular Raleigh skyline view and pick out his office window in Wachovia Capitol Center. He tried calling Ashlyn but got her voice mail.

He stuck the phone into his pocket, and it immediately rang.

It was Caroline Kramden. "My editors are in love with me now, so thanks for the break. The TV guys didn't have it."

"It was a win-win. What's up?"

She waited a second. "I've got a document you may want to take a look at. It might help your investigation."

"What is it?"

"You have to see it. Where are you?"

"Near downtown."

"Me too. If you've got a minute, drop by my place. I live in Cameron Park behind St. Mary's Episcopal School." The sprawling campus of the 160-year-old girls' school near North Carolina State University reminded Jeff of Taft. Caroline gave Jeff the address. "Park on the street in front of the main house, walk down the alley, come through the wooden garden gate. I rent the apartment above the garage."

* * *

The house at the address was an odd combination of gothic and Craftsman styling, with tapered porch columns atop stone piers, semi-circular attic windows and copper gutters. Ivy covered a bank at the front of the property. The main house was dark, and a Realtor's sign stood in the front yard. He walked down the alley, unlatched the tall wooden gate with his thumb and stepped inside the privacy fence.

Caroline's voice shouted, "Over here!"

He made a right turn. She was coming down the steps from her apartment, wearing white cotton shorts and a tight T-shirt and carrying a tote bag. She led him across the brick patio, which had a hot tub sunken into it.

"Should be warmed up by now." She crossed her arms over her stomach, grabbed the T-shirt hem and pulled it over her head. It caught him completely by surprise. He couldn't stop his eyes from darting to her heavy breasts bundled in the lemon-yellow bikini top, but he tried not to alter his expression.

"I should have told you to bring your suit so you could come with." She bent toward him and pushed her shorts to her ankles. She was some kind of amazing flirt. The bikini bottom was actually pretty modest. She was a size or two larger than Ashlyn, a lot curvier. But he thought they both had great bodies. Caroline was clearly comfortable enough with hers.

"You from the Midwest?" Jeff asked. "Everybody at Northwestern from corn country said 'come with.' "

"Maryland. Went to school in Missouri, though." She daintily dipped a toe, then walked down the steps. To hide the effect her display had on him, Jeff kicked off his sandals, sat on the edge of the tub and dipped his feet into the warm water. She sat diagonally across, maybe three feet away, and reclined so her hair pooled on the surface behind her. "I wanted to go to school far, far away."

There was a story there, but she started firing questions before Jeff could find out more.

"Where'd you grow up? Tell me the story about the aristocratic family that gave you that name and made you 'the third.' "

"It's a pretty weird story."

He told her he'd grown up as Jeff Davis Swaine The First in Charlotte, a namesake of the president of the Confederacy. But a trip to Disney World with his Baptist church choir at age 13 had altered the direction of his life. In line for Space Mountain, he'd met a girl named Ellen from Rye Brook, New York, and they'd become pen pals. She'd suggested he was smart enough to get a scholarship to her boarding school, Taft, in Watertown, Connecticut. He'd applied, been offered a free ride and had a big fight with his folks over it. They were dead against it until one of the executives at the uniform company where his mom was a payroll clerk had told her what an incredible opportunity Taft was. Mom had talked Dad into shipping him off to boarding school.

In a clerical error – or maybe as a parting gift – Taft had printed his name on his transcript and diploma as J. Davis Swaine and added the Roman numeral III. So he'd applied to journalism school at Northwestern University that way and picked up another diploma with it. When he realized he couldn't survive on what the TV gig paid and didn't like the work anyway, he'd found the job with CB Allison through a schoolmate. The firm had gotten Jeff's name legally changed to match his diplomas. Now many colleagues and clients called him Davis, he told her. Friends called him Jeff. His parents still called him J.D.

He didn't tell Caroline that Ashlyn had taken to calling him Jeffrey. And now he noticed that, like a good reporter, she was nodding, listening and keeping her mouth shut as he went on. Because of Ashlyn and professional boundaries, Jeff was now feeling like he shouldn't be talking like this with her. He hated to be on the wrong end of the interview, especially when he found the woman asking the questions so sexy that it threw him off his game. He ended the press conference by asking her how the cancerous dog story had turned out.

"Great. And since you mention it, now would be a good time to look inside that envelope." Her foot broke the water gently, and she smiled and pointed to the tote with her dripping big toe.

He took the envelope, tore it open and removed a two-page computer printout, an e-mail to Caroline from the Raleigh City Clinic, thanking her for a gift of $9,300 "in loving memory of your beloved dog, Beatrice."

"I bet you didn't give the clinic $9,300."

"Excellent guess. If I had that kind of money, I'd pay off half my Visa. I didn't get that message until after their office was closed today. It could be some wiseass reader who saw the dog's name in my story. But I thought it might mean something, and that you'd like to have it."

He instantly decided not to mention the e-mail he'd gotten from the Triangle Children's Medical Fund. He looked up from the note to thank her. She was fixing him with a drowsy, brazen stare.

A line popped into Jeff's mind. Inside his head, he practiced saying it with a smile of his own that would certainly make it work: *Why don't we go upstairs? I'd like to see your place.*

Really, he needed to leave right away. Caroline was like a two-scoop ice cream sundae when you hadn't eaten a real meal for a week. "Thanks for this," he said, picking up the envelope, "I ought to get home."

But as soon as he began the sentence, she stood and waded to his edge of the tub. And before he'd finished it, she'd pressed her dripping breasts tightly against his belly, laying the side of her head just under his chin and wrapping both arms around him. He could feel her outline soaking warmly through his polo shirt and shorts.

"Uh-uh," she murmured. "Stay."

WEDNESDAY

Fourteen

The office trailer blocked the rays from the construction site's single, anemic security light, so Leonard had to feel around in the dark to find the heads of the screws. The Phillips bit slipped satisfyingly into place. The tool screamed and then stopped, screamed and stopped – a variation on the siren sequence of notes from the last track, he realized – until he'd undone two rows of screws. At 2:30 a.m., no one was around to hear the serious racket he was making, and there had only been three sets of headlights on Rocky Falls Boulevard since he'd parked here five minutes ago.

He had again limited himself to one mouthful of sanitizer, but thankfully the pure taste lingered in his mouth.

Leonard put on leather gloves and peeled back the trailer's skin, pulled out glass-fiber insulation and threw it onto the ground. Then he kicked at the sawdust paneling that made up the interior wall until he had a hole between studs big enough to crawl through. Not his most glamorous burglary, but this was just the first step.

He found himself underneath a countertop on a vinyl floor littered with chunks of dirt. He pushed a rolling chair out of the way, then stood and brushed the grit from his hands. He pulled out a small metal flashlight and shone the beam, finding a sign on the far wall with the name of the contracting company that was building this new shopping center.

Tonight was the perfect moment for this track. A dozen flatbed trailers loaded with structural steel beams stood parked in rows on the muddy, graded shopping center site. The Freightliner road tractor bearing the erecting contractor's name was still hitched to one load. But the crane hadn't yet arrived at the job-site. Leonard found a row of brass cup hooks near the door to outside, and a pleasant sparkle greeted his light: keys. He looked them over until he found one that said Freightliner. He pulled it from its hook and kissed it.

He unlocked the door with the little diamond-shaped window and walked down three wooden steps. He froze at the bottom when a car's headlights appeared out on the highway. When it had passed, he strode toward the truck, grabbing and dragging along a couple of the orange caution barrels with those flashing lights he'd always thought of as "blinkies." He wedged them onto the trailer with the steel beams.

The truck cab wasn't even locked. He climbed into the springy seat and bounced up and down. He clutched and turned the key to fire up the diesel engine. He figured out how to release the air brakes and wrench the shifter into low gear with the help of handy diagram stickers. This truck was fancier than the ones he'd driven in the Army.

He let out the clutch, and the engine coughed as the truck began to move almost imperceptibly, changing the patterns of light inside the cab. He chuckled at the orange blinking through the rear window. He upshifted as the back of the trailer cleared the front edges of its mates. He pulled hand over hand to steer the heavy load of steel onto Rocky Falls Boulevard.

After half a mile, at the I-540 overpass, Leonard stopped on the shoulder to let a following car zoom past. When it was out of sight again, he backed and pulled the truck – almost jackknifing it once – until he had it where he wanted it: perpendicular across the southbound lanes. He shut off the engine, turned on the truck's emergency flashers and climbed down from the cab, locking the doors behind him.

He placed the blinky barrels on the dividing lines between the southbound lanes so no one would crash into the friggin' thing and get decapitated. That wasn't in the spirit of this composition at all.

Leonard checked again for cars, saw none, and pulled the .380 from his coat pocket. He'd kept the blue-steel semi-automatic from the load of stolen guns. It reminded him of one he'd admired in a pawnshop case as a teenager. He got a nervous little thrill from the cold steel and turned on his heel to face the truck.

He fired. Fluid drained onto the ground, looking dark as blood in this light.

The diesel fuel wouldn't catch fire, since it only exploded under the pressure inside an engine, but they'd probably bring out a HAZMAT crew to clean up the spill, and that would take a while. Excellent.

And they'd have a harder time moving the truck without fuel. And with 18 flat tires. His ears rang from the shot, and he cursed himself. A musician had to be smart about his hearing. He stuffed in yellow foam earplugs, almost burning his cheek on the gun barrel in the process.

He fired slugs into the tires in succession with a drummer's perfect rhythm, seeing his written score for the piece in his mind, counting out the measures to time the leaps of the pistol. He worked around the truck methodically until he'd created a 40-ton roadblock.

The traffic engineers around here were clearly no military strategists. Making all the traffic in an area rely on one big-ass road made it plenty easy to bring traffic to a stop, either by accident or on purpose. *Why, thank you folks; thank you very much. This next tune is one I call "Choke Point." It's off "Stolen Inspiration," and there are autographed copies on sale out in the lobby...*

He bet they wouldn't have this road cleared until lunchtime or after. They might need a crane to unload the beams onto another trailer, and then they'd have to change all those tires, then tow the road-tractor. He could hear the horns honking, the bass line of the heavy engines that would be idling ...

He walked the half-mile back to the construction site smiling as a single car approached the roadblock and its brake lights lit up the pavement in red. He surveyed the empty lanes that would soon stack up with these useless automobiles, thinking how hard it would be for most of them to turn around across the landscaped median, hearing how the notes screeched to a halt at the end of this piece.

Leonard started up his station wagon and drove one mile to the hauling company headquarters where there was always a dump-truck load of gravel ready to go out the next morning. He stole the key from that office, then loaded his 10-speed bike from the wagon into the passenger side of the truck cab.

He cranked the truck and drove to Creek Crossing Way at its intersection with Rocky Falls Boulevard. No cars. He used the hydraulic levers to dump a mound of gravel across three lanes with the sound of a massive snare-drum roll, blocking the only logical workaround for the roadblock he'd made at the interstate. He backed the truck into a utility pole, pulling down wires onto the intersection.

He left the truck next to the gravel pile, shot holes in its fuel tank and tires and got his bike down. For once, a bike would be the way to travel in Rocky Falls. His breathing quickened as he worked the pedals, and as he began to coast down a slight grade, he tossed both sets of truck keys into a storm grate. He was back at the hauling company to pick up his station wagon within a couple of minutes.

Leonard was home and in bed by 5:30. He set his clock radio to wake him at 7:37 for "traffic on the sevens" and drifted to sleep with his music looping through his head in an endless encore.

Fifteen

Jeff made it back to his loft to shower just after sunrise. It occurred to him that he had to get rid of more of these vintage soft drink bottles before he could complete the renovations. For some reason, the building had come stacked with hundreds of cases of them, all from the '50s and '60s, mostly Mint Cola, Cheerwine, Big One and Nugrape. At first, he was kind of annoyed at having to dispose of them. Then he realized he could sell them in batches to antique dealers and one by one on eBay for an average of five or six bucks apiece. He'd raised an astonishing $50,000 so far, money he was using toward the renovations. He planned to build a few hundred bottles that weren't in collectable condition into a cool-looking glass wall to partition off the kitchen.

Ashlyn's call came just after he turned on the shower. "Hi, sexy. I miss you up here. It's weird sleeping by myself."

"Hey." He shut off the water again, walked out to the living room and sat down cross-legged in the center of his air mattress. Concentrating his weight made him sink to the floor. He wiped his eyes and stared across his cavernous, unfinished loft.

Ashlyn said, "So?" and Jeff realized he'd been quiet too

long. A stomach cramp nudged at him.

"I miss you, too, cutie." He imagined Ashlyn in some hotel room with framed prints of flowers, dark wood veneer furniture and a mauve bedspread.

"Are you at my place?"

"No. I'm in the donut factory."

"Aww. Your first night there. I bet you were lonely. I can't wait to join you. I wish I was there right now. Did they deliver your furniture?"

The guilt cramped Jeff's stomach like food poisoning.

"Nah. I'm urban camping." He struggled for something else to say. "I think you'll like my new couch if they ever do bring it."

"I bet I will," she purred. "It's nice to be with a man who stays away from the cheap stuff."

That made Jeff wince. "I tried to call you last night to tell you how beautiful the skyline view is here at night."

"I bet it is. I got your message. But you didn't pick up when I called back."

He remembered silencing his phone without looking at the caller ID at Caroline's.

Ashlyn's conference was going fine; she felt lonely; she really missed him.

He told her he wanted to talk longer, but he had to get to work on the case. He folded his phone shut and wiped his hand back across his hair.

He opened his wallet and pulled out a picture of him and Ashlyn at the North Carolina State Fair in Raleigh. She held her face pressed against his shoulder, her own shoulder nestled under his arm and her small left hand pressing a cone of cotton candy against his stomach. He had rushed into the frame after balancing the camera on the window ledge of a funnel cake trailer and setting the timer, he remembered. She looked really pretty, but the picture was somehow wrong. He tossed the snapshot across the room like a Frisbee.

He was pissed at himself. He didn't owe Ashlyn an extension of their relationship, and yeah, it might not last much longer. But he did owe it to her to do things in order.

And he didn't feel any less lonely this morning. That was for sure.

Jeff shook his head, palming his scalp. He remembered he had a coffee maker here but no coffee or filters. He took the quickest shower he could in the curtainless stall, then stopped on the way to the office to give $3 to the ubiquitous green chain.

He got to his office feeling – for some reason – kind of angry. Sarah wasn't in yet, which surprised Jeff. He'd heard something about a traffic snarl in Rocky Falls on the radio on the way in, so that was probably it.

He stuck his head out his office door and asked Annie.

"She just called. There's some big truck stalled across the southbound lanes of Rocky Falls Boulevard, right by the freeway interchange. And on top of that, a dump truck wrecked and spilled its load on Creek Crossing Way. Traffic's backed up five miles. Some people can't even get out of their subdivisions. Sarah would just work from home, but there's no place to turn around."

Jeff shrugged and checked out the Progress-Leader website. He went from angry to furious.

Fucking Caroline Kramden! This time, the stories were on the main page of the site, played with large headlines: "Subdivision project linked to pet deaths." And there was a sidebar: "Golden retriever Beebee had beaten cancer."

He read the first paragraphs:

> Beatrice, an 11-year-old golden retriever, survived being hit by a car as a puppy. Just last year, she also beat cancer, which went into remission during an expensive course of chemotherapy.
>
> But early Monday, the owners of the dog they called "Beebee" returned from an evening out to dinner to find their Mill Run Estates home ransacked by burglars – and Beatrice dead on the kitchen floor, apparently poisoned. It was the first of two apparently connected burglary/pet executions...

Jeff pulled up the main story:

> The heads of the two families whose Mill Run homes were burglarized early this week are both major players in a controversial plan to turn a Rocky Falls mobile home park into an upscale subdivision on Drying Barn Road.
>
> Mickey Reuss, the subdivision developer, lives at 105

Mill Run Way. Dean Hegwood, owner of the framing subcontractor Reuss has hired to work on his homes, lives at 111
Mill Run Way.

The Hegwood family's cat, Porcupine, was discovered
dead Tuesday after a burglary. The Reuss' golden retriever
Beatrice, was found dead after a burglary at the Reuss home
the day before (see sidebar).

Sources close to the investigation refused to comment
on the possible connection.

Jeff cursed and threw his wireless computer mouse against
the window, and it bounced into the foot well of his desk. He
snatched up his phone and called her desk number, which he'd
written on the yellow legal pad by his phone. She picked up on the
first ring.

"You fucking piece of shit."

"What the hell is your problem?"

"You broke our deal."

"What?"

His hand strangled the phone receiver. He spat the words
through gritted teeth: "I gave you the doggie cancer angle. In exchange, you agreed to *wait* on the trailer park thing!"

"Our *deal* was before the framing contractor, two doors
down from Mickey Reuss' place, turned up with a dead cat of his
own, graffiti of his own, and another solid connection to the same
subdivision project. I didn't end up needing confirmation from
you."

"That doesn't mean it has anything to do with the burglaries!"

"It doesn't matter, and that's not what I wrote. I wrote that
they're both connected to the project and that you and the freaking cops won't say boo about whether it has any bearing or not."

A sour coffee taste backed up into Jeff's mouth. When he
realized she had a point, it only made him more furious. She had
been clever not to mention last night that she was going to print
the trailer park angle, and he hadn't confirmed with her then that
the arrangement was still intact.

"I want that correction."

"You already got it. Page 2 of today's Rocky Falls Progress. 'A story Tuesday gave an incorrect title for J. Davis Swaine of the Cross Baker Allison law firm. He is a legal investigator.' I sucked it up. You don't have to call my damn editor. And I can't *imagine* how you can sit there this morning and act like I've been anything but *extremely* sweet to you."

Jeff sat in silence, angry at himself, he realized.

Caroline spoke first. "Look, I really want you to know that I wasn't trying to screw you." She said it without a trace of irony. "Remember, I gave you the e-mail."

He looked over at the envelope with the charity e-mail. "Look, never mind. I got to go."

He slammed the handset into the cradle.

Sixteen

Morning sunlight sneaked through gaps between the leaves overhead, and Leonard used his trowel to scoop up another trout lily and the dirt that held its roots. He carefully pushed it into a quart-size plastic pot, then added it to the plastic tray behind him – beautiful plants, dark greenish leaves with purplish specks, and a salmon- or yellow-colored bloom during this part of spring. He potted two more lilies, which filled the last slots in the tray. A hundred trays lay scattered in the woods around him, filled with different woodland plants: phlox, trillium, Sweet Betty, purple coneflowers.

Leonard had to laugh at himself. He had never thought that the media would cover his burglaries. Burglaries happened every day, he reasoned, and as far as he knew, they weren't in the paper unless someone got hurt. But his had that certain little touch. It was mostly the pets, he realized. And the messages on the walls.

He was disappointed in his *Progress-Leader* neighborhood newsroom. Those squares had completely misrepresented his work – some type of retaliation for a land development deal? They were trying to turn him into some rival condo-building Republican? He had no idea where they'd gotten that. And the TV reporters were even worse: "Is there a serial killer of pets lose in Rocky Falls?" They'd made him out to be some kind of torturer. The *whole point* was that the pets *hadn't suffered, wouldn't suffer any more.*

They were so wrong, and so far behind. The album had totally moved on. It was to be expected, Leonard figured. Critics never understood great compositions right away. It might take decades for the many of the subtleties to be appreciated.

The TV reporters were hopeless, he figured. But maybe he could give the girl from the newspaper a little assistance. She seemed pretty sharp.

The main point though, was that he had The Soulless Bitch's attention now. The way to a lawyer's heart was through her most lucrative clients, and Leonard felt like he'd heard every detail about the bigshot developer across the McHouse's dinner table, along with how happy his wife was that the divorce was so messy and complicated and producing so many billable hours.

Then, his wife had referred him to the new Mrs. Reuss when she needed a piano tuner, and the woman had told him about the sick dog and what they were spending on her care – and how *everybody* in the neighborhood "took care of their pets," including the neighbors and their cat. When he decided to do the album, it was the first suburban outrage he decided to write a song about: "Rich Pets, Poor Kids," even though it ended up as Track Two.

J. Davis Swaine III. That was another dude Leonard had heard too much about over dinner. The more Leonard thought about it, that was probably who Jacob's father was. One of those nights when Sarah was "working late at the office" something had happened... Leonard had scrutinized J. Davis' photo and bio on the Cross Baker Allison, PA website. Good looking. Fancy prep school. TV news background. Elite college. Pretty much everything Sarah was and Leonard wasn't.

Well. Now, Leonard would get to see whether this smart, young zero's chops were any match for almost 50 years of life experience. J. Davis Swaine Three might at least understand the themes Leonard was working with here.

Leonard gulped some water from a plastic bottle. He decided to work on Christmas ferns for a while. He used his spade to transplant several dozen into gallon pots.

It was uncomfortable to be the one digging up native plants. By right they should just keep growing in these woods, which had been theirs for millennia. But better he preserve them than let a bulldozer plow them under.

Leonard had moved into the century-old, wood-frame house on this 40-acre parcel, which had been a family tobacco and vegetable farm until 10 years before. These 15 acres were densely wooded with birches, maples, tulip poplars and shagbark hickories along a little creek.

The rent was just $400 because the lease was month to month. The county had re-zoned the land for a new subdivision, and as soon as the construction financing was approved, he'd get two weeks' notice to leave. Then the bulldozers would push over the house and carve the land into cul-de-sacs. Not one tree in 50 would survive. None of these understory plants would after their habitat was altered – not without his help.

Leonard had no idea why dudes wanted to turn this kind of beautiful country into Dallas. He stuck the shovel blade into the ground and leaned on the handle to rest. Suburbs.

Cities, he understood. He'd never been happier than right after he'd left the military, 19 years old, and moved into a tiny apartment in pre-yuppie Greenwich Village. There was something efficient and vibrant about all those people and buildings packed so closely together, where you could jump onto the subway and get wherever you wanted to go, where there were enough people in one area to really support the arts. He especially loved New York, where he and America's classical music – his music – jazz, had gone to grow up.

Leonard was tired. And he had to work again tonight. He left the shovel sticking in the ground and went inside to shower and get some sleep.

His score was sitting here on the kitchen table, open to the page for tonight's track. He had it all memorized, but he had a weakness for enjoying his own art on the printed page. The top of the sheet of music said, "The Natives are Priceless," and under that, in small capitals, "L. Noblac ASCAP Bassburbanbourbonturban Music Group. All rights reserved."

Leonard sang the opening bass riff, his fretting hand's fingers moving subconsciously as his vocal chords hummed the notes and he read the italicized words underneath. But these weren't lyrics. They were the plan – the meticulously composed dance movements, so to speak, that went along with this track.

Seventeen

Jeff called Cooperton. "I guess you saw the press is onto the connection between our pet burglaries. What'd you find out about that minivan license plate?"

"Hell, I figured you'z callin' about the traffic sabotage thing."

"'Traffic sabotage?'" Jeff heard a swish and pictured Cooperton contributing dark spit to a foam coffee cup. "The snarl on Rocky Falls Boulevard?"

Instead of answering, Cooperton put the receiver down on his desk hard enough to hurt Jeff's ear. Computer keys clicked. Soon, a new e-mail dinged into Jeff's inbox. Cooperton picked up the phone again. "Take a look."

"So y'all think the traffic tie-ups are deliberate?"

"Yep. Somebody stole a semi and a dump truck, dumped them at major intersections and shot holes in the gas tanks and into every one of the tires. Hard to do that by accident. Big damn mess."

"Graffiti?"

"Nuh-uh."

"But it could be our guys again, too?"

"Hell, buddy, I don't know." It took Cooperton about three minutes to explain the basics, say that the Sheriff's Office had no suspects and report that the roads wouldn't be cleared until mid-afternoon. They were driving a crane to the site to clear the flatbed.

Jeff shook his head in amazement. "Thanks, buddy."

"Anyway, the van tag is kind of interesting," Cooperton said. "Lady said she wasn't in our neighborhood the night the dog died. Sent an officer to see her, and he saw the tag number on her van was totally different from the one you gave me. Somebody had switched her license plate for another one."

"So where's her plate?"

"Ran that plate and called the owner and found out her van's being repaired at a body shop right down the street from the dead pet cases. Sure enough, it has the other license plate on it."

"Maybe somebody who works at the body shop?"

"What I was thinkin', too. Except they said the van wasn't there the day the lady said she dropped it off overnight. It showed up a day after that. I assigned my two best detectives, but that ain't sayin' much. They ain't gotten much goin' so far, and we're covered up with all this other shit."

Jeff felt like the investigation was gaining momentum. Unfortunately, the photo of the van was useless now, since the burglar wasn't using that vehicle any more. "Any results from the pet necropsies?"

Cooperton told him that the lab work on Beatrice showed she had been killed with an overdose of sodium phenobarbital, a drug used as a veterinary anesthetic and anti-seizure drug – and in larger doses, to euthanize animals.

The phenobarb screen had been run on Beebee only after other tests for the cause of death came up negative. Now that the phenobarb hit had come back, the same test was being done on tissue from Porcupine.

Jeff hung up intrigued. He did some quick Internet research and found that phenobarbital overdose was considered one of the most humane ways to put an animal down. So killing the pets wasn't an act of sadism. Maybe it was simply a way for the burglar to keep them from attacking him or making noise. That made sense for the dog, but how much resistance would a house cat offer? Killing Porcupine seemed gratuitous, unless killing the animal was the whole point. But if so, why steal anything?

When he dug through his inbox, there was the e-mail from the Triangle Children's Medical Fund again. He put in a call to the Peter Wallace who had sent it, pulling the e-mail Caroline had given him from its manila envelope before Wallace picked up.

"Appreciated the quick e-mail," Jeff told him.

"Least we could do. And let me tell you thank you again. How may I help you?"

"It looks like I don't have a record of which account the donation came from," Jeff said, choosing his words carefully. "Could you double-check that for me? Clearly, I didn't handle it personally."

Wallace put him on hold for a moment and came back. "The money came in a series of convenience store money orders in various denominations. The amount I listed in the e-mail was the total. I assumed you had a good reason to do it that way."

"Strange. I didn't give instructions for money orders to be sent. I'll have to check with folks in the office about that. How did they arrive?"

"Well, they were in an envelope with a typed page with your name, telephone number and e-mail address, with your instruction that the donation help inner city children with diabetes. The envelope had been slid through our mail slot when we arrived at work yesterday morning."

Children with diabetes. "Fine, fine," Jeff said, and he could tell the guy was nervous he'd ask for the money to be returned. "Well, thanks again for your assistance."

"My pleasure. I don't believe I've met you, so I'd love to host a tour of our facility at your convenience. Also, we'd love to have another attorney on our board of directors."

"I'm not an attorney. I just work for a law firm," Jeff said.

"Oh, I'm sorry. I saw the 'esquire' under your signature..."

Jeff raised an eyebrow. "Got to run." He called the Raleigh City Clinic and asked for the development director. She was a friendly, soft-spoken woman.

"I'm calling for Caroline Kramden to verify that you received her donation. A stack of money orders in an envelope?"

"Oh, yes, sir. A generous donation. The largest we've received in some time."

"And you are clear on how to use the funds?"

"To help children with cancer. Yes, sir. We have a great need in that area."

"Good. I wanted to make sure the note was included."

"Yes, of course. In fact, I sent Ms. Kramden an e-mail. Has she not received it?"

"Ms. Kramden is a busy woman," Jeff said. "Thanks for your help."

The burglars had killed the animals, stolen merchandise they could sell to raise the approximate amount spent on their medical care, then donated the proceeds to two charities to help children with the same ailments, Jeff guessed. And they'd given the donations in the names of two people they'd gotten from Caroline's story about the dog, one of whom was erroneously listed as an attorney.

* * *

So one thing Caroline knew she had to figure out was what in the world was the Knox Family Trust, and who were the real people behind it? That was the legal entity that owned the trailer park that Mickey Reuss was turning into a subdivision. State records listed a Raleigh attorney as the registered agent for official mailings, but that guy had refused to put her in touch with or identify any of the trustees.

Neither her editor nor the newspaper archives seemed to know about any well-to-do family around Raleigh with that surname. It wasn't some old tract of farmland that had stayed in the family, either. The Knox Family Trust had bought the trailer park just five years ago. And the previous owner had died, so she couldn't ask him.

Odd – and frustrating. Her reporter's intuition said that once she found a member of the Knox family, she might learn more about who would seek revenge on the builder. It was in the trust's interest to expose that person, get them in jail and move the transaction along – the sale of the land hadn't yet closed, public records showed.

Caroline noticed a new e-mail in her inbox just as she was about to stand up from her desk for the day. She tucked her hair behind her ear and clicked the subject line.

"Pretty good story about the dog today," the message began. "That's the good news. But I bet there was more to it than what you wrote. And I'm not sure you're on the right track about the real estate development angle. If you want my opinion, there's an artist at work in Rocky Falls and he is using these crimes and these pets for making a statement. I am a artist myself and I may be able to help you get ensight on what is occuring."

Caroline flinched at the syntax and misspellings but kept reading.

"I think you are a very smart and bright reporter, and I would be happy to give you an interview. I am looking forward to reading what you write in the paper tomorrow. Write me back at this address. -- Leonard."

The guy's e-mail address was bassburbanbourbonturban@aol.com. Another Raleigh good 'ol boy who liked to fish and drink whiskey and probably sculpt bears out of tree trunks – but who couldn't string a sentence – thought he could offer insight on the crime of the decade. She deleted the message, powered down the computer, and waved at her editor as she headed for the door.

Eighteen

Leonard Noblac drove a Ryder panel truck – his vehicle of the day – to his new job at DIY Warehouse. It was a regional chain store that competed with Lowe's and Home Depot. He parked the truck near Lawn & Garden and went inside.

He punched his code into the electronic time clock. He was early. The digital readout said, "21:55, ARRIVE E. GRANT." He walked past the customers who hadn't heeded announcements that the store was closing.

In Receiving, his new supervisor, Robert, greeted him. "Hey Eddie."

Leonard had been hired a week before to drive a lift truck part time under the name of Eddie Grant, after the dumbass pop single "Electric Avenue" that had been popular when he was first trying to make serious jazz music in NYC. He had a fake Social Security card in that name that he'd bought for $100 from a guy who sold them mostly to Mexican illegals.

"Hi Robert. What we got tonight?" Robert was king of the zeros. Sold stuff to yuppies and yupettes for their McHouses for 11 bucks an hour.

"Load of dehumidifiers need to go into overhead storage.

They're on that trailer right there." He pointed through the open loading bay. Overhead storage meant the tiers of the racks above customers' reach.

"Bunch of cases of framing nails need to go to Aisle Three for the stockers, and in Appliances, I need you to take down these items and bring them back here to Customer Pickup." He handed Leonard a list. "Check back with me when you've got all that done."

"Will do, chief." Leonard turned his DIY Warehouse ball cap backward so he'd be able to see up the tall racks he'd be moving merchandise onto and off of. He hopped onto the forklift and started it up.

He dragged ass through the tasks, taking just one more small assignment from Robert before his shift ended at 2 a.m. Then he punched out on the time clock and sneaked back to Kitchens. When he was sure no one was looking, he opened a door on a display set of maple cabinets, climbed inside and shut the door behind him. The melody to Track Four played inside his head for the next hour as he waited, the smell of his spearmint chewing gum eventually filling the small space.

He pushed the door open a crack when he figured everyone should be gone. He was just in time to see the blue-tinged lights flip off in succession. After another 15 minutes, he stood. He sat on a cool granite countertop and waited 20 more minutes. It was quiet.

He pulled out the list of things he needed and began gathering them. He carried them to an empty shipping pallet he'd placed near the front cash registers. Finally, the stage was set. He went to Receiving and cranked up his forklift again, rolled forward –

"Eddie!"

Leonard jerked the lift to a stop. Robert was still here! Leaning out of the little office in Receiving holding a clipboard; must have stayed late to do some paperwork –

"What are you still doing here, Eddie?"

This wasn't in the plan. Leonard's mouth filled with sourness, the whole project now in jeopardy. Now Robert was walking straight toward him.

Leonard went with his impulse – he gunned the throttle and

pushed the lever to raise the big metal fork, and the front edge of the blade, sharp from scraping against the concrete floor, easily penetrated Robert's abdomen.

Robert's eyebrows arched over frightened eyes. A line of drool dropped from his mouth when the momentum doubled his torso over. Leonard veered left and aimed for a pallet stacked with cardboard boxes. The fork punched the rest of the way through Robert and into a carton like a thumbtack pinning a note to the bulletin board.

Leonard stopped the truck and just stared. The cat was straightening himself up, gripping with both hands the steel shaft that impaled him. The dude was fully conscious. And barely bleeding.

"Eddie ..." Robert muttered.

Leonard put the lift truck into reverse. It started to beep – a perfect C sharp, he was amazed to realize. A feeling of calm energy flowed into his fingertips and toenails. He slowly backed 30 feet, looking behind him instead of at the man he held skewered. The tops of Robert's shoes scraped disagreeably against the concrete floor. Leonard brought the lift to a gentle stop, and raised the fork another foot.

He put the lift into forward gear, accelerated, slammed on the brakes. Robert slid off the fork and thumped onto the floor. Without the pressure of the metal inside the gaping wound, Robert's intestines and blood gushed onto the concrete around him.

Leonard sat and watched him die. He threw up a little inside his mouth. Look what he had done! He felt like a little boy, waiting for his mother to come and scold him for being so stupid, for making a mess, to call him a little idiot, her moron child, and to beat him with the sole of her shoe.

But Soulless Bitch No. 1 wasn't really part of his life any more. And suddenly he realized he'd made a breakthrough.

For the first time in his life, he had done what she, what TSB Two – what everyone – had always told him he couldn't do, was no good at:

He had improvised.

Now inspiration hit him again.

He used the fork to scoop up the body. It threatened to fall off, so he set it down on an empty pallet and lifted that.

He putt-putted out to Lawn & Garden, crashing through the double swinging doors. Once he was in the fenced outside area, he stopped and set the pallet with the body at the end of the long tables filled with plants for sale, the same stupid petunias and pansies and crapola you could find at any DIY Warehouse in four freakin' states.

This was going to turn out even better than what he had composed! Now he understood what other musicians had been trying to explain for so long. A brilliant written score could be your jumping-off point for something even better... He not only saw what they meant, but for the first time he was able to make – to let – his mind do it.

He got off the lift for a second, searched through Robert's pockets, keeping a few things that inspired him.

Then he picked up another empty pallet with the red half of the fork, so that the rough wood protruded to the side of the lift. He raised the fork to the level of the display tables, and he used the empty pallet to shove whole rows of plants off the ends and onto the ground. The lift beeped each time he backed to make another run; he liked that. He would have to work some C-sharps into his score for a little dissonance... He used the lift and the empty pallet the best he could as a bulldozer to mound the spilled soil and pots and managed a 5-foot pile over Robert. Pretty friggin' poetic. He got down from the lift and set a single, orange gerbera daisy upright on the pile. He had to laugh.

Now he dropped the empty pallet and drove the forklift to the registers, where he picked up his pallet of merchandise, which he trucked back to Receiving. He rolled open a dock door and jumped to the ground. He pulled his Ryder around and backed it until it banged into the rubber bumpers.

Leonard used the forklift to unload the 10 pallets of plants he had brought from the woods. He trucked these out to Lawn & Garden, where it took him nearly three hours to display them on the tables in neat rows. He put out the signs he had printed on his computer. They told what each kind was, what growing conditions it liked and how much it should sell for.

Finally, he hung up his banner: "Plant Native Species in Your Yard." He smiled.

He loaded his pallet of merchandise onto the Ryder. Then he found some bags of the granules that Robert had trained him to use to soak up spills. He dumped them onto the bloody puddle. After they absorbed the liquid, he swept them up and poured them into a trash bin. He closed the loading bay door, started up the panel truck and drove toward home. He was exhausted.

But improvising for the first time was unquestionably the great victory of this album. He realized later that he hadn't even thought about taking a shot of sanitizer all night. He understood now why everybody made such a big deal out of it, why they called it the essence of jazz. It was exhilarating.

Nineteen

Caroline arrived at the Progress-Leader bureau just after dawn to find a new e-mail from bassburbanbourbonturban: "Don't you think that thing on Rocky Falls Boulevard had something to do with the previous day's story about the dog and cat? Write me back."

"No," Caroline said out loud. At the risk of beginning a correspondence with the guy, she hit the reply button and typed: "Thanks for your thoughts on my stories. If you have some evidence to show that a criminal fixated on killing pets would also stage a traffic jam, I'd like to see it. Why would any one person do all of that? Best, C. Kramden."

Five minutes later, Caroline got two new e-mails. One was a news alert from the Sheriff's Office about a homicide at DIY Warehouse. The other was a note from Bassburbanbourbonturban with the subject line, "Good question." The body of the message was blank.

* * *

As soon as Leonard hit the send button on his computer, he

was certain he shouldn't have sent the reporter the e-mails.

The weight of a realization tightened his chest: He was a violent felon. A murderer.

The police would find him, and they would throw him into jail or prison with a bunch of homosexuals and after years and years of them raping him, the court would give him the death penalty.

He gulped down two mouthfuls of sanitizer and sat to think. It took longer than usual for the fuzziness to cleanse his mind.

But when the stuff worked, it worked. In one beautiful instant, Leonard gained an entirely new inspiration for the album. It would just have to be renamed – to *Everything Comes Due at Once.*

He did a quick Internet search for "violent felonies" and found a neat table. Of course, murder was at the top of the list. But he hadn't realized that burglary met that standard. A First Degree Felony. He'd already done two. This must have been where the album was leading all along…

He looked at the others:

Aggravated assault.

Kidnapping.

Arson.

Stalking.

Rape.

Robbery.

Criminal Use of a Firearm.

Leonard felt a sudden clarity. He decided to rename the album again: *In the First Degree.*

Suddenly, a cacophony of new melodies filled his mind, yet he heard each one in individual clarity playing alongside the others. He pulled out fresh sheets of composing paper and started setting down the notes, and in the exhilaration of the task, he didn't worry any more about being arrested.

* * *

Sarah Rosen reached toward the rear of the top shelf of her maple pantry and felt for the box of cherry Pop Tarts she knew was back there – exactly the junk breakfast she was craving this morning. Her fingers found a flat, triangular shape, and she gave an exasperated grrrr.

How the hell had a guitar pick wound up way back here? She slid the little piece of plastic toward her. She had been finding dozens of these since the separation: orange Dunlop picks. Medium stiffness, a characteristic that fit her ex-husband perfectly.

After everything, he had never gotten rid of the guitars, and she'd realized that to get rid of them, she had to get rid of Leonard, too. The man bought guitar picks by the gross. After he'd given up playing the bass, he played the same guitar scales and three songs seemingly every night of their last months of marriage, just over and over and over.

He always had two or three guitar picks mixed in with his pocket change, and he had kept two different electric guitars and an acoustic on stands in various corners of their house, where people would see them when they came over.

She grabbed the steppy stool from between the refrigerator and the wall to get a better angle on the Pop Tarts.

The wall phone rang when she put her foot on the first step, so she sighed again and climbed down to answer it.

It was Leonard. But he sounded like he was in a better mood than she'd heard since the very beginning of their relationship.

"I'm calling because I want to settle the division of property without a fight," he told her.

"You do?"

"Yes. Just cut me a check for $50,000 and, ah, take the rest. No alimony. You take primary custody of Jacob. Then we go our separate ways."

This offer was ridiculously favorable to Sarah. Their combined net worth was close to a million dollars, not even counting her stake in the firm, which was worth at least that much again. She'd earned most of that wealth, not him, but she'd done it during the more than 12 years they had been married. She was pretty sure Leonard didn't even know how much there was, since she managed their investments, but any decent divorce attorney would find every asset, total them up for Leonard and tell him the courts would be inclined to split it more or less down the middle. She'd advise the same if he were her client. She also guessed the court would make her pay her ex-husband alimony to help him continue the upper-middle-class lifestyle to which he'd become accustomed.

She felt a sudden, odd surge of compassion for the man and said, "That doesn't seem fair to you, Lennie," before her lawyer's instincts could stop her. She fingered the guitar pick in her palm.

"It doesn't matter," he beamed. "I don't care about money. I just don't want us to fight any more."

Sarah was concerned about him. This was the first time she'd heard form him in more than a week. She was fed up with being married to him, but she had been nervous about his state of mind ever since they'd separated. He had seemed abjectly depressed every other time they'd talked. Now he seemed over the freaking moon.

"Let's sign everything tonight," he said. "Can you meet me at Rocky Falls Crossroads at 8? Near the food court? Bring the papers."

"They really need to be notarized."

"Just have the girl in your office do it tomorrow. Or bring your camera and videotape me signing it or whatever, so you can prove it's legit."

Sarah sensed she shouldn't jeopardize this by insisting on anything right now, so she just said, "Okay." She'd figure it out later. She paused, then said it: "Lennie, are you okay?"

"I'm great," he said. "I've been composing. The pieces I've been working on? I'm playing them tonight at the mall. You could show up at 5:30 p.m. and hear it. If you want to. I'll be done around 7."

It was a risky thing for him to ask of her. His insistence that he would make it as a jazz musician had been the central, recurring fight in their marriage. Ready to raise kids, she'd argued for them to move from Manhattan to Raleigh so she could accept the job managing this firm. He'd said that amounted to giving up his dream, that leaving New York meant leaving the best opportunities in jazz. As if the best opportunities in law lay in North Carolina ...

The truth was he'd been playing smaller and smaller clubs

every year, and finally, just background-music gigs for tourists. Gigs like this mall thing, which couldn't be paying him a cent. Countless record executives and band leaders had told Leonard he was a technically skilled player but lacked the spontaneous creativity to make it as a jazzman. And he was getting too old to break in, anyway. He should become a studio musician or something, they said. But Leonard had always refused. He wanted to be famous.

"Come on," he said, sounding friendlier and less bitter through the phone than she'd heard in a long time. "Nobody will know you're my wife."

As soon as he'd moved out, he'd bought his bass back, she knew. And now he was asking her to come hear him play. That was what he wanted more than his half of two million bucks.

"I won't point you out from the stage or anything," he said now. "Just sit through one last set, and then I'll sign my life away."

The whole thing broke Sarah's heart, but she knew a fair deal when she heard one.

Twenty

Today, Jeff decided, he would track down the phenobarbital angle, something he bet Cooperton's boys hadn't been sharp enough to try. He looked around the office for a reasonably up-to-date Yellow Pages. He finally found one less than a year old. He opened it to the "Veterinarians" section and made a quick count. There were more than 40 businesses listed, including one veterinary dermatologist. If you had an itchy dog, you probably wanted to get that taken care of, Jeff reasoned. He decided to start with the vets in Raleigh or Rocky Falls and work his way down the list.

The first place was a veterinarian inside a national pet supply chain store. Jeff identified himself and asked for the vet listed in the display ad. The clerk put him right through. She sounded like a nice person, the playful, joyful sort you'd want to care for your dog or cat. He introduced himself as an investigator and asked if any sodium phenobarbital was missing, and a cabinet squeaked open as she checked. She said she didn't think there was. The office kept just one vial on hand; it was still here. They didn't put down too many animals. Because she was so nice, Jeff interviewed her a little about how the drug was used, and she seemed happy to help when he explained why he was asking.

"Has the Wake County Sheriff's Office already called to ask you about any of this?"

"Nope. Haven't heard from any police officers."

"Thanks." Jeff put a black dash next to that entry in the phone book. He dialed the next number. He had to leave a message for the vet. Same at the next place. He worked his way down the listings to a big private practice on Rocky Falls Boulevard with several vets, called PetHealthPlex. The receptionist put him on hold, saying she would have to figure out the right person for him to speak with.

Before the receptionist came back on, Jeff's mobile rang. Cooperton. Jeff hung up on PetHealthPlex and answered the call.

"Buddy, you might want to show up to the big-ass hardware store out here at Falls Commons."

"What you got?"

"Suspicious death. Impaling by forklift."

Jeff had heard of death by drowning, lightning strike, electrocution, hanging, beheading and what coroners called "fall from height," but never an impaling. "A person?"

"Yeah, for a change. Deceased was supervisor of all the guys that drive forklifts at the store."

"I'm there." Jeff assembled his briefcase and told Sarah where he was going. "Cooperton seems to think it might tie in." She looked at him with amazement.

Cooperton saw Jeff arrive at DIY Warehouse and eased up to brief him: The Lawn & Garden staff had found the department's normal stock of plants in piles on the ground, with different plants and price signs on display in their place. A banner that said, "Plant native species in your yard," lettered in black marker, was what led Cooperton to believe the crime was related to the residential burglaries. "I can't take you back there, but trust me, the writing's the same."

When the DIY staff had found the disruption in the garden department, they had closed it to customers and spent two hours cleaning up while managers debated calling the police. It looked like an outlandish employee prank of some kind, and they were leaning toward handling it in-house. Then a 19-year-old clerk named Eileen got to the bottom of her pile and found the body of

Robert W. Claypool. He was 47. His wife was being notified.

"Where was he impaled?"

"In the gut. Employees found pieces of his intestines in the main aisle of the store by the paint department first thing this morning. They didn't know what they were and didn't connect them to the Lawn & Garden thing until – shit, until a hell of a long time after they should've. We had to fish them out of the trash. There are red circles the size of a nickel every five feet from the back to the front of the store."

"You think an employee did it?"

Cooperton nodded vigorously, smiled and said, "No comment."

"Who's your suspect?"

"Can't tell you that, either." Cooperton dipped his clipboard, and Jeff could read the tab of a personnel file underneath it: "Grant, Eddie."

"New guy started part-time a couple weeks ago," Cooperton said. "Only forklift driver working last night. Bullshit address. Bullshit social."

"Bullshit name," Jeff said. "Remember that '80s song Electric Avenue? That was Eddy-with-a-Y Grant."

"Interestin'. I listen to country... Anyhow, these jackasses they send me for detectives up here ain't gonna be able to find out shit. If you can figure out who it is, and it leads to an arrest, I'll take you along to pick him up. Hell, I'll let you question the suspect or whip 'im with a belt and snap pictures if you want, whatever it takes to make your client happy."

Jeff hoped the whipping part was Southern cop bravado. He raised his eyebrows expectantly. Cooperton slipped him a copy of the employment application "Eddie" had filled out. Jeff tucked the sheet underneath the blank pages of his legal pad so it would look to an observer as if he were reading his own notes. To Jeff's surprise, Eddie's Rocky Falls address was not on any avenue that sounded even vaguely electrical. A number on some local street called Upsal. He didn't recognize it, so he assumed it was made up. Maybe something spelled backward? Laspu? Didn't make sense.

"Got his photo?"

Cooperton's jowls quivered as he shook his head no, then changed mid-movement to make a half nod. "Kind of. There's some grainy, longshot stuff from the security cameras last night. He knew where they were placed, and he kept a cap pulled down low whenever he was around one. Was supposed to have a close-up taken for his permanent ID badge, but never did it, apparently."

"What about older security-camera footage?"

"Possible. But they only save a week's worth, then they tape over them unless there's been some kind of incident. He only worked one other night this week. And it's the kind of system where it records four cameras on one divided screen, so the picture's shitty."

Jeff let the notepad pages fall to conceal his copy of the employment application as an underling approached Cooperton.

This time, the TV crews didn't show up until 15 after noon, too late to get onto the air before the 5 p.m. newscast. They'd have to type up a blurb for their websites and then go live at 6. The body had already been hauled to the morgue, and they didn't have a clear view to the end of the plant display table where Claypool had been found. The only decent video for them to shoot was the sign on the front door that read, "Closed due to emergency. Shop DIY Warehouse for everything you need to make your house a home."

* * *

"Come on, Jimmy." Caroline crossed her arms under her boobs and pouted at Detective Norton. She had guessed he was one of the ones inside the DIY Warehouse all afternoon investigating, so she'd been waiting out here, figuring he'd duck out sooner or later for a smoke break. "You're my buddy. Make a girl happy. Just give me a 10-second peek. Just for background."

He leaned against the loading dock bumper, looking more uncomfortable the longer she held his eyes. He wanted to make her happy, she knew, and he liked standing here with her. He was just afraid of getting into trouble. She knew she almost had him.

When the pink color drained from his face, she let her lips slide into a smile. "I promise I won't put anything in the paper that could lead back to you. You'll be my secret source."

The detective checked around and saw no one. He held his clipboard face up at a level even with his crotch. "Ten seconds."

Caroline scanned the form, labeled as an employment application, and memorized Eddie Grant's name and address. Norton pulled the clipboard out of her view a little before ten seconds was up, but she'd gotten it all. He said, "White male, shorter than average height. Beard. But don't you put any of that into the paper unless the lieutenant gives it to you."

Caroline met his eyes and mouthed, "Thank you," brushing her tongue against the underside of her front teeth. As she walked around the outside of the store, Norton told someone, "She'll have to get the lieutenant to brief her."

When she turned the corner, she leaned against the wall to write it all down in her notepad.

Twenty-one

No matter what angle Jeff worked, he couldn't find any connection between poor Robert Claypool and Mickey Reuss. Claypool lived in Durham County and commuted to the store job in Raleigh. Reuss had never heard of him, didn't care a thing about the guy. Reuss's crews never even bought building supplies from DIY Warehouse.

Back downtown in his office, Jeff got Robert Claypool's wife on the phone for a wrenching interview. Her husband had been saying he didn't think his employees liked him. He hadn't been happy since being promoted to supervisor. He really just wanted to be a front-line, regular workin' boy, not the boss man. She felt guilty because she'd told her husband he was getting too old for physical work and that they needed the extra money from his manager's job.

"I've talked to a lot of people in your situation," Jeff told her. "And let me tell you, Mrs. Claypool, you ought to stop thinking like that and try to be nice to yourself. No matter what happened, you'd be able to find some way to blame it on yourself if you were determined to. You have to keep yourself from doing that."

The idea that these diverse crimes might be connected fascinated Jeff. His gut told him they were. As the sun set outside his office window, he went into a fugue-like state, writing everything he knew on 3x5 cards, taping them to the giant panes of one wall of windows and drawing lines among them on the glass in three different colors of dry-erase marker, trying to find the connections, to identify some pattern.

None of his online databases had come back with anything usable on Eddie Grant; the name was so common there were a few hundred of them around the country, though none in the Triangle. It was a fake name anyhow.

He was coming up with nothing.

On the second, empty window, he transcribed in black marker each piece of the burglar's graffiti – and the alcohol smell of the marker reminded him of how the paint itself had smelled. He couldn't find any coherent message.

Twenty-two

Leonard picked up a pair of jeans from the front table in Abercrombie & Fitch. They looked like they were about to fall apart – holes in the knees, frayed cuffs, even brown stains on the ass. $159. They were the kind of thing you'd buy only if you had grown up out here in the burbs with brand new, perfect clothes all your life. You'd pay that for a pair that had been through some fake danger and friction and life experience to make it seem like you had, too. He looked at the tag and wondered what the $1 a day garment worker in Macau thought about being paid to ruin a pair of jeans he really needed so that they would fall apart in six months for someone who was so rich they were just looking for new stupid shit to spend their money on.

All these mall stores acted as if they could sell you a personality, an identity – or as they put it, "a lifestyle." The most ironic ones catered not to the hottest kid in school like Abercrombie did, but to the outcast nonconformist skater kid. Buy into our edgy corporate brand, and you'll be making a statement.

Leonard tossed the jeans onto the floor and stepped out into the mall concourse. There was almost no one standing in front of

Center Court Stage. But Leonard walked 50 feet across the granite tile, mounted the stage and nodded at his bandmates as he launched into the bass lead-in for Track One.

He was debuting his masterwork at 5:30 p.m. on a weekday night at a crass shopping mall. It was like some legendary Charlie Parker gig at a rent party Harlem in the '40s. Few would have the experience of being there, but everyone would wish they had, imagine they had – say they had. He hoped someone would be smart enough to save the vinyl banner attached to the stage that read, "Rocky Falls Crossroads Presents: New York Jazz Composer and Artist Leonard Noblac."

As the track reached full swing, two wandering couples stopped to listen, and by the end of the piece, a few dozen people were standing there clapping. Leonard pretended he didn't see them. The band knew to head straight into Track Two after eight beats of pregnant silence. The crowd was expanding. When Leonard opened his eyes after a long solo, he nearly had a stroke when he saw how many people were listening.

He was grinning and sweating by the end of the fourth track, exhilarated by the attention, by the power of his music to STOP PEOPLE COLD, the now huge audience completely hooked, people even looking down into the atrium from behind the chrome-topped glass railing around the mall's second level. Bennie the drummer, whispered, "Hey man, flog the CD."

When the cut ended, Leonard bowed to applause and walked to the microphone.

"Thank you very much, folks." His voice sounded embarrassingly squeaky over the PA. People looked as if they might drift away, like they thought this was a set break. Well, it wasn't. "I'd like to take ten seconds before we start the next piece to let you know that if you like what you're hearing tonight, our CDs are on sale right here at the corner of the stage." He pointed to Bennie's girlfriend, who held up a cardboard box of their old albums and waved. "They're $10, and based on the fantastic response you're giving us tonight, it seems like they may become a collector's item."

He gave a winning smile, and Bennie's girlfriend sold three CDs on the spot as a line formed leading toward her.

"Two, three, four!" Leonard shouted, and he and the drummer opened the final track.

"I don't see you out there, honey," Leonard said into the mic before stepping into the background, "but wherever you are, this one's for you."

* * *

Yet the second set, after the break, was totally different. Leonard seethed about two things: His bitch of an ex-wife wasn't here even though she'd promised. And now the band wasn't as in the groove; most of the people were just walking by the stage like there wasn't even a band up here; just a dozen people sat on benches actually listening.

When he looked at his watch and realized it was almost 7, Sarah finally walked up with a thick file folder filled with papers. She gave a mild smile, but Leonard was pissed. He ended the song they were playing with a flourish, and Sarah started clapping, inducing a couple of mall customers to join in.

But he'd already set the bass down on its side and charged down the two steps toward her. "Where the hell have you been? What makes you think I'm going to sign now? You didn't come when you said you would!"

She looked at him like she was surprised, saying something about how her paralegal had been late getting the paperwork all set and printing it out, and then how there had been traffic on Rocky Falls Boulevard and she was sorry. She had intended to be there.

"Fuck your damn excuses," Leonard told her. "Forget it. You had your chance. I asked you for something really easy. And you didn't do it."

* * *

Now, in the car, Leonard was listening closely to the new melodies in his head, realizing that some of them were the same ones he had already composed for the burglary album – well, almost the same. A few notes were different. A new musical bridge between sections had appeared, that kind of thing.

At any rate, the plan for tonight's track was almost the same; he'd just play it with a little more verve. He hadn't thought about it before, but this performance always had required Aggravated Assault.

So Leonard went to his job at a takeout driver as planned. His first run was to drive an order of fried chicken and potato salad to a '50s ranch house, and that wasn't right for this track at all.

But he would perform the first half of "Emptiness and Fullness/Aggravated Assault" at the first obscenely large house that ordered a gourmet meal.

* * *

Jeff didn't leave work until 7:30. The images of his evidence windows stayed inside his head as he stopped on the way home for a take-out plate of Eastern North Carolina pulled pork barbecue soaked in a sauce of apple cider vinegar, crushed red pepper and powdered mustard.

He got back to the loft and realized the moving company hadn't ever returned his call about bringing his stuff from storage. Not that he had really had time to deal with it, but one night on the air mattress had been enough. There was a note from the cable company, though, that his service had been activated.

So he unboxed the new TV that waited in a corner and connected the coaxial cable that his electrician had installed to the back. He tracked down The Colbert Report on Comedy Central, and he laughed his ass off. That, the savory barbecue, two beers and letting a call from Ashlyn go to voicemail made him sleep more soundly than he had in at least a week.

* * *

The honest truth was, Sarah certainly hadn't wanted to sit in an audience and hear her husband play jazz again – at a mall. She was afraid she'd embarrass herself by weeping through the entire set, mourning over her broken marriage as she remembered the night she'd fallen for Leonard as a young woman at the Viceroy Hotel. That she would mourn the loss of her ability to form a reckless crush like that ever again. She would mourn raising a son mostly by herself for the next 18 years – she understood how severely stacked against her the odds of remarrying were. Men her age would marry a 28-year-old with no kid. Sarah didn't want to cry like that in public, or pour out all that emotion in front of Leonard.

But she damn sure had tried to get to the show on time, anyway. And not just because he'd agreed to sign the settlement. Because she had once loved the man and wanted to do it for him.

Naturally, Leonard wasn't empathetic enough to understand that she legitimately couldn't get it together to be there on time. All he registered was that Sarah hadn't showed up, didn't believe in his music, didn't care about what was important to him.

She sniffed, cleared her throat and called Leonard's mobile phone number. She got his voice mail greeting. She left a message in a gentle voice explaining all of it the best she could. "I am so sorry. I want you to know I really tried to make it." She told him that if he still wanted to settle, he could come to the small law office of a friend of hers to sign the papers. It was near his house. "Neutral ground," she called it.

"Leonard, I'm sorry not to be there tonight like you wanted." Then she told the computer recording her words what she'd said to Leonard 500 times or more as he'd left her alone for an evening to go play some smoke-filled bar: "Have a great show."

She replaced the receiver in its cradle, turned out her office lights and locked the door.

Twenty-three

Walter Ellis flipped through the channels looking for something besides CNN. You didn't want to see that depressing stuff on a high-definition, 42-inch screen.

In the kitchen, Janet was clinking around with plates and silverware, which in his mind defeated the whole point of ordering Chef-2-U. Sure, you didn't have to cook, but there were still dishes to clean up. The containers the meals came in were perfectly fine. Whatever; when you'd been married as long as he had, you didn't start fights over piddly stuff. You just let it grate on you.

He found a landscaping show on one of the cable channels. They were building a pretty neat flagstone terrace in a steep back yard like his. They were showing how the workers chipped and set the stones, but he didn't care. If he put one in his yard, he'd get a crew of Mexicans just like the folks on TV had.

The doorbell rang, and the show cut to a commercial. Good timing, because when they came back from the break, the host was just going to reveal whether the homeowners liked the finished project or not. The odds were on "Oh my God; thank you so much! We *love* it." He could skip that and eat.

He felt his back pocket, fished out his wallet and pulled out two twenties as he padded across the Brazilian cherry floor in his blue dress socks. He looked through the window set into the Craftsman-style front door. The delivery guy wore a tweed, snap-brim cap and a salt-and-pepper beard that could use a trim. He was a good bit older than these fellows usually were. Probably a real sad sack to be delivering takeout in his 40s. Walter depressed the brass lever and pulled open the heavy door.

The man mumbled toward the floor: "Janet Ellis; wine-braised sage and thyme turkey breast with cranberry couscous, mixed baby field greens salad with toasted pine nuts and balsamic mustard vinaigrette. Times two."

Walter nodded. "Sounds like us."

The man pulled two plastic-domed dinner plates from a green insulated sleeve. "$29.50."

As a wastewater systems engineer, Walter could easily afford it. But it did bother him to pay for a prefabricated dinner when his wife was home all day and could have cooked it for them. She'd hardly been cooking at all since Katie had left for college.

Walter handed him the twenties and just asked for five bucks as change. The man blushed as if the five-dollar tip were more than he was used to. Walter would've liked to believe the guy was squirreling away money to make himself a better life, but he guessed he'd blow it on science fiction books or something.

The food was delicious as always, and he and Janet each had one glass of pinot noir – their strict weeknight limit. He told Janet about the flagstone patio over dinner. She liked the idea and even suggested that he get the new stainless gas grill he wanted when it was done. As they chatted about their days, a smile cracked into Walter's tight cheeks. Janet was sweet to him, and he was damn lucky to have her, judging from the number of miserable guys his age at work. His problem was that he came home from work in a bad mood every night.

They headed over to the living room sofa ready to relax and watch a movie. He opened the drawer and pulled out the stack of red Netflix envelopes. He decided to go with the one Janet had placed on top.

As Walter put in the DVD, he realized he was feeling powerfully sleepy. He'd felt pepped up before dinner, so he was surprised to be yawning. He kind of welcomed the feeling; he often struggled with insomnia. Must be what they always said about that chemical in turkey...

The movie was *Blood Work*, based on the Michael Connelly book they'd both read and liked several years back. He stretched an arm around Janet's shoulders. One of the neighbors had told Janet it had a different ending than the novel... Janet was yawning, too...

FRIDAY

Walter's lower back was really killing him. He rolled onto his side. The bed felt super hard somehow. He opened his eyes, and the morning sunshine coming in the windows seared his eyeballs.

Why hadn't the alarm gone off sooner? He could hear it beeping now; it hurt his ears. Dang. He was supposed to be up before dawn to make it to work by 8 ... He *never* overslept.

He threw the comforter off. Ho boy, his body ached. It smelled like some kind of solvent in here... Ginger barked her head off, but she sounded far away...

He forced his eyes open again. He felt like he had the morning after his bachelor party 25 years before. He pushed himself upright. The texture was strange on his hands – carpet instead of bedsheet, he realized.

His vision finally cleared. He looked around the master suite and couldn't believe it: He was sitting in the middle of the floor in his briefs and undershirt with his ankles under the bedspread. Besides the spread and the clock, the room was completely empty. Nothing hanging on the walls, no furniture, and there was some kind of crazy black design and writing all over Janet's peach-colored walls, black-painted graffiti that started above Janet's walk-in closet and dressing room: "1BR APT, FULLY FURN," and two painted shapes that looked like vases or something?

His heart throbbed faster. He felt dizzy. This was some sort of screwed-up nightmare!

Walt squeezed his eyes shut and opened them to the same

scene. He turned to his right, and there was Janet, under her half of the spread, on the floor, her head on the pillow and the alarm clock beeping into her left ear. It said 9:30 a.m. He jostled Janet's shoulder to wake her.

He couldn't get her to move.

He threw back the covers. Instead of her usual nightgown, she was naked except for her underpants. Oh, Lord! He put his palm near her mouth because he thought she wasn't breathing; then he turned his hand over and felt the slightest movement of air. Sobs shook Walt, and his tears fell onto Janet's skin as he shook her completely limp body. He had to call an ambulance! He couldn't find the phone that was normally on the bedside table next to the clock.

He leapt up, felt nauseated. He stumbled into a wall and slid down it out of control with a pathetic yelp, until his butt rested on the floor and he was looking up at more paint above where their headboard had been: "U WON'T REALLY MISS IT."

Was he having a stroke or something? He'd never felt this way before; his temples pounded with his heartbeat as if he'd just run a sprint. He made another frantic attempt to stand, then half staggered, half crawled to the bedroom doorway, his vision watery with the tears.

He forced himself to concentrate, crawled through the open first floor to the kitchen counter and used it to pull himself up. He snatched the phone from its hook on the wall.

He punched 9-1-1. "There's been a burglary. My wife won't wake up!"

As he tried to explain, he realized how confused and slurred his words sounded through his blubbering. He felt furious that the old-fashioned looking wall phone had a cord, that he couldn't go back to Janet and stay on the phone at the same time. The lady on the other end of the line was firing questions at him, and he answered each one the best he could.

The door out to the garage stood open slightly, and the cooler air blew against his bare ankles. He hoped no one was still out there. He stretched the cord to its limit, slammed the door and turned the lock and then told the dispatcher he had to go. The lady said not to move Janet; she was sending the Sheriff's Office and the paramedics, but Walt dropped the receiver on the floor and stumbled back into the bedroom and fell down next to Janet. Her pulse was weak and slow underneath his fingertips, and her naked chest rose and fell only faintly. He clasped her moist hand. The possibility of losing her flashed across his mind.

He beat back the thought and prayed for Janet, massaged her cool hand, cried into her hair until it was soaked. She took shallow breaths a couple times more, but she never responded to him.

Finally, the paramedics were banging on the door, and the doorbell chimed, too, and Walt sprang to his feet. He bashed his head good against the thermostat as he lost his balance again on the way, through the foyer, but he wrenched the lock open, and the paramedics pushed their way in. Walt collapsed onto one of them, a young guy who looked ex-military.

"She's in the bedroom!" Walt pointed the way, and three of them scrambled over there while the guy wrestled Walt to the living room sofa. Walt tried to pull away, "Janet, my wife…"

"Sir, you need medical treatment, too. They'll take good care of her. Sit here."

The blood-pressure cuff pinched Walt's upper arm, the medic's fingers hot fingers on his wrist. The guy shined a bright penlight into each eye. Walt tried to look past him at the doorway to their bedroom, but he couldn't tell what was going on in there.

Walt stood to go to Janet, but the man said, "Sir, sir," and urged him back onto the couch. The others already had her strapped to an orange, plastic board and were hurrying toward the front door. "They're taking her to the hospital. She needs you to be calm and patient. We'll bring another ambulance for you, and then you'll be able to see her."

Walt's gasping sobs turned to weeping. When the paramedic got a report on his walkie talkie that Janet was still alive just one minute from the hospital, Walt finally raised his gaze.

The television was on. But the image on the screen was still. The DVD player was paused at 20:35. Walt realized that he couldn't remember past the opening scenes of the movie.

Twenty-four

Just as Jeff was stepping out of the shower, Cooperton called about another weird break-in: "More black spray paint. No homicide, but damn close. Woman is at Wake Med unconscious in ICU. Meet me at the convenience store outside the main entrance to Country Estates, and I'll drive you in. We'll say I'm giving you a ride-along today."

Jeff spotted Cooperton's Crown Victoria at the gas station, parked the Audi and opened Cooperton's passenger door. He squeezed into the small space next to the police radio and laptop computer that were mounted to the dash on flexible stalks. "I thought this was supposed to be a safe place to live."

Cooperton had the car running, but he didn't put it into gear. "What'd you find out about Eddie?"

"I ran him through every database the firm subscribes to, but fake people aren't in those. Came up with nothing. Sorry to let you down. I'll keep trying."

Cooperton spat. "Sounds like that little newspaper reporter's got both of us beat. Her story today says 'employees who wished to remain anonymous' said the suspect's name was Eddie Grant."

"Where'd she get that?"

"Hell if I know."

Jeff frowned. "Any prints or DNA or anything from the store?"

"Pretty good set of prints from the forklift," Cooperton said. "But they're not any that match ones we got on file. DNA takes a while, and really, you need a suspect in custody to match your sample to. We had popped the dead guy once for DUI..."

"Maybe it's somebody from out of town," Jeff reasoned.

Cooperton sniffed. "Shit, all I know is, we've had a year's worth of crime up here in four days. There's some motherfuckers around here somewhere who need a screen check." Jeff knew that meant cuffing a suspect in the back of a patrol car with no seat belt, then slamming on the brakes so he slammed face-first against the partition between the front and back seats. Cooperton spat into the opening of a plastic soda bottle, then replaced it in the cup holder as he repositioned the wad in his jaw.

"There's all the spray paint – includin' this one today. I'm thinkin' maybe some kinda liberal terrorists."

"Well, what's the deal with this new one?"

"You got to see this." Cooperton shifted the Crown into drive and rolled out of the parking lot.

A wooden sign near the brick entryway advertised "Custom Homes 350s to 420s." Jeff liked the look of this neighborhood; the houses showed real attention to detail and varied in architectural style – though they had identical mailboxes, and the dominant feature of each façade was a double garage door.

"Come on inside," Cooperton said.

They parked the car, and Cooperton led Jeff up the cobblestone driveway where a Chevy Suburban was parked at an odd angle with one wheel on the lawn. "Homeowner parked it in the garage last night before dinner. When he woke up this morning, it was out here. Apparently, they moved it."

They walked up a path still illuminated by a row of tiny lights staked into the ground, though the sky was bright by now. Cooperton kneed open the oak front door. A couple of deputies straightened when he entered, and Cooperton said, "Meet our friend Jeff, fellas." He walked Jeff across the living room past beautiful granite countertops and a kitchen full of restaurant-grade appliances. They stopped at an open door.

"This is the master suite where our Mister and Miz Ellis woke up this morning. Norton, will we fuck up any of your evidence if we step in?"

"No, sir, L-T, but could y'all stay right inside the doorway?" Norton wore tan slacks and a short-sleeve dress shirt. He was on his hands and knees inspecting the carpet. He looked younger than Jeff. "I think they mighta even vacuumed before they left, if you can b'lieve that."

"Ahh-ite. Ain't nothin' too weird for this one." Cooperton shrugged and stepped in. Jeff followed and noticed the light-dark-light argyles that a vacuum combs into plush carpet.

The master suite was the size of Ashlyn's whole apartment—or bigger—and empty of furnishings. There were dents in the carpet where furniture had stood. "They stole all this? Was it antique or something?"

"Naw, nice stuff, 'parently, but new and from Haverty's right down the street. Plus, they took all the pictures off the wall and all the clothes that was in the drawers. Last thing Mr. and Miz Ellis knew, they was watchin' a movie in the living room. This morning, Mr. Ellis wakes up here on the floor. His wife's half naked and damn near dead. We think both of 'em was drugged. You're gon' like this: Hospital done a tox screen on the woman. She just come to. Small amount of diazepam, a.k.a. Valium, nothing she'd ever been prescribed. A shitload of sodium phenobarbital, just like them pets. If she'd got a little bitty bit more of it than she did, she'd be just as dead. We're gettin' Mr. Ellis checked out, but we bet it was the same thing. Only, he's bigger so it didn't affect him as bad. He woke up feeling like he'd drunk a fifth of Jack. Both of 'em have little injection marks on their shoulders."

"Lieutenant, have y'all checked into where the suspect could get hold of the phenobarb?"

"Hell, probably on the Internet. We did look through our reports, and nobody's reported any stolen in the past year."

Interesting, Jeff thought. He had to get back to his calls to vets as soon as he returned to his desk. Now he looked at the black letters on the wall. And the two large painted shapes, sort of cone-shaped, one an outline, one solid.

"Yeah, read that," Cooperton said. "I ain't no prosecutor, but sounds like enough for attempted homicide. These are some sick fuckers. Let's step back out. Downtown's comin' in on this, and I can't let them see you in here. Right, Norton?"

"Yes, sir."

Jeff made notes so he could add this writing to his office window. He felt strangely lightheaded as he followed Cooperton back through the living room – the paint fumes, maybe. Cooperton paused to point out diamond-tread tracks in the living room carpet where a hand truck had again been used to wheel items to the garage. "Tires match the dolly from your clients' house. We think they loaded it all on a truck inside the carport. Must have moved Mr. Ellis' SUV out to make room for it."

Jeff nodded, still feeling a little weird and not sure why. He was probably shy a cup of coffee or two, edgy and foggy at the same time. "Anything else missing from the house?"

"Dunno, but all the TV sets seem to be here. They didn't have no guns to start with. And buddy, their little Penkanese was just fine, shut inside an upstairs bedroom barkin' her ass off most of the mornin'. We're having her blood tested for that stuff, too, though."

Cooperton took Jeff back to his car. On the way back to the gas station, Jeff acted on instinct. "Lieutenant, I want to trust you with something."

"Ahh-ite."

Jeff told Cooperton about the charitable donation thank-yous and his theory that the amounts matched the value of the items stolen in the dead pet burglaries.

"Seems way out there, but still, I like the way you think," Cooperton said. "Keep on thinkin' about it."

Cooperton dropped Jeff back at the convenience store, where Jeff went inside for coffee, then sat for a few minutes sipping it in the driver's seat of his car. He still felt really funny, and he still couldn't say why. It was as if his mind had figured something out without telling him.

* * *

Signs inside the hospital directed Jeff to Intensive Care Family Waiting. Jeff had learned the hard way, when his grandfather had died at Presbyterian Hospital a few months ago, that families of ICU patients formed a little fraternity in these waiting rooms, keeping up with each other's loved ones, relaying messages and so forth. He decided to tap into the network.

So Jeff introduced himself by name only to a haggard woman in her early 40s. He'd let her assume any official title for him that she wanted. "Is Walter back with Jan right now?"

She nodded. "They won't let him stay back there long, because she's so delirious that it upsets him. And when he's upset, that agitates her. You a friend of theirs?"

"I'm investigating what happened."

Now a man opened the blonde oak door and stepped in, rubbing the corner of one raccoon-circled eye as he pinched the bridge of his nose. His untucked shirt didn't match his pants, and he had bedhead.

"Walter, this is Jeff Swaine," the woman said, and Jeff stood silently to shake Walter's hand. The woman asked, "How's Janet?"

"She's still pretty mixed up, but the doctors say she's through the worst danger already. They're just giving her fluids and watching her, and they are hoping she'll be fine. I can tell she's getting back to normal. Any news about Harvey?"

"He's still sleeping, and the medicine seems to be helping. Supposed to hear more right after lunch."

Walter nodded.

Jeff looked him in the eye. "You must be so relieved to hear she's doing better," Jeff said. "You've had a hell of a night."

"Yeah, I am. And I have. Thanks."

Jeff could see by Walter's expression that the older man approved of his manners. "I'm J.D. Swaine, and I'm one of the investigators trying to find out what had happened and who did it." If Walter Ellis thought he was with some government in some capacity, that was an error, but not Jeff's fault.

Ellis looked at Jeff with a needy gratitude. He sat in the next chair and spoke softly about waking up on his floor, about the terror of not being able to wake his wife. He told about calling the police, about coming to the hospital in another ambulance not knowing whether his wife was still alive: "I've never felt my love for my wife more than this morning, when I had to think for the first time in 25 years about how life would be without her."

Jeff let silence hang in the air. It turned out to be the perfect move.

"I didn't have the chance to tell the other police this," Walter Ellis said, "but the more I think about it, the more I think that food delivery guy must have had something to do with all of this."

Twenty-five

Leonard pulled the rented white cargo van into a street being cut into the woods for a new subdivision. Once he was out of view of the main highway, he threw it into PARK and did a mouthful of sanitizer.

Then he reached into the back seat for a package of blue vinyl letters he'd bought at Office Depot and got out. Within a few seconds, he'd spelled out "BBT Painting" on the side of the van, with a random phone number that began with a real local exchange.

He hopped behind the wheel again and drove a couple of miles to a subdivision called Ashley Woods. The road into the development ran beside an easement for high-voltage power lines.

He made a left turn onto Pleasant Lane. He was sure this was where he'd noticed the pretty blonde girl and her brown-haired friend walking home from the school bus about a week before, before his new inspiration had written them into a composition on the album. He hummed the new melody that had leapt into his mind the other night. Leonard wiped his damp palms on his coveralls and swallowed a mouthful of citrusy saliva.

The yellow bus had squealed to a stop right at this corner, by the house with the plastic picket fence, and when it had disappeared, there they had stood.

They were probably in junior high, just past the cusp of adolescence, the girls' narrow frames blooming with the first signs of womanhood, the blonde in particular smiling with self-assurance and tossing her long, platinum hair, pressing her lips together and smirking at her brunette friend as they passed two gawky, slightly older boys messing with a car stereo in one of the driveways, thrusting their chests and swinging their hips, trying out their new bodies, lording their power over the boys, just teasing them with what they couldn't have.

Leonard had sat parked by the curb and watched them down the sidewalk. He'd seen each girl disappear into a different door a little farther down the street. That house. And that one.

And Leonard had realized that his string of problems in life stretched back to Carley King, the girl with red hair and blue eyes in the eighth grade that he'd sat behind in algebra.

He sat here now in the driver's seat with his eyes wide open, amazed at himself. His mind was amazing. This was virtuosity, wasn't it? That your mind got so fluent with your art that it worked on it even when you weren't trying to. Man, he hadn't even realized it until now – this was the kind of subconscious inspiration that made a great story to tell on a talk show to Oprah or David Letterman:

"So, Leonard, where did you get your ideas for the great tracks on this album?"

"Well, Dave, you might enjoy the story behind the track, 'Babe Watching.' When I was in middle school, this pretty girl named Carley King overloaded my mind. She turned around one Monday when the teacher wasn't looking and whispered that she always matched her socks to her underwear. That day, she had on polka dot socks. The next day, she wore hot pink ones; Wednesday, zebra-striped, Thursday, tiny anklets with lace around the edges. Each day I'd ask her if they matched, and each day she'd grin and nod and slide down in her seat and pile her great-smelling curls on my desktop. Friday, she wore sandals on bare feet, and my imagination nearly sent me into a coma."

Here was where Leonard knew the studio audience would laugh – and Leonard realized he wouldn't ever tell the story on TV.

Because the following Monday (sheer black trouser socks) the teacher had left him and Carley alone in her classroom when they'd both gotten study hall for the talking during class. And he'd tried to kiss her, but Carley had squealed at him, banged her palms into his chest and shouted, "Why don't you give it up, you little loser! Are you so stupid you didn't see Maggie back there laughing at you every day in class when I was making you drool? How could you think I liked *you*! Get over yourself!" Mrs. Klosky had come back in after hearing the squeal and let Carley out of the rest of study hall when she'd whined, "Leonard tried to kiss me," and given Leonard after-school detention and a humiliating parent conference with his mother about appropriate interactions with girls...

Leonard stopped the van in front of the blonde's house and threw it into PARK. He opened the double rear doors so anyone passing by could see all the dropcloths and cans of paint and roller handles and brushes he'd loaded in there from the shed behind his farmhouse. He had carefully smeared a few colors of paint down his white coveralls, and naturally he wore one of those disposable hats.

He took a 6-foot stepladder he'd lifted from DIY Warehouse, a brush and a can of paint that had hardened completely and walked around the side of the house like he belonged there. He set up the ladder next to a window on the side of the house that had a Mylar balloon with a pink star – a mighty fine indication that this was her room, he figured – and dangled the can from the ladder's little hook. He popped out the screen and pulled a putty knife from his coverall pocket as he climbed up to look inside. Yep, it was her room. Pop CDs mixed with little-girl princess leftovers.

Then Leonard's body went on full alert, and he nearly pissed himself. The glass reflected the danger just a foot from his nose: A Wake County sheriff's cruiser crept down the street on patrol straight toward him. Leonard told himself to stay calm. This would work perfectly. He belonged here. He so totally belonged here. He fit in. He was a guy painting windows for The Man. If the officer challenged him, maybe Leonard had stopped at the wrong address. Or maybe he didn't speak English.

He leaned in close toward the window, started whistling loudly and scraped the frame with his putty knife until it threw off flakes of paint. Sure enough, the cruiser kept right on going past his van without the deputy even giving him an extended glance. Leonard breathed again.

Leonard scraped for about five more minutes after the car disappeared, just to be safe, but the cop never came back. Leonard gave up on slowing his heart rate, which was in the grip of both fear of the cop and excitement about this composition.

He slipped the putty knife into the slot between the window's upper and lower sections. He wiggled it around and bit his lip. Finally, he worked open the toy brass latch inside. Just. Like. That.

He pushed up the sash, scrutinized his reflection in the upper window, then, using it again as a rear-view mirror to make sure no one was watching, slipped inside. He lowered the window quickly – but not suspiciously quickly – behind himself.

It smelled like watermelon bubble gum in here. He grabbed the open pack of Bubblicious from the white lacquered desk, unwrapped a piece and sank his teeth into it.

Shit! The little dog gave Leonard a freaking heart attack, skidding through the girl's bedroom door and across the hardwood floor barking as if it were some kind of Doberman. Miniature Schnauzer, Leonard guessed. Stupid little thing. He opened a plastic baggie in his left pocket and tossed a ball of pork sausage with Valium onto the floor.

He petted the dog's silvery fur as she munched down the treat. He looked at his watch and nodded: School would let out in about two hours. He took off his shoes and wiggled between the covers of her unmade bed. The cool sheets were unspeakably soft on his rough toes.

This was timing out perfectly.

* * *

"Several large boxes just arrived for you by private courier, Sarah." Annie's voice was musical, even with the distortion of the speaker on Sarah's desk phone.

"What are they?"

"They're heavy. I think depositions or discovery or something."

"Can you bring one in?"

"Sure."

Sarah took a sip of bottled water, then went to the door to help Annie lift the box.

"Thanks."

"Let's put it down on the floor behind my desk."

There was no return address, so Sarah used the letter opener from the cup on her desk to pop loose the packing tape.

The carton held several rows of identical looking, unopened envelopes. She pulled one out and realized it was a credit card bill. All the others were similar, but addressed to different recipients. All were from Citibank. The makings of a class-action suit from a tipster who didn't realize how many federal laws this violated?

"Huh," Annie said.

"Yeah. Let's check the other boxes."

There was another box of Citibank bills, and two boxes from MBNA, and one from First USA. Inside the top of that box was a letter-sized sheet of white paper. In large, computer-printed letters, it said, "1. Everything Comes Due at Once."

Twenty-six

The school bus was such a stinky, yellow piece of monkey shit. EmmaJane Porter stood there next to Katie and watched it drive away, puffing a black cloud into their faces. That *could not* be good for your skin, she thought, rubbing her cheek. She *hated* riding it home every day. It seemed like forever before she could take driver's ed and then get her permit. She had just turned 13 four months ago. Almost two more years, and then Catherine and Ray would never let her have a car for, at least, another two years, *if ever.*

She gathered her blonde hair, all getting in her face from the gust of wind from the bus, and twisted it around a finger behind her head.

The sixth-graders on the bus, Seth and Jason, were so immature. She turned to Katie: "All they did, like the whole way home, was drool and look at us?"

Katie laughed and squinched up her cheek.

No matter what, the goobers always sat near her and Katie. And her and Katie couldn't wait to get off the bus every day and go home and do homework or whatever. Just anything to get away from them.

"That thin fuzz they tried to grow on their lips just looks totally gay, and I don't think they even get that, you know?" Emma-Jane told her.

Katie totally knew. She just shook her head and rolled her eyes. "Heh. Later, girl. Call me; we'll go to the pool tomorrow."

EmmaJane smiled and put up her hand in a slacker wave, and Katie waved back and pulled out her house key as she started up the sidewalk to the house.

EmmaJane stared two doors down at her house, the siding of which her wench of a mom had decided to paint *peach*. Seriously, Catherine? That's very attractive. I *love it*. It looks like your husband's giant Caucasian ass.

EmmaJane rolled her eyes, delighting in her private profanity as she walked up her driveway, pulled out her own key and shouldered through the front door.

She nudged it shut and then walked into the kitchen to sneak a Diet Coke.

Oh. My. God. She froze in the spot, and her legs wouldn't move. A creepy man with a beard was standing leaning against the island.

EmmaJane's mind froze for a second. She wanted to scream and run back toward the front door, but as she started to move, he did, too – a hand closed around her ankle, and that tripped her up and then, like, a bee sting on her thigh, and she must have blacked out or whatever.

Twenty-seven

As soon as Jeff got back to his office, he called in the physical description of the food delivery man to Cooperton, who said he would talk to Walter Ellis again himself.

"And check their kitchen trash for the food," Jeff said. "I bet the lab will find it was full of diazepam. The delivery guy knocked them down with that, then the burglars hit them with the phenobarb either intending to kill them or keep them unconscious long enough to haul out the furniture."

Jeff wrote the description of the food delivery man above the graffiti on his right-hand office window. It fit the descriptions of Eddie Grant. He drew a red line to the card on that crime.

He looked up the phone number for Chef 2 U, dialed it and asked for the manager. He got the owner.

"Davis Swaine from Cross Baker Allison," Jeff said. "I'm working in conjunction with the Wake County Sheriff's Office. We're looking for an employee of yours who walked off the job last night after a delivery. Would have been two dinners for Walter and Janet Ellis."

"Wow," the guy said. "How'd you know?"

"I'm sorry," Jeff said. "I can't discuss the investigation, but your former employee is a person of interest, and it's really important that we talk to him. Are you going to be there for a few minutes? I'd like to stop by and get a copy of your records on him."

"Those are supposed to be confidential."

"I know. We'll get a court order eventually, so you'll be covered. Mrs. Ellis, your customer, is in the hospital, and we think your guy put her there by poisoning your food and delivering it to them. For the sake of mitigating your civil liability alone, I'd think you'd want to help us catch this guy as quickly as possible."

The owner was quiet a few seconds, doing the math and coming up with the right answer. "You think Tommy did that? He's about as shy as you can get. Little fella, too."

"Can I stop by?"

"Yeah. I'll be here 'til midnight."

Now Jeff started working the vets again. The phenobarbital would be key, he thought. He left several more messages. And when he got to PetHealthPlex, he apologized for hanging up before on the receptionist, a woman named Marinna with a great phone voice.

"That's okay," she said. "Our practice administrator said to tell you we can't answer any questions like that about drugs unless we know who we're dealing with. But if you want to come down here and show some ID, they'd probably help you out."

"I'll be there at 4:30."

Jeff drove to the gourmet delivery business first. It was stuck in the back of an industrial park and also offered catering services. The owner showed Jeff an employment application for a Tommy Tutone. The guy had been working there, "very part time," for about a month. He'd been a good worker, and he'd made three deliveries without incident last night before heading to the Ellis' and never coming back. They didn't have his picture.

The sprawling, single-story building that held the veterinary office was glass and stucco and reminded Jeff of a California plastic surgery practice from a TV show whose name he couldn't remember. Inside, the waiting area was skylit and done in slate tile. There were separate alcoves for dogs and cats and people with other animals. Each had toys and jars of treats appropriate to the species.

The place smelled like litter box, hamster food and wet dog, yet Jeff suspected it wasn't cheap. The vehicles in the parking lot were high-end, and so were the owners. One dachshund wore a long, skinny green sweater. A retired woman caught him looking and volunteered, "He has a cold."

At the nexus of the waiting rooms, a young woman sat at the center of a circular desk at least a dozen feet in diameter. She looked Scandinavian, with pale skin and woolen hair that seemed to range naturally from white to straw.

"You must be Marinna. Jeff Swaine. We just talked on the phone." He pulled his laminated legal investigator card from his wallet and showed her.

She stood, smiled and nodded, then picked up the phone in front of her. She wore a breezy white blouse and a sleeve skirt made of some sort of unbleached natural fiber. "You can talk with Dr. Maddox."

She put a self-standing sign on the desk – "Back in two barks and a meow" – and ducked underneath a section of the desktop that probably hinged open when there wasn't a stack of papers on it. Marinna's long hair brushed the floor. She smiled. "Hard to do that gracefully."

"Yet that's exactly how you did it."

She smiled at him again, open and friendly. Jeff wondered if she delighted everyone she met like this, whether an identical twin without her effortless way of being would strike him as so pretty.

Marinna led Jeff to a narrow corridor of offices, knocked on the door of one and then let him in to speak with Dr. Maddox, a silver-haired fellow with lines in his face that indicated he spent a good bit of time frowning. Marinna touched Jeff lightly on the shoulder while making the introduction, then left and closed the door behind her.

"Just move those files to the floor," Maddox said. Jeff cleared out the guest chair he indicated. The rest of the office was just as cluttered.

"Dr. Maddox, you may be aware that two pets were killed with sodium phenobarbital during burglaries this week. This morning, a woman woke up after her home was burglarized, and sheriff's investigators I'm working with have determined she was injected with the same drug. I'm trying to help figure out where the burglar may have gotten it, so I'm asking veterinary practices in the area if they're missing any."

"I have no idea."

And, apparently, no desire to find out.

"Would you be willing to check? This woman had been stripped mostly naked. She is in the ICU at Wake Med right now. She nearly died overnight."

Maddox silently stood and opened the door. Jeff decided to follow, even though he hadn't been invited. Maddox took them to a suite of exam rooms. In one of them, a brown-skinned woman was examining a border collie.

"Rena, are we missing any sodium phenobarb? This guy is looking into those pet killings that were in the paper. He says a human was injected with it overnight."

The woman turned to the dog's owner. "Try to keep him still for a moment, if you don't mind. I'll be right back."

Dr. Rena Nagra shook Jeff's hand and then led him and Maddox to the next room. She held open a swinging door. It looked like a hospital operating room, with bright lights mounted on the ceiling above a metal table. When they were all inside, Dr. Nagra pulled open a drawer. Glass tinked. She pulled out a box with a plastic liner in the bottom, like an egg carton, with circular slots for 12 vials of the drug. Jeff counted five vials.

"Uh oh," Nagra said.

Maddox activated his facial creases. "What?"

"We just got this in last week, enough for a couple of months, but half of it is already gone. I used two vials, and I can't imagine that the rest of you guys would have used more than one other one."

"We have to call the police," Maddox said, apparently never having assumed Jeff fell into that category.

"Definitely," Jeff said. "Actually, it would be the Sheriff's Office, and Lt. Randy Cooperton is in charge of this part of the county. Let me give you his number."

Maddox called using a phone on the wall.

Nagra looked pale. "Those stories about that dog and cat were horrifying. I treated that golden retriever myself. She had returned to perfect health and could have been expected to live happily for years. I can't believe we had some part in this happening." She stopped and looked around the room. "How could someone have gotten in here to take it?"

When she looked at the floor, Jeff waited a couple of beats. "Does anyone here have a salt-and-pepper beard, stand about 5'8? Maybe wear a snap-brim cap?"

Nagra shook her head at first, but then she stared at Jeff and her eyes opened wide. "Corey. Just started part time. In fact, he helped me put down some sick animals yesterday."

"With sodium phenobarbital."

She nodded and covered half her face with her right hand.

Jeff's senses aroused. He was close. "What was his last name?"

"Hart."

Jeff knew his '80s music. Corey Hart was another pseudonym. The "I Wear My Sunglasses at Night" singer.

Maddox hung up the phone. "He's on his way with some detectives. I'm going to have to ask you to leave or to wait out in our reception area ..."

"Did Lt. Cooperton say that?"

"I'm saying that."

Maddox had Jeff by the triceps now and was pushing him down the corridor toward the reception area.

Nagra spoke to calm her colleague, but Maddox told her, "I just figured out why I recognize this guy – from the picture on the back of the Yellow Pages. He works for a fancy law firm downtown that loves to do pharma liability cases, and I figure he's here because he intends to sue us."

Jeff realized there probably were grounds for a negligence suit here, but the presumption still offended him. He wrenched himself free from Maddox and gained two steps on him. To his surprise, Maddox turned and disappeared back down the hall.

Jeff decided to make the most of the opportunity. When he reached the reception area, he extended a hand across Marinna's desk, and she shook it with another unwavering gaze into his eyes.

"Thanks for your help," Jeff said. "One more question: Is Corey working today?"

"No, he was scheduled, but he didn't show up. Didn't call in sick, either. He's a sweetie. Loves animals. Do you know him?"

"Dr. Nagra mentioned him," Jeff said.

"He's kind of shy. I think he has a little crush on me."

Yeah, who would't, Jeff thought. He fished for more information about "Corey," but she didn't really seem to know much. Soon, Cooperton pushed through the glass front door.

He spotted Jeff. "Shit fire, son. I'm gonna have to get you a damn junior deputy badge or somethin' if you keep doin' our job for us." Then to Marinna, "Here to see Dr. Maddox, young lady."

Jeff waited an hour in the reception area until Cooperton re-emerged. The big lieutenant showed Jeff "Corey Hart's" employment application.

This one listed an address of 13 Germantown Ave., Rocky Falls, N.C., and Cooperton confirmed that he he'd never heard of that street, either.

"They said he had a staff ID badge for this place with his damn picture on it, but when they check their computer, there isn't a copy of the photo on file like for everybody else. He mighta made his own."

"What about security cameras? I saw one mounted over the receptionist's desk."

"Good thinkin'. We'll get his picture off that."

Twenty-eight

When she woke up, EmmaJane was in some stinky old house in the country, locked inside a teeny bedroom with dirty brown carpet and an old couch and no other furniture and with, like, steel mesh over the one tiny window. All she could see outside was pine trees, woods. And her head hurt so bad

And her clothes were wrinkled and stretched from him all dragging her around and her shoulder was sore but she thought she was okay. He hadn't like, molested her yet.

But he'd stuck his head in the door a few minutes ago and said, "Wait here. There's something I want you to do for me later."

So she was really scared and alone, and she wasn't even sure whether she could trust these bottles of Aquafina standing here on the floor even though it seemed like they were still sealed from the factory. And she was *soooo* thirsty.

This was, like, really bad.

She sat with her back against the wall and just cried, sooo hard for at least an hour, and the sun went down, and she thought he must have left.

So she tried screaming a few times, but nobody came.

And what the hell: She twisted open the bottled water and took a couple of sips, and it tasted regular, she thought.

Twenty-nine

The Boston Market roasted chicken dinner smelled so delicious that it took all Jeff's discipline not to start eating it in the car – but he didn't want to grease the Audi's steering wheel or sacrifice a dress shirt. What the plastic plate held was far from a home-cooked meal, but it would be the closest thing he'd had since Ashlyn had been gone. He turned over the moral implications of staying in a relationship with a woman who wasn't right for you because she was pretty and fed you well. Many a marriage had been built on less.

But he had cheated on her. The very same day she'd left! He had to end it soon. He would have to go up to Baltimore and see her, end it in person, but certainly not tell her about Caroline. When? Sometime...

When he pulled into his alley, Jeff squinted at new black scuffs on the temporary plywood garage doors. He'd gotten the padlock key back from his general contractor after the walls were done, so no one should have been inside the loft since Jeff had left this morning.

He had to push harder than usual to get his key into the lock. He parked the car and got out balancing the dinner carefully on the fingertips of his left hand. He rode the freight up to his apartment. When he opened the heavy steel door, the lights were on.

Jeff looked toward his living room and flinched at the ears-boxed sensation of sudden fear. He dropped the plate to the floor without meaning to, and the lid popped off, spilling food across the concrete.

His living room was full of furniture.

A leather loveseat stood under a framed Edward Hopper print centered on one of the new walls, grouped with a glass-top coffee table, recliner and floor lamp. His new TV stood opposite the sofa in an expensive armoire. What the fuck? The remote control now rested on the alien coffee table at a casual angle.

Jeff's vision narrowed to a tunnel, and his body's systems seemed to be shutting down one by one. He hurried down the short hallway and into the main bedroom. It was furnished too: An ostentatious walnut queen-size bed, neatly made with a plaid spread. A dresser, nightstands and chest. He pulled a nightstand away from the wall, and a drawer slid open, spilling knicknacks he'd never seen. He looked at the back panel: a Haverty's Furniture label.

The Ellis burglar – or maybe burglars.

The panic prickled in the balls of his feet.

Jeff ground his teeth. The room was neatly arranged, with a bedside phone, lamps, even a book called *Blink* he knew had been some kind of best-seller left open to a middle page next to a glass of water on one bedside table. The air mattress where he'd slept the previous night lay deflated on the other side of the bed, long slashes cut into the vinyl.

Jeff breathed fast and shallow. Someone could still be in the building. He got an extra jolt of adrenaline. He had no weapon. He turned back toward the doorway, trying but failing to see into the shadows outside the bathroom. Then he bolted down the stairs and outside.

He juggled his mobile phone, found the record of Cooperton's call that morning and hit SEND. The phone seemed to ring 10 times before Cooperton picked up.

Jeff's voice broke: "I think I found the Ellis' furniture."

Thirty

The Rocky Falls Value Warehouse Club closed at 6:15 p.m. on Fridays. At that moment, Leonard was lying on a stack of brand-new queen-size mattresses on the top rack of overhead storage, probably 25 feet off the floor.

Dozens of little birds – sparrows or finches something – lived up here in the rafters. He watched them fly short trips from steel beam to steel beam. He figured there was plenty for them to eat in a place that sold carbs by the ton. He had a lot in common with these birds, making his way in the world by stealing crumbs.

The first birds must have flown in through the loading bays. Then they must have bred in here, because there were a lot of them. Leonard figured the store manager either didn't know how to get rid of them or was too pansy to poison them. He loved that the birds had reclaimed the territory after their forest had been turned into a 10-acre rainwater collector.

Down in the aisles, Leonard could hear the store employees hastily "zoning," tidying up the sections of the warehouse they were responsible for, just like the guys at DIY Warehouse always had to do before the managers would let them go home. Leonard's mood darkened. He would make sure no one was here this time before he came out of hiding. At least Robert had been an asshole who deserved it; he had no such assurance about anyone he would run into here.

* * *

The mattress was so comfy Leonard actually dozed off for a few minutes. He woke and looked at his watch. The lights were off, and he didn't hear movement. But he lay still and waited 15 more minutes anyway. Then he pulled on latex gloves and stood on his mattress. Its heavy plastic covering crinkled, giving him a vague feeling of shame. He remembered how being screamed at didn't make you less likely to piss the bed.

Leonard's head was just below a ceiling beam. He could see to the far walls of the store, though he didn't have the angle to see into every aisle. He stood perfectly still and waited for the A/C blower to shut off. His heart was thumping. He didn't hear anything or see movement. He concentrated as he climbed down the end of the rack. He laughed at the idea of falling to his death, cracking open his skull on the concrete floor and having them find him here in the morning. They'd think he was the latest victim of the DIY Warehouse burglar! They'd be right.

On the floor, he crept from aisle to aisle along one side wall, looking down the length of each to the opposite end of the store. It was dim, but about a tenth of the overhead lights stayed on all the time. So he could see. He went to the loading bay area in back, and the only little office he could find was locked up tight. He checked the crack underneath the door. No light. He exhaled loudly and walked down one of the main aisles to the registers at the front, where he grabbed one of the gigantic shopping carts. He had worked up a powerful thirst, so he slid a case of bottled water onto the lower rack of the cart, wrenched one bottle free, cracked the top and downed it in a messy series of gulps, liking the cold splashes on his chest. He stuck the bottle back into the case in the empty space.

He rolled his cart to the personal care department, where there were vats of contact lens solution, bricks of deodorant soap and cylinders of shampoo heavy enough to break your foot if you dropped one in the shower. He stopped the cart and grabbed one case of VWClub diapers, size 2, one case of baby wipes and a case of formula. He grinned at the symbolism, the brilliance, the personal significance of this composition for him.

He wheeled this little load toward the back of the store. He left the cart near the rollup door the managers used to bring cars inside for display up near Customer Service. Leonard went back to the front for a new cart. He salivated even before he reached the entire pallet stacked with 2-liter bottles of name-brand waterless hand sanitizer, shrink-wrapped into packages of two.

Nearly a gallon of the stuff being offered for $12.47. It didn't taste as good as Kroger's but that didn't really matter. It was such a good deal. He stripped away the plastic overwrap from one bottle and depressed the big pump on top – it reminded him of the containers they kept ketchup in at the ballpark.

He tilted his head sideways and squirted it into his mouth, and it drooled down his cheek and dripped off his earlobe and onto the floor. He grimaced at the taste, but the prickly burn on the way down was – fiery. Fiery and good.

Leonard stacked the cart with dozens of bottles of the stuff, the weight of the load making it hard to get the thing rolling after he was done.

He made it back to the roll-up door and carefully unscrewed the alarm sensor, keeping it in alignment with its other half on the doorframe, then taping the two pieces together to make the alarm system think the door was always closed. He opened the door, and the harsh rattling of the metal hurt his ears.

It looked dark outside beyond the bluish-white parking lot lights. He hummed the appropriate tune. He ran out to the plain white van he was driving today and pulled it through the open bay door, the only one on this side of the building, and the only bay in the building that was level with the ground. He shut the door behind him and thought its metallic boom sounded like an orchestra's kettle drum. The thought gave him a rush. An orchestra, playing his music ...

This sanitizer tasted all wrong – the aftertaste of the non-ethyl alcohol ingredients was overpowering. From the van's floorboard, Leonard grabbed one of the bottles of Haut-Brión he'd brought along, uncorked it with his Swiss army knife and turned it up. The first mouthful of that was harsh against the sanitizer bite, but the second tasted fantastic.

Damn, was he thirsty. He'd chugged down a third of the wine before he realized it. Didn't want to have too much. Lots more to do tonight. Needed to keep his edge, plus, he had to remember not to take this fine wine for granted, no matter how plentiful it was now that he was famous. He swallowed like a cartoon character and held the bottle over his head. "To a brilliant new jazz album."

He was feeling playful, so he stuck the cork back into the bottleneck, took off one glove and deposited a perfect set of fingerprints on the shoulder of the bottle. He carried it to the wine department and placed it in the second row of a bunch of $7 bottles of Australian shiraz. He didn't think anyone would find it or realize what it was, at least not right away, but if they could, more power to them. To promote a new album, you had to create buzz. A month from now, someone would pay big money for that bottle on eBay. The stage was set, and now it was time to perform the rest of the album with a little solo that had occurred to him along the way.

Thirty-one

Sarah and Annie were both still at the office when Jeff called to tell them what had happened at his loft. Soon they were both standing with him on the sidewalk outside his place. After more than an hour, Cooperton walked over with a Raleigh Police detective holding a clear plastic bag containing a piece of paper and a separate baggie with an empty Carolina Blonde bottle.

"We got his prints."

"From where?"

"That's the thing. They musta touched everything in the place, movin' the furniture in there like that, but prints were just on this beer bottle. It was sitting on top of your little refrigerator. Big mistake. They match the ones from the forklift at the home center. Might get DNA off the bottle, too."

Jeff's throat tightened. The person or people who had skewered the DIY supervisor had been in HIS HOME. "He drank my last beer?" He looked at the baggie.

"Yeah," Cooperton said, his face tight. "He left this note under the bottle."

Cooperton angled the baggie under the streetlight so they could read the permanent marker scrawl beneath the moist ring the bottle had left:

"ITFD:

5. EMPTINESS AND FULLNESS."

"Beats the shit out of me," Cooperton said. "Aw, damn, 'scuse my language, ladies."

Sarah glared at the sexist remark masquerading as chivalrous. "Sounds like an acronym."

"I don't know what the hell it means, but I know it ain't no joke," Cooperton said. "Be right back."

"Annie, would you bang on doors and see if neighbors saw anybody moving the furniture in?" Sarah said.

Annie looked around, and Jeff guessed she was wondering where she would find any neighbors, but she headed down the sidewalk, without a word, to try.

Jeff wandered around the outside of the bakery for another hour or more in his own personal fog as evidence techs and cops went in and out with cameras and equipment. About 11, a Ford Explorer pulled up to the curb, and Caroline Kramden stepped out.

Now she was going to write a story about him. He turned his back on her and strode the opposite direction down the sidewalk, fuming.

Her heels clicked quickly against the pavement, and he felt her hand on his shoulder. He whirled around to face her.

Before he spoke, she said, "I'm not here for work." She said it with a softness that made him believe her instantly. "When Cooperton got called down here, I heard it on our police scanner. I checked in with him on the cell, and he told me off the record what had happened. I didn't tell anyone in our newsroom, and they won't ever catch on tonight that it's anything other than a routine burglary."

She grabbed his right hand with both of hers. "I'm sorry about before. I'm just on my way home. I wanted to stop by and see about you."

She waved her hand toward the police cars. "These guys aren't going to let you back in there tonight. You need someplace to stay. When you get done with them, why don't you come back to my place. I may be asleep, but you just go on and let yourself in, okay?" She pressed her apartment key into his palm and squeezed his hand with long, cool fingers to close it around the key. "If you want to sleep on the couch, that's okay, too. But you can ..."

She broke eye contact and looked at her feet, "Crawl in next to me again. That was nice."

Jeff hadn't seen this sincere side of her, and the gentleness felt good to him. But before he could reply, she had turned her shoulder and was walking toward her car.

SATURDAY

Thirty-two

The crunch and buzz of the coffee grinder woke Jeff. He looked around at the stylish cherry bedroom furniture and smelled Caroline's shampoo on the linens. He piled the blanket and pillow by his feet and sat up, his gaze following a shaft of sunlight streaming into the bedroom from the small living room.

"I thought I heard somebody stirring." Caroline emerged from the tiny kitchen and crossed the living room to the doorway. Her smooth legs disappeared underneath a thick, white, terrycloth robe above the knee. Her hair was wet from a shower. "What time did you finally fall asleep?"

"No earlier than four. It didn't seem like I disturbed you."

"No. You felt nice." She smiled at him. "As always. Coffee will be ready in a minute."

Jeff realized he had felt oddly comforted, too, nestling into Caroline's back. It was completely different from their other night together, which had been no warmth, just sex. This night had been no sex, just warmth. He felt a multi-dimensional attraction to her now, maybe the beginnings of a real connection, and he wanted to make love to her again with that on his mind.

"Caroline," Jeff called after her, and she reappeared in the doorframe. "Thanks for letting me stay here. Seriously."

"I didn't want you out on the street." She grinned. But as if she knew what he was thinking, she added, "I have to get dressed. I'm going to be late for work. Mugs are to the left of the sink. Help yourself."

"It's Saturday."

"I'm busy and ambitious."

With newfound modesty, she'd apparently taken her work clothes for today into the bathroom to dress there.

Jeff exhaled and walked toward the kitchen. The coffee pot was still brewing, and he decided it would be bad houseguest manners to hold his mug under the dripping filter to pour an early cup, so he just stood there as the European coffee maker spat and hissed. He noticed her work satchel on the dinette table. A folder was open, and he could see she'd been going through some notes before he'd awakened.

A page of handwritten bullet points said, "Knox family trust sold parcel to Reuss firm in August. Wake County Planning and Zoning approved plan of subdivision December. Tenants told to vacate MHs by Mar. 31." The list ran several pages.

Caroline rustled down the hall, so he carefully edged toward the sink and the coffee pot. His mobile phone rang, and he jumped backward a step. Damn, was he still edgy. He made himself take a breath: Probably Cooperton.

Instead, it was the trucking company ready to drop off the furniture from his storage unit at the loft. "We're at your address with your items, but we can't find a front door, and there's tape that says it's a crime scene."

Jeff cranked his neck backward and stared at the ceiling as he blew out a breath.

"I'm in an unusual situation," he told the driver. "How many more stops do you have to make?"

The driver agreed to do his other deliveries first, and he gave Jeff his mobile number. He could take the furniture back to the warehouse if he had to, he said.

Jeff shook his head and stared at the ceiling, and the coffee maker sighed and exhaled loudly as it conveyed the last of the water from the tank to the filter basket.

Caroline reappeared — dressed — holding his khakis by one beltloop. She reached into his front pocket, fished out the house key she'd given him and slid it into her own pocket.

Jeff raised his eyebrows.

"I can't let you move too fast on me," she smiled. "But stick around as long as you need to this morning. The door will lock behind you when you pull it shut."

* * *

Jeff went to his place, intending to shower there.

He found the spilled dinner right where he'd left it by the elevator. Jeff bent and scraped most of the meal back into its container, resenting Cooperton's men for not cleaning it up. His face felt numb and stiff, as if he'd walked 15 blocks on a frigid day. He stood and rubbed his cheeks with his hands.

A note on pink paper on the coffee table said the Sheriff's Office would send a crew on Monday to "recover" the Ellis' furniture. There was gray fingerprint dust on nearly every surface.

He realized suddenly that he couldn't stay here long enough to shower. The place was making him so anxious he wanted to peel off his skin. He filled a duffel bag with clothes, threw in his razor and deodorant from the bathroom and got the hell out of there.

He backed into the alley, stopped, jerked the parking brake and got out of the car. He paced down the alley a little way, hoping to calm his runaway pulse. The damn Scranton thing wouldn't go away; that was the problem — the experience had been fucking with Jeff's sense of security ever since it had happened, making it hard for him to settle down and go to sleep some nights and waking him with nightmares most of the rest.

Even when his conscious mind put it aside for months, it seemed his body remembered that someone could break in while he was most vulnerable, so his mind tried to keep him on hyper-alert all the time. He had been working to teach it to relax again. Jeff took a deep breath, blew it out, as he often did.

What had happened here at the loft yesterday was the *same thing* to his primal brain, the same gray outline of danger, proof to his mind that it had been correct to guard so persistently against this threat.

Jeff panicked at the thought that he might never be able to relax again – and he found himself glancing around the alley for threatening figures. He had the brief impulse that what had happened at his loft might be the work of the same gang from Scranton. He worked to attack the ridiculous notion with reason: He would've had trouble from them before now. He'd lived in Scranton another two years without problems. One of his attackers, the one Jeff had tackled against his dresser that night, was dead, another paralyzed, and the other guy wasn't up for parole for five more years. He was being completely irrational.

Jeff looked up at the roofline of his building and wiped his hand across his face. He probably felt as much guilt about the episode as he did residual fear.

That the stupid fucks could make him feel guilty about what had happened especially pissed him off.

It had been nearly five years now. Jeff had done a TV report on Scranton's gang problem. A gang he had neglected to mention on the air alongside its rivals had sent three guys – three stupid kids – to break into Jeff's apartment and put the organization onto his radar.

When Jeff had wakened and fought off the guy upstairs, the two guys downstairs had hollered to each other to "jet." The neighbor in the other half of the duplex had heard the yelling, called 9-1-1, and a Scranton cop patrolling one block over had arrived almost instantly, in time to see the first two kids bolt across the lawn.

The kid Jeff had fought was stupid enough to point a pistol at the cop, who fired seven shots from his service weapon, hitting the boy in the chest with two lethal rounds and crippling his 13-year-old cousin with a stray bullet that nicked his spine.

Fourteen. Thirteen. Thirteen. Born with no advantages. Already that hardened and dangerous as young teenagers, their highest ambition to be demonized on a brainless TV news report.

That one night had ended or irretrievably ruined each life. That was the pathetic reality of the situation. Jeff had been lucky to come out of it with just a broken nose and mild concussion.

Thirty-three

Protection Armaments stood in an aging shopping center with an awning made of corrugated metal. The gun shop was the only store with steel bars across its windows and doors. As he turned the knob to walk in, Jeff prepared himself for somebody like his uncle Drewry, a guy with a camouflage shirt, facial hair and a beer gut.

A brass bell attached to the door rang when he opened it, and a voice said, "Well hey there, honey."

The woman behind the counter was the only person here. She was in her early '30s with blonde hair, a great smile, tight jeans and a cropped top that showed off her flat stomach and navel ring. "I'm Trinity. What you lookin' for this mornin'?"

For the first time in 18 hours, Jeff smiled. It made perfect sense for a firearms dealer to make an attractive woman its salesperson, he decided. "I'm interested in a pistol."

"What've you got in mind?"

"Not sure."

"Well, what's it for?"

"If somebody breaks into my apartment, I want to kill him."

"In the gun business, that's what we call 'home defense.'

Most people will probably never have to use their gun, but they just sleep better knowing it's there if they need it. And that's worth every dollar you spend."

"I must not be very lucky," Jeff said. "I could have used one twice in the last five years."

She raised her left eyebrow as he looked through a glass-top case. Pistols stood on clear plastic stands with manila tags dangling by white strings from their trigger guards. The gold velvet underneath made the black, chrome and blue-steel guns look like pieces of sculpture. The saleswoman reached in and grabbed a silver pistol with a $199 price tag. She aimed it at the floor, pulled back the slide and looked through the ejection port to make sure it wasn't loaded. She pressed it into Jeff's palm with the action locked open.

From his work covering crime in Scranton, Jeff recognized the brand as a cheap one favored by cracktown shooters. The guns often misfired. He gently set the gun onto the cork mat that seemed to be there for the purpose. "Something higher-end."

He raised his gaze to a poster behind the counter that said, "Glock PERFECTION." He smiled again. Cops usually carried Glocks, Sig Sauers or Smith & Wessons. "What about a Glock nine-millimeter?"

She raised both eyebrows and glanced toward the other end of the case, where the Glocks stood in rows with price tags above $500. "The Glocks are real nice. But you want a .40-caliber."

"Why?"

"You know, knockdown. Stopping power."

She pulled out two identical-looking guns. "This one's the model 19. Holds 14 9 mm rounds." She made sure it was unloaded and set it on another cork mat. This is the .40, and it holds 13. The bullets are bigger, so not as many fit. But you don't have to use as many to get the job done, neither."

She smirked and put this gun into Jeff's hand. The handle felt like the same plastic as Ashlyn's plastic cutting board, yet sturdy somehow. He pulled back the slide slightly and pressed a lever with his thumb so it sprang closed.

"You look great holding it." She smiled. "That's the one for you."

"Okay, I'll take the .40."

Trinity smiled. "Great. Your permit?"

Jeff shook his head. She explained that under North Carolina law, he had to go to the Sheriff's Office and fill out an application for a $5 handgun purchase permit. The sheriff would run a background check, and in about two weeks, he'd have the right to buy a handgun if it came back clean. Pretty tight ship for a Southern state, Jeff thought.

"Lot easier to get one if you're a criminal," she concluded.

"I have a good friend at the Sheriff's Office," Jeff said. "I promise you I'll come back with a permit if you let me take the gun today."

"Who is it?"

"Lieutenant Cooperton. You can call him right now."

"Then go get the permit, and bring it back here tomorrow or whenever. We'll sell you the gun."

"I can't wait for a permit," Jeff said. "Somebody broke into my house last night. I'm afraid they'll come back."

Trinity searched Jeff's face, narrowing her eyes. When they widened again, she took a breath, started to speak, closed her mouth again and then said, "Walk out to my truck a minute."

Trinity locked the shop's door behind them and led them around the side of the building, where her brown Ford F150 was parked. She opened the glovebox. "This is a Glock Model 22. It's a .40-caliber, just like the one in there; it's just not the compact model like that one is. There's an ATM inside that quickie mart." She pointed across the highway. "I'll give it to you for $600 cash. You go on and take the pistol – if you'll go get you a permit and bring it back to me to make it all legal. That gun's registered to my daddy, and he'll say he loaned it to you."

Jeff nodded and crossed the highway to the ATM with the strong feeling that he was making an unwise decision, though the best one available to him. He withdrew the daily maximum of $300 from his checking account. Next he put in his Visa card and took a $300 cash advance.

When he brought Trinity the cash, she grabbed the gun by its barrel and handed the butt to Jeff. Loaded with ammunition, the pistol was twice as heavy as the one Jeff had handled inside the store.

He was careful to keep his finger outside the trigger guard. He pressed the button to drop the magazine of bullets from the handle, then racked the slide, which flung the unspent round from the chamber to the asphalt as his feet.

He remembered his father taking him to the pistol range while he was home from Taft during summers, felt keenly how incongruous his peers there and at the firm would find it that he knew his way around a handgun.

"Ain't too handy without no bullets." Trinity stooped and picked up the one Jeff had ejected. "Don't worry; it won't shoot unless you pull the trigger. It's a safe weapon."

Jeff re-loaded the ejected round into the magazine and slammed it into the handle of the pistol. But he didn't retract the slide to chamber a round.

"I need collateral," Trinity said.

Jeff squinted at her. "Like what?"

"Whatever you can convince me you'll come back and trade that permit for." She looked at Jeff's wrist. "That watch."

Jeff's wristwatch was the Bulova his Pa-paw had treated himself to after fighting in the Philippines in World War II. "This was my grandfather's."

"Then I'd say you'll be back. I'll lock it up in our safe in the back."

"I can't do it."

She pulled the gun from Jeff's hand and reached into her jeans pocket to return the money.

Jeff thought of trying to fall asleep without the pistol. He reached to unbuckle the leather band.

Thirty-four

Jeff ended up showering at Ashlyn's, which for all of its psychological discomfort seemed like the best option. He felt more like himself wearing a clean Polo shirt and khakis.

Cooperton called, asked how Jeff was doing and told him about another apparently related crime. "Another big-box store was vandalized. This time, the Value Warehouse Club. Last night after closing, somebody scattered a bunch of granola and trail mix in all the aisles, and this flock of birds they got living in there was eating it and then shittin' all over everything all night. Same kinda eco-terrorism-type stuff like at the DIY. Looks like they broke in through a roll-up door on one side. Jimmied the alarm sensor and drove some kind of vehicle in. They can't really tell if anything was stolen without doing a whole inventory, 'cause they keep so much shit in that place all the time."

Annie called Jeff's mobile on his way back to the office, the new pistol within reach under a blue sportcoat on the passenger seat. "I was here catching up on some stuff, and your line rang, and I thought it might be that sheriff's lieutenant, so I picked it up. But it was a woman named Margaret who said she's an old friend of yours from college. She'd like to see you, but she's only in town for two more days."

Margaret Samuels had been Jeff's girlfriend his senior year at Northwestern. They'd been great for each other. Only the different locations of their after-college opportunities had pulled them apart: he'd gotten the TV job in Wilkes-Barre, and she'd stayed an extra summer and fall quarter for a master's before taking a job as a second violinist with the Cincinnati Symphony Orchestra.

He'd always had the sense that Margaret would become part of his life again.

"She said she's playing with her orchestra at Raleigh Memorial Auditorium," Annie told him.

A pleasant nervousness in his stomach verified Jeff's residual feelings. As soon as Annie said Margaret's name, he'd wanted to see her.

"She leave a number?"

Annie gave it to him, and he thanked her as he wrote the digits on the back of a Taco Bell receipt. "I'll be in around lunchtime."

"Sarah said she told you to take the weekend off."

"I'd rather work."

Jeff went back to the donut factory, parked, and held the new pistol at his side as he rode the freight up to his loft, reminding himself it was irrational to think an intruder would be here now. The doors opened, and he stepped over the greasy spot on the floor and took a closer look at the strange furniture. He couldn't come up with any useful information. He made a mental note to ask Cooperton whether the furniture was arranged here the same as it had been at the Ellises'.

He checked again, but nothing was missing after the reverse-burglary besides the 12 ounces of beer, as far as he could tell. He tried to figure out what it meant that there wasn't any graffiti, despite long, tall stretches of wall that should have looked like a ream of blank paper to this guy. He'd just left the little paper note.

Jeff gathered up his few clothes and toiletries and decided he would stay at Ashlyn's until the police could retrieve the Ellises' stuff. As he locked the makeshift garage doors, he ripped down the scrap of crime scene tape and wrote a note in ballpoint pen on the plywood: "To Contact Owner:" then the number of Ashlyn's apartment where he planned to stay and his own cell number. He sat behind the steering wheel holding the pistol awkwardly. He stuck it behind the passenger seat and wedged it so it wouldn't slide around, then he drove back over to Ashlyn's.

On the way, Jeff touched base with Sarah. He could hear little Jacob fussing in the background. Sarah asked how he was doing. He said he was okay, realized he was lying, and realized he had to get his shit together and catch this guy. Sarah thought what had happened was horrible, and she was sorry for it. He should be careful and call if he needed anything. She offered to take Jeff off the investigation, which irritated him, and he could tell she knew it. She insisted again that Jeff take the weekend off, and he said he would think about it, though they both knew he wouldn't.

He climbed the stairs to Ashlyn's carrying his junk, set it on the floor, then sat cross-legged on the freshly shampooed and still crunchy carpet. He pulled out Margaret's number.

"Hey." There was a smile in her voice when she realized it was him. They were both quiet for a second.

"Annie from my office said you tried to call me."

"Yeah. We're playing a pops show tonight in Raleigh, and I saw your name in a newspaper that was lying around in the lobby. In a correction. 'J. Davis Swaine is a legal investigator. A story misstated his occupation.' Sounds like you're in the middle of something exciting."

"That's definitely been true," he said. "This case is a lot more immediate than a bad pill that damages your heart valves or rots out your liver," and left it at that.

She told him she was still putting in time with the Cincy Symphony. She was already the associate concertmaster, and as soon as the concertmaster found a job with a better orchestra, she'd been told, his job was hers.

"Until then, no second fiddle jokes. Come see the show tonight. I'll warn you we're on a paying-the-bills tour, as our conductor puts it. But there's one nice Vivaldi piece on the program, plus a lot of show tunes and patriotic stuff that sells seats. I'll leave you two tickets at the box office."

Jeff needed to get away from all of this for a few hours. It would be nice to hear some music, nice to see her.

"Okay. But I just need one ticket."

He heard the smile in her voice. "Well. We'll have to get a drink afterward and catch up. It's been a long time. Meet me by the bus. I've missed you, Jeff."

And before he agreed, she ended the call.

Thirty-five

Jeff wore a tan linen sportcoat with a white dress shirt. He picked up his ticket at the Will Call. Margaret had scored him a box seat, and an usher led him to his perch to the right of the stage.

He stuck his forefinger into his collar, which was pinching his throat, and leafed through the program. A few musicians milled around on stage as the timpanist ran through some licks. Ladies in evening gowns laughed loudly but with great dignity in the aisles below.

"Margaret Samuels is a masterful violinist who began her career with the Cincinnati Symphony and rose rapidly to associate concertmaster," her program bio said. "She holds both a bachelor's and a master's degree in violin performance from Northwestern University."

She was half Italian and a quarter Japanese, which made her striking. She looked glamorous in the photo, with a serious, smug expression, magnificent cheekbones, teeth to make an orthodontist cry, wavy raven hair with a slight widow's peak and penetrating eyes. Jeff could perfectly picture their shade of green, though the photo was black-and-white.

Just before the program was scheduled to begin, three other men joined Jeff in Box A and sat with a nod. The smell of scotch wafted off them. Spouses of musicians, Jeff guessed.

Orchestra members filed onto the stage. There was Margaret.

She took her place in front of a chair that faced his box head-on, perpendicular to the floor seats. Her strapless black gown showed off porcelain shoulders, which he remembered always feeling slightly cooler than his hands. Her face was even more handsome than it had been in college. She looked directly at him while the audience applauded, smiled to reveal those beautiful teeth, then gave him a wink with her backstage eye as the conductor entered to a gale of applause.

Then she sat, tucked the violin between her chin and collarbone and fixed her gaze on the conductor's hovering baton.

Electricity danced across his skin as she performed. She was more expressive, more confident than before. She closed her eyes through quiet passages, the bow delicately between her thumb and forefinger as she drew its length languorously across the strings. She jerked her whole body through staccato phrases.

The Vivaldi piece ended, and Jeff and a few audience members stood quickly to applaud. Everyone else belatedly succumbed.

Margaret raised her gaze to Jeff's box, saw his reaction. A blush washed over her face, and she arched her eyebrows. It felt as intimate as being naked with her.

As Margaret had warned, the rest of the program was fluff. But the orchestra executed each piece well and drew lots of applause. A Phantom of the Opera overture, some Rogers and Hammerstein. John Williams Olympics anthems and a little Gershwin salvaged the final half-hour.

Jeff stopped by the restroom, then picked his way through the crowded parking lot to the stage door. A luxury motor coach painted in a purple geometric design waited to take the musicians back to their hotel. He stood near it and waited, as he often had outside Pick-Staiger Concert Hall at Northwestern. He felt nervous. He didn't let himself think too much.

The plain steel stage door opened several times before Margaret stepped out. She carried her violin case and a little sequined handbag. She still wore the black gown. She smiled as they closed the distance and fell into a tight hug.

He remembered her scent as soon as he detected it, a rich vanilla that seemed to come from every square inch of her skin. He'd never known whether it was shampoo or perfume or something else. She seemed surprisingly tall, and he realized it was because she was a good six inches taller than Ashlyn. He took a step back from her and said hello.

"You look great. I thought you'd throw on sweatpants and a T-shirt after the show."

She scanned him up and down with those eyes. "I knew you'd still have that on, and I didn't want to be the slob hanging around with the sharp-dressed Southern beau. Who broke your nose?"

Jeff fingered the little ridge. "I got this working in TV back in Pennsylvania. Just a little difference of opinion with the subject of a story."

"Who prevailed in the end?"

Jeff forced a smile. "Like a lot of arguments, I think: No real winner."

"Too bad. But I like the scar – looks tough." She was smirking at him. "Well, where are you taking me? Does Raleigh have anything to offer besides that one mall they keep driving us to?"

"I'm sure we can find something decent. Have you had dinner?" As soon as he asked, he remembered she never ate before performing.

She just looked at him and cocked her head.

"It's got to be The Duck and Dumpling," Jeff said.

She hooked her hand over his elbow in a way that could have been flirtatious or simply upper-crust Northeastern formal. He led her to the Audi, opened the passenger door for her.

She settled into the seat, glanced around the car, and said, "You've done well for yourself." He shut the door for her.

Though neither of them had had a car at school, it felt perfectly natural to have her in the passenger seat of his now, Jeff realized as he turned the key and put his hand on the back of her seat to back out of the space.

She said she was resisting recruiters from more prestigious

orchestras because she was sure she'd get concertmaster in Cincinnati. Besides, she was pretty happy there. She had a loft condominium with a view of the Ohio River. One of the orchestra's patrons, an old man who loved her playing, had loaned her use the of the 200-year old Cremona violin from his collection that now rested at her feet. Jeff knew that having a collector lend you a violin was a compliment reserved for the world's best violinists.

"You always said you'd know you'd made it when your violin had a name. Does this one?"

She pursed her lips in an attempt to be modest, but a grin stretched across her face. " 'The Marquis de Savigny,' after the Spanish nobleman who owned it for most of the 19th century."

He stretched out his hand so she could give him five. "How much is it worth?"

"Depends on the mood of the market when you're ready to sell, but at least half a million, maybe double that."

Jeff whistled and glanced down at the instrument's undistinguished molded plastic case.

"So tell me the story behind that schnoz."

He told her about the gang kids. He thought about telling her how his apartment had just been forcibly furnished and how much it was bothering him because of the old experience. But he was unwilling at the moment to face that reality or burden their conversation with it.

They parked the car in a parallel street space, and Margaret took the violin case as she stepped onto the curb.

The downtown restaurant faced a large public park. They got a little table in a corner and spent three hours drinking wine and eating a series of appetizers but no entrees. He could still make her smile, and the tip of her nose still wrinkled whenever she had a mischievous thought. She looked fantastic. Jeff felt much better tonight.

With a series of gentle questions, Margaret soon got Jeff talking about the Rocky Falls burglar. He told her almost every detail, including that the furniture had been placed in an empty apartment. But he left out that it was his loft. The case made her smile with fascination, and she tried to shape a theory that would explain all the oddball crimes.

The waiter came to clear dessert. Jeff set down his empty coffee cup. When he looked up from the saucer, she'd already pulled out a credit card and was sliding it into the leather folder. She shook her head to pre-empt his challenge.

"You make this Rocky Falls sound like the most generic place in the world. It can't be that bad. Give me the grand tour."

She was extending the evening, and Jeff wondered how Margaret expected it to end. He read her as being open to going to bed with him. That brought back his chronic guilt about Ashlyn, whom he hadn't mentioned, and made him determined to salvage some small sense of personal morality by not sleeping with a second woman until he could speak with Ashlyn.

So an uncomfortable moment potentially lay ahead tonight with Margaret, but he wasn't quite ready yet to ruin the connection they were sharing. Or to be alone.

He took her back to the car. They drove north on Glenwood Avenue. They picked up Rocky Falls Boulevard just south of I-540, and when they crossed the freeway, he started pointing out landmarks, mostly shopping centers, he realized. They passed the newspaper bureau, and when they came to The Rocky Falls Brewery & Grille, she pointed. "Let's get another drink."

That seemed a safe enough idea.

She brought the violin inside again, and the hostess led them to a cocktail table.

When the bartender spotted the instrument, he grabbed a bottle of wine and two crystal stems, ducked under the bar and came to their table. "The band is late, and the crowd's getting antsy. I'm afraid they'll start to leave. This is on the house if you'll play for 10 or 15 minutes."

The bottle was a nice Burgundy, and Margaret looked at it and raised an eyebrow. "Pretty nice. How'd you know we were red wine drinkers? And how do you know I'm good enough to play in public?"

"Two questions; one answer: The dress."

She grinned and shrugged. "What kind of thing do they like to hear?"

Jeff checked out the crowd, lots of couples in their 30s and up wearing sweaters, polo shirts or Tommy Bahama button-ups with khakis or dress slacks.

"Band plays jazz, but I'm sure you'll be a hit with whatever."

She looked at Jeff, and he nodded and leaned against the cushion of the booth. Margaret unlatched the case. The instrument's worn, bourbon-colored wood glowed under the pendant light.

The bartender smiled, set the glasses upright on the table and pulled a wine key from his back pocket. "I really appreciate it."

Margaret stood with the violin before he poured, and Jeff realized she was protecting it from a potential spill. Jeff tried a sip. It was velvety; Ashlyn would like it, he realized, again feeling guilty.

Margaret took a quick gulp, waved to Jeff and mounted the little stage near the bar. The televisions switched off and people quieted down and looked her way as she tuned.

She launched into an Irish reel. The last voices fell away. She closed her eyes and swayed as she moved from the microphone so that people would hear the instrument's pure tone acoustically. She captured each eye in the room until no one touched a drink. When she finished the piece with a flourish, the people stood and hollered.

Margaret bowed from the waist, then held her bow ready until they quieted again. She started a bluegrass tune that got them clapping along. When they applauded that, she said, "This next one is an old one, something a little different. I hope you like it."

Tears collecting along Jeff's his eyelids at the first notes. She was playing the Bartok solo piece she'd worked to master her senior year while she and Jeff were together. He refrained from blinking and was glad she didn't look at him. The sonorous vibrations of the fine violin were other-worldly, and her playing amazingly better than when he'd last heard her.

When it ended, the audience didn't clap. It didn't move. The room was still, as if people hoped to experience just one more sound wave.

Margaret quietly stepped from the stage and returned to the table. People watched her. A guy with red hair started an awe-struck round of applause. Jeff lifted his glass and mouthed, "To you." She tapped her glass to his, gave a slightly sad smile and took a sip.

A three-piece jazz combo hustled onto the stage from some corner where they'd assembled. Margaret smiled at Jeff and re-filled his glass. The tangle of conversations resumed, and people stopped by the table and left tips for Margaret.

"I have to remember to supplement my income with bar gigs next time we go on strike at the CSO." She grinned, smooth-ing a five-dollar bill and adding it to a discreet stack near the wine bottle.

Jeff felt unsure what to say, so he was glad when the bassist started into "Gloria's Step," a tune he recognized from Bill Evans Trio *Sunday at the Village Vanguard*.

They sipped their wine and chatted, pouring the last few drops from the bottle as the first set closed with the pianist intro-ducing the band.

"Leonard Noblac on bass, everybody." There was more ap-plause, but the bassist didn't step out of the shadow at the back of the stage. "And folks, you can hear all of us plus a couple of other local musicians on Leonard's forthcoming CD, 'Everything Comes Due At Once.' We've been in the studio all day. When's that coming out, Leonard?"

The bassist with the porkpie hat was too far from the mi-crophone, so when he mumbled something, Jeff couldn't hear. The pianist said, "To be announced, everyone. We'll be back after the break, and we're back here again next weekend. Stay tuned. And how about another hand for our opening act."

The people clapped, and a minute later, Jeff and Margaret stood to leave. She left one of the five-dollar bills she'd earned in the band's tip jar as she passed the stage.

Thirty-six

Leonard pushed out through the side door of Rocky Falls Brewery & Grille into the parking lot, unlocked the door to his station wagon and sat behind the wheel. It was a small damned world. J. Davis Swaine, his nemesis, had come to his steady Saturday night gig in Burbland. Leonard paused in a shadow and watched Jeff and the girl laugh their way across the parking lot.

And that wasn't enough. No. Davis Swaine had upstaged him times two. He had brought in some brilliant violin player to make his band look like crap, some girl who could play like that without even trying, and who would be famous with those looks even if she sucked. And that was the other thing: Jeff had rubbed it in Leonard's face that he could get with such a fine looking lady. And damn! It was a different babe than the one in the picture he'd found on the floor at the kid's apartment.

The sarcastic bitch had tipped him five bucks like he was the hired help, like you'd pat a dumb little kid on the head for trying his hardest. Insult!

Maybe Davis Swaine had figured him out! Maybe this was payback for the furniture thing. Leonard chastised himself for letting Davis Swaine fall off his radar just because Track Five was finished. Just because the name hadn't been in the last couple stories in the paper.

Leonard had a moment of panic when the light reflected off the girl's teeth as she smiled at the investigator. Directed at Leonard, it would have been enough to paralyze him. Then she folded herself into the hot little sports car.

Leonard looked at his watch. The set break would last another 12 minutes, but he was the band leader, so he could stretch it if he needed to. He slumped in the seat to straighten out his hips so he could reach into his pants pocket for the car keys. He took off the hat and set it on the seat but kept on the chick shades, which weren't too dark brown, especially with all these street lights.

He pulled onto Rocky Falls Boulevard behind the little convertible. He followed it for about ten minutes, the Audi seeming to hug the right edge of the lane, until it suddenly turned into the driveway for Laurel Lake Apartment Homes. He passed the driveway, made a quick U-turn, then entered the apartment parking lot in time to spot Davis Swaine's taillights going dark. He killed his own headlights and parked in a handicap spot.

Fury burned in his chest. This gorgeous brunette, this musician, this *string player* – the type of girl who should be all over Leonard – sashayed down the sidewalk, moving that great little butt for Jeff, pressing her violin case against her tight little tits.

Leonard started with the naked shoulders he could see and mentally extended the idea downward until he could picture those tits. Feel his tongue bump over each one of her lower ribs, then slide smoothly up the little hill to her nipple, which he imagined small and pointy, like a man's, then up her sternum to her magnificent neck. Man, she was a perfect musical instrument. Leonard immediately heard the beat for a new composition. Throbbing, hungry percussive notes in a quick tempo...

He watched Jeff walk around her, lead her to the door in no hurry. And why should he hurry? He knew he was about to get some.

Yeah, he would get some. Leonard took a deep breath and glanced at his watch. They were expecting him back at the restaurant to start his second set.

SUNDAY

Thirty-seven

The rubs and scrapes, exaggerated through the speaker of the baby monitor on Sarah Rosen's nightstand, half-woke her. She listened, only partly conscious, to judge whether the boy would whimper and settle himself to snooze again or melt down and demand a bottle now.

Now someone hummed a melody, something Jacob wasn't even close to being able to do. She leapt upright in bed, snagging a fingernail on the coverlet. She yanked it free and grabbed the plastic box, pressing its speaker to her ear.

The louse! Electricity pulsed every nerve in Sarah's body. Leonard was here to hurt Jacob.

"Twinkle, twinkle little star," Leonard now sang in a whisper, "How I wonder what you are."

Sweat pricked Sarah's back under her nightgown, and now it felt like she was having a heart attack. In the speaker, Jacob's scrapes and social coughs turned into distress whimpers and now a full-throated scream, and she pulled the monitor away from her face and forced herself to go slowly enough to move quietly in the dark. She set the monitor on her nightstand, groped for the drawer pull, slid it open, reached inside it and closed her fingers around the pistol she had bought after Leonard left.

She knew in that moment that she would kill her son-of-a-bitch husband without hesitation – if she could do it without jeopardizing Jacob.

She felt the revolver's weight in her right hand, crept to the door of her room and forced her screaming mind to *shut up*. She had to *be quiet*, because if he heard her coming, he might hurt the baby.

Sarah moved nearly silently on bare feet into the hallway, her breathing ragged, the sweat making the gun feel as if it might slip from her grip, stepping carefully over the section of floor beneath the nightlight, the spot that always creaked. It creaked now. She kept going.

The soft humming from the monitor she'd left on her nightstand had faded from her hearing, and she couldn't yet hear Leonard in person around the corner. She struggled to draw a breath into her constricted chest as she took the last three steps to Jacob's door.

She shoved the half-open door. It banged against the rubber stopper as she curled around the corner, flipping the switch to turn on the overhead light and screaming – for some reason – "Hey!"

She was pointing the gun just to the left of Jacob's empty maple crib. Leonard wasn't in the nursery.

JACOB WAS GONE.

Sarah gave an anguished grunt. She darted through the rest of the house, swiping on every light switch she passed and pointing the gun into empty rooms. In the living room, she grabbed the cordless phone from the end table and punched 9-1-1 with her right index finger, banging the pistol against the phone in the process.

Instead of the ringing she expected, Leonard's voice babytalked in the earpiece of the phone, sounding just as he had through the baby monitor: "Listen to that, little Jacob. It looks like mommy's discovered you're with me. She heard you crying, didn't she? Say bye-bye."

Then, in the acid, adult tone he had used with her for the past year: "Um, hey honey, how's it going; Listen, I didn't make it by that place to sign those papers, and I'm not sure when I will. I meant to, though, but one thing led to another, and anyway, I just didn't make it. You know how it is. Anyway, don't worry about dropping Jacob off at day care tomorrow, okay? I'll, uh, take care of him. Got to go."

"Where are you!" Sarah screamed into the phone, but the call went dead, and when she tried to hang up, she got no dial tone, just electronic near-silence. She scrambled upstairs and found her mobile phone in her room and called the police on that.

* * *

The first Wake County deputy who arrived at Sarah's house found her on her front lawn in her nightgown clutching the pistol, pacing, half crazed with panic. Not knowing for sure who she was, he pointed his own weapon at her and ordered her to drop hers.

After Sarah explained what happened, the deputy found the transmitting module of the baby monitor – the part with the microphone that normally sat on the changing table next to Jacob's crib and beamed his cries to her bedside receiver – plugged into an outlet on the front porch of the house. Next to it was a cheap desk telephone with a speakerphone function. A 100-foot cord stretched from that phone around the corner of the house to the gray phone company box screwed onto the siding. The box's door dangled open, and the porch phone's cord was plugged into the jack inside. Leonard had wired a new extension to the front porch.

Then other cops arrived and found that the ringers on the front-porch phone and every other phone in the house had been turned off. Leonard must have turned off the power to the whole house to disable the baby monitor temporarily while Sarah slept. Then he'd used his key to sneak inside, abducted the baby and flipped the switches to silence the phones, since he knew where they all were.

Then, on his way out, he'd moved the baby monitor transmitter to the front porch and plugged it in there and turned the house power back on. He already had the new telephone installed and waiting. So when he'd called Sarah's house line on his cell, none of the phones rang, but he was standing on the porch to press the speakerphone button to receive the call.

After he'd driven away with Jacob, the phone had piped everything he'd said into his cell phone into the baby monitor via the speakerphone. By the time Sarah had picked up the telephone to call the police, Leonard was already miles away – and tying up her phone line.

Thirty-eight

Ashlyn steered her VW down the I-95 exit ramp somewhere south of Petersburg, Va. She pulled under a gas station's giant canopy, and she could see the first hint of dawn along the horizon under its opposite edge. She filled the tank, went inside for a pit stop and bought a 16-ounce cup of surprisingly good coffee – and some peppermint gum to chew after she finished it.

If she didn't hit bad traffic, she should be at Jeffrey's door in a little more than an hour. She was looking forward to surprising him. A bunch of the people in the seminar had been going out to dinner together every night, and last night she'd had a long conversation with a woman about her age who was planning her wedding. That had inspired Ashlyn to surprise Jeffrey by visiting him a week early. Ashlyn had gone to her hotel, packed a few things, slept for a couple of hours and left at 3 a.m.

She wore the baby-blue halter top and tight jeans that had gotten Jeffrey's attention last year at Club Oxygen. She hoped he'd still be in bed when she got there, because that was where she wanted him. She savored her naughty thoughts and licked her lips. The boy really got her going.

Since she was feeling seductive, she listened to a Norah

Jones CD, and the time passed quickly.

The sky brightened as she picked her way through light traffic in downtown Raleigh to the donut building, drove into the alley where Jeffrey was going to put his garage door. She'd probably have to honk her horn to get him to come let her in…

She found the wooden doors. Writing said, "To Contact Owner," then gave her own phone number and his cell number. Apparently, he was at her place after all, which was even better, because she had the key and could sneak into bed next to him.

It wasn't far to her place. There was Jeff's car parked by the building. She turned off the engine, pulled down her sun visor and retrieved her purse from the passenger floorboard. She glided on lipstick and touched up her mascara as best she could in the little mirror. She shut the door and locked it. She savored the emotional anticipation of seeing him mixed with the little bit of horniness that only Jeffrey could make well up so reliably.

She tiptoed to the door and pressed her ear against it. She didn't hear any sounds. She smiled as she put her key into the deadbolt as gently as she could. It seemed dead quiet inside.

Ashlyn had an intuition something was wrong.

She pushed the door open. No one.

Now the sound of sudden movement.

"Yes?" A pretty, skinny, young brunette in a huge T-shirt and pair of drawstring shorts appeared around the half-open door, holding a mug of coffee – staring out of Ashlyn's own apartment at her.

Ashlyn actually checked the number on the door, even though the key had just worked in the lock. Now she noticed the mug in the woman's hand: Ashlyn's own Health Education Association mug. She felt a rush of embarrassment, then a little nausea. And only when Jeff said, "Who is it?" – fury.

The brunette looked at Ashlyn as if to ask, *yeah who are you?*

The door started to close, but then Jeff appeared behind the woman. "Ashlyn!"

Ashlyn was just absolutely stunned by this. She hung a smile on her face while she struggled to figure out what she should do. She'd been apart from Jeff for a week, and he was already cheating on her in her own damn apartment? Her first impulse was to turn without a word, get into her car and drive back to Baltimore. She would not cry here on this doorstep, that was for sure.

And now she decided she would not let Jeffrey Swaine off that easily, either. This was her apartment, and she had some cleaning to do. She stiffened the smile.

"Margaret, this is Ashlyn I was telling you about." Jeff was trying to act casual, but the boy knew he was in deep damn trouble. His hair was wet from a shower.

"Oh my god," this girl Margaret said, reflexively smoothing her hair and looking down at herself. "This is your apartment." Then, "This must look pretty terrible." She blushed, switched her coffee to her left hand and extended her right to Ashlyn. Now Ashlyn recognized the clothes Margaret wore. Jeff's. Ashlyn pushed forward to gain entrance, and the woman awkwardly stepped backward, nearly sloshing coffee over the rim of the mug but still talking: "I'm an old friend of Jeff's, and we met for dinner last night because I'm in town for work, but I had a little too much to drink, and he was nice enough to let me stay here. On the sofa."

"Yes," Ashlyn said, imagining that her smile looked crazed. "You're his girlfriend from college."

Margaret took another step backward, all pedicured bare feet and smooth, toned legs. Ashlyn pushed aside her insecurities about her own legs. Her hand vibrated as she finally extended it to touch the woman's fingers. She drew back quickly, both as a snub and to hide her trembling.

She stepped in and looked at the man she'd felt closer to than anyone else in her adult life and wondered whether she really knew a damned thing about him. She'd never been so mad and hurt at the same time. Ashlyn scrutinized the sofa, realizing she was desperate for evidence the little slut had actually slept there.

Past the far end, a blanket was folded on the floor with a bed pillow on top.

After an initial surge of relief, Ashlyn realized that even if there had been no sex, which she would be a fool to believe, this was all a huge violation of their relationship. It was even more heartbreaking if Jeff was having sleepovers with old girlfriends than if he'd met some slut in a bar.

Jeff seemed to be deciding whether he should approach Ashlyn for a kiss. His cluelessness was infuriating! Ashlyn stepped around Margaret, walked to her boyfriend, and threw her arms around him. "Hello, sweetheart," she said, a name she never called him.

He tensed. Margaret managed an uncomfortable smile. Then Ashlyn walked around Jeff into the kitchen, searched through the cabinets for another clean mug and poured herself coffee. She walked back to the living room and sat at the end of the sofa with the pillow. Now she could smell the woman's perfume on it. Another favorable bit of evidence, she admitted.

Both of them just stood looking at her for a second before they realized they should sit, too. Margaret sat on the front edge of the opposite end of the couch, and Jeff did some more calculating before he finally pulled a chair over from the dining table. The black dress that hung over the back of another chair puddled onto the floor when he jostled the table.

"I would be so pissed off right now if I were you," Margaret said, trying to cultivate girl-to-girl chumminess.

Jeff set his chair at the end of the couch nearest Ashlyn.

"Why?" Ashlyn said breezily. "You slept on the couch."

"Still, it's so embarrassing." Margaret turned toward her, making eye contact. "He was telling me all about you, that you were at that conference in Baltimore, how you met, how long you've been dating. I was in town playing a concert – I'm a violinist. I invited Jeff to dinner afterward to catch up. We had some wine, and I was worried about him driving too far, so he offered to let me sleep here so he didn't have to take me all the way downtown. I slept right there. I have a boyfriend myself."

Ashlyn suppressed a sneer, nodded and reached over to pat Jeff on the knee. She thought, well, what's the big deal if all you were doing was taking my boyfriend out to dinner in that sexy dress and drinking to excess together before coming back to *my* apartment in the middle of the night?

Ashlyn smiled at Margaret with her mouth and frowned with her eyes. "Why don't we all go to brunch? You and I can get to know each other."

Jeff took a breath, started to say something, then simply

breathed out and shut his mouth.

Thirty-nine

EmmaJane sat in the filthy, tiny room and cried. She had done this lots of times before, and really, she was kind of good at it and liked it. But no one had ever forced her to do it before. So this was totally creepy. The weird, bearded guy was making her.

This was why he had kidnapped her, EmmaJane realized. To babysit.

To, like, stay here at this old house wherever and take care of this little baby. Why was this baby here?

He was cuuuuute. And he was hollering. She snuggled the sweetie on her lap the best she could and tried to figure out why he wouldn't stop crying. Probably because EmmaJane was crying, she realized as one of her tears dropped onto his forehead.

She didn't even know the baby's name, so she just decided to use the boy name she'd picked when she and Katie'd come up with names for their future children.

"Dylin, honey, it's okay. I'munna take care of you." She wiped her nose and eyes on the sleeve of her hoodie. She really needed to take a shower. She had slept in these same clothes. Gross.

The big creeper had opened the door about 10 minutes before, and EmmaJane had curled herself into a ball in the corner, afraid he was a pervert and was going to, like, assault her, but he hadn't paid any attention to her. First he'd laid the screaming baby on the carpet in the middle of the room. Then he'd dragged in all these boxes of baby supplies.

EmmaJane bounced Dylin on her knee a little and scooted over to the boxes on her butt. She would start with the diapers. She'd never sat for a baby this tiny, but she had changed a lot of diapers. She opened the big box and got one out. It took a while, but she finally got the baby's butt clean and a new diaper on him (she folded the nasty one together with the tabs and put in the bucket the guy had left for her to, like, pee in or whatever), but Dylin was still crying, maybe a little bit louder than before.

The sound made EmmaJane feel different than she ever had before. Somehow, she just knew that Dylin must be hungry. So she picked up one of the big cans of the powdered milk stuff. Next to it, there was a baby bottle still new in a box. EmmaJane read the instructions on the can and the bottle box, and it said to like, boil the nipple, but she didn't have any way to do that. Dylin needed to eat. She hoped it would be okay. She scooped out powder from the can, poured in Aquafina from a new bottle, measuring by the scale on the side of the Avent Nurser, and shook it up.

She curled Dylin against her chest and put the nipple to his lips. He shut his eyes, stopped crying in a second and stretched his lips around the fake boob and started suckling.

EmmaJane sniffed up the last of her own tears. Somehow, giving the little guy his milk made EmmaJane feel safer, too.

Forty

Leonard yawned broadly and scooped up a marigold with his trowel, then re-buried it upside down. He wore train engineer overalls and a ball cap. He had the wagon stashed in front of a different apartment building in the complex. People who saw him would think he was just some nameless contract landscaper some nameless real estate investment trust had hired to maintain franken-plants at its just-like-everywhere-else Class-A apartment complex. He dug up another marigold and buried it bloom-down. It cracked him up.

His heart was still beating kind of fast. Acting like the gardener was his backup plan, and he had been forced to resort to it right away. The blonde woman from J. Davis' photo had showed up at the apartment door right as he was about to walk up the steps. They had nearly bumped into each other on the sidewalk. Then the brunette had answered the door in her nightclothes. And there hadn't been a fight! The girls had shaken hands, and now they were all still inside together. Maybe the blonde was Swaine's sister, but he didn't think so from the way he'd seen them standing in that picture ... The brunette definitely wasn't.

At any rate, Leonard had to stay put. Three against one wasn't good odds, even if two of them were chicks.

After learning where the investigator was staying last night, Leonard had calmed down and gone back to the brew pub and played his second set. He had known Mr. Investigator and the brunette would be inside all night. Leonard was no pervert, so there was no reason to waste his time watching the place when he had the gig and then other important elements of his composition to attend to. He felt like a conductor – he had J. Davis staked out; The Soulless Bitch would be totally freaking out by now, and he'd kidnapped the little hottie from the subdivision and had her taking care of J. Davis' bastard child. Everything was in harmony, Leonard figured. He would introduce dissonance at just the right moment.

Leonard thought about how humble, frightened and submissive the teenager was locked in a room at his house, the total opposite of when she had been prancing down the sidewalk in her neighborhood. Yes, her knowing who was in control was a good feeling. It reminded Leonard that it was about time for the rape track. He started thinking about the composition.

He re-oriented five more marigolds – a definite improvement – before the apartment door finally opened again. He stole a long glimpse at the chicks under the brim of his baseball cap. Mr. Smooth brought both of them out to the blonde girl's car, and the brunette put her violin in the back seat and climbed in after it.

He pulled the brim of his cap low, stood facing away from them and brushed soil off the overalls as he eased toward his station wagon. When their car doors closed, he shimmied under the steering wheel.

He took off the cap so they wouldn't make the visual connection. He caught up to them at the first traffic light, two cars behind. With those two to look at, he was certain J. Davis Swaine would never notice him following, anyway. Leonard kept them in sight all the way to the Statesman Hotel near the capitol, where the one with dark hair went inside.

* * *

Jeff buckled his seatbelt in the passenger seat of Ashlyn's car – Margaret had insisted on riding in the back – dreading the worst brunch of his life. But now Margaret was explaining to Ashlyn she was scheduled to play a matinee concert before leaving town, so she didn't have time to eat.

"Too bad," Ashlyn said. "Let me drive you back to your hotel" – and the sentence hung unfinished in the air, with Jeff imagining, *where you belong.*

They drove downtown stone silent, and when Ashlyn pulled up to the hotel, Jeff pulled the lever to slide his seat forward. He didn't think it would be wise to stand and hold the door while Margaret climbed out.

So she squeezed out, said, "Bye – nice to meet you," and walked toward the hotel door, turning to wave, her eyes fixed deliberately on Ashlyn's, not his. Ashlyn waved back, and Jeff slid the front seat back into position, leaned back and shut the door.

Jeff knew the key was not to admit that he'd been anywhere close to sleeping with Margaret, to work his way up to a righteous oratorical offensive. Even though he hadn't slept with Margaret, there was Caroline. He didn't deserve a prize for one out of two.

And the truth was, there had been a perilous moment just after he and Margaret had walked through the door of the apartment. The lights were off. He could smell how the wine that legitimately made it a bad idea for him to drive her back downtown sweetened her breath.

He gave himself credit for this much: standing still for ten seconds when he normally would have entwined his mouth in Margaret's and located the tab of her zipper. Yet he thought things had stayed platonic mainly because Margaret had spoken up just then: "There's something I should have told you that I haven't."

Her drowsy smile had turned to a pained one. "I have a boyfriend back at my condo who's waiting for me to call and say goodnight. He's kind of a shit, and we could break up any day, and Jeff, you don't know how much I want to, but I just can't. I'm sorry to lead you on."

Jeff had stepped backward, exhaled and flipped on the overhead light. Margaret had sheepishly gone to the terrace to make her phone call, and he'd retreated to the kitchen to pour himself a glass of water, the evening's spell broken. He'd brought out the pillow, blanket and spare clothes for Margaret and told her all about Ashlyn.

And Margaret had smiled her Renaissance-painting smile and said, "Normally you wouldn't have given me the time to raise an objection. But I'm glad you did. It's the right thing, and you're a good guy, and that's why I've always been so crazy for you." They'd exchanged something like a handshake, a hug seeming too risky, and he'd lain awake for an hour in the bedroom, knowing she was just 14 steps away on the couch.

Now Ashlyn unclenched one fist from the steering wheel and rested the hand on her knee. "She's really stunningly pretty, Jeff. Beautiful."

Jeff recognized the conversational trap and kept quiet.

"And very intelligent and charming. I don't blame you for keeping in touch with her."

Now was the time to speak. "We haven't been in touch. She saw me mentioned in the newspaper and called yesterday and offered me a ticket to her concert."

Margaret had said all of this, but Jeff figured Ashlyn was going over it again, like any good interrogator, to look for inconsistencies. She'd probably check the trash for used condoms, count how many were left in the box in her top dresser drawer and then question her memory of how many there had been.

Ashlyn glanced over. "It wasn't the reunion I had in mind for us this morning."

"Me, either." Jeff sighed.

She smiled a little, though it looked forced. "Were you going to tell me she'd stayed with you?"

"Of course." Jeff felt the guilt of telling her the first ever 180-degree lie. And the real transgression was what had happened with Caroline. Jeff felt guilty for violating the rules of the relationship, but somehow he had the odd sense of being within his rights. His mind had already begun to think of him as single again. He heard himself still talking: "But I realize even though she and I are both with other people and nothing was going to happen, it was out of bounds to let her stay over. When I look at it from your perspective, I realize why you're upset. It was your apartment. I would be pissed too."

"I feel stupid for being mad about it," Ashlyn was saying, really warming up to him again. "I know I have to trust you. If you're going to cheat on me, you're going to cheat on me, and there's nothing I can do about it."

She stopped at a red light, and he looked her full in the eyes. He wondered why he was putting her through all of this, anyway. She gave him a little half smile.

"I'm not thinking straight right now, Ashlyn. Night before last, someone broke into my loft. It really freaked me out. I tried to call you, but you had your phone off, and I didn't want to leave something like that in a message because you might worry."

"What happened?" She was alarmed and sympathetic now.

"Remember that burglary Friday where the woman was nearly killed with the drug they use to euthanize dogs? Well, that guy broke into my place night before last."

Jeff told her the story of finding the Ellis' furniture at his place, and by the time he was done, they were within a couple blocks of the loft. He asked her to stop there so he could show her.

They rode the freight up and he flipped the light switch for the upper floor, even though light was streaming in the windows. "This is all their stuff. The burglar brought it all here, broke into my place, and arranged it like this." He pointed at the greasy spot on the floor. "That's where I dropped the takeout I was planning to eat right after I got off the phone with you. That's why I wasn't staying here, and that's how Margaret ended up at your apartment instead of here."

She threw up her arms, and her face suddenly flushed red. "Good – otherwise, she would have slept in your new place before I did. Why didn't you call me and tell me some criminal had broken into your apartment?"

It was surprisingly enraging for her to accuse him of sleeping with Margaret when he hadn't while he was feeling guilty because he had slept with Caroline, something Ashlyn had no inkling of.

"I told you!" Jeff snapped. "I tried. I knew you were busy, and I figured you were probably having a great day yesterday, and I didn't want to spoil that for you. I was going to call you this morning." Jeff realized how stupid this sounded, how his decision not to call her said everything about their relationship.

She raised her voice to a scream. "But you weren't too upset to meet your old girlfriend for dinner, and let her talk her way back home with you. I can't believe this! I'm your girlfriend!"

As Jeff looked at her, his own anger erupted. He was getting an insecure tantrum. No wonder he hadn't called her. He couldn't imagine her reaction if she knew about Caroline. He would never tell her, and even if all the other problems somehow went away, he had irretrievably fucked up the relationship. He would never be able to feel good with Ashlyn again. He would never be worthy of her trust.

"I am your *girl*friend" – she was shouting, and squeezing her fists, her voice echoing off the concrete floor and walls. "Do you hear me? Don't you understand that? *I* am your girlfriend."

And before he even thought, Jeff said it: "Yeah, you're my girlfriend, even though I know this relationship isn't right." He said it so softly that her anger faded in an instant and she took an apologetic step toward him. His face hurt. "And I've known it for a while. That's the real mistake I've made. And I can fix that."

Jeff turned away from her and said it louder: "Let me fix that right now."

* * *

Leonard waited in the station wagon at the end of the alley behind the old donut factory.

The plywood doors lunged open, then bounced halfway closed. The little blonde screamed in frustration and pushed them open again. The car they'd showed up in came backing out too fast, and Leonard started his engine. He didn't see Davis Swaine, and when the car started moving forward, Leonard made a snap decision. He crept forward too and followed it to the end of the block, turned right to stay with her, keeping well back.

At the next stop sign, a Raleigh Police cruiser filled up his rear-view mirror. He nearly swallowed his own tongue. The little Volkswagen headed straight through the intersection. Leonard turned on his right blinker, turned, and the cop turned right, too, hard on Leonard's bumper.

Leonard started to panic. The cop was definitely radioing in his tags now. The station wagon shouldn't be listed as a wanted vehicle, but what if someone had seen him out working on "Choke Point" the other night and written it down? It seemed like too many coincidences to Leonard. He signaled left, turned left. The cop did the same. The guy followed him all the way back to Capitol Boulevard. Leonard kept expecting to see the siren, the blue lights. He wondered if he was swerving or anything from being so nervous.

But they never came on. On Capitol Boulevard, the cruiser accelerated, changed to the left lane without signaling and blasted past Leonard's station wagon.

Leonard shivered and calmed himself. He thought about going back to the donut factory but realized he'd be a fool to do that now. Besides, he had a gig in a few minutes. He kept heading north toward Rocky Falls.

He was still addled when he got to Rocky Falls Boulevard. He fought the compulsion to steer his Chevrolet Estate Classic into the Catholic church near his farmhouse and light one of the tall candles. Robert's death had just been one of those random things in life. Not a Mortal Sin. Church stuff was bullshit, but it was hard bullshit to let go of. Damn, The Original Soulless Bitch had really ground that crapola into his brain when he was a little kid. It was about half his problem. Now he realized he felt guilty for calling his mother a bitch. He wanted to scream. She *was* a bitch! BITCH!

And Robert had reaped what he'd sown.

Leonard breathed out and steadied his grip on the hard plastic steering wheel, looked at his watch. Still on time. He *was* on his way to a church, but to him it was just a gig.

He pulled into the Rocky Falls Community Church's Worship Campus. He unloaded his bass case from the back of the car. He played in the Jazz Praise Band. These cats had finally given church a makeover. The place looked like a stadium-seating movie theater inside a private school, or maybe an office park. Nondenominational, no crucifixes, no kneeling. You didn't even have to say any creeds or prayers or sing. Just sit and groove out to some lite jazz by yours truly and the band, listen to a little talk by a school counselor-type minister – and nothing about hell or anything – nice chats about how to feel better when you're depressed or be a more compassionate spouse.

Leonard rolled the bass fiddle past the stand where they sold $3 fair-trade, shade-grown lattes in the lobby. All the proceeds supported the church.

A little market research had taught the minister how to give the zeros what they wanted, and they wanted easy-listening church, more than a thousand of them, 50 of which were already clustered in the aisles of the auditorium, chatting. For Leonard, this was good for some stage time and 200 bucks a week. He always enjoyed the applause, too, even though the minister said it was for the Lord.

Leonard thought back to the groovin' studio session yesterday. He'd improvised on the bass, though he'd had a hard time letting himself do it in the formality of the studio. He'd put some nice, extra flourishes on what he'd composed, gotten thumbs-ups from the guys. That had been a rush, but not as intense as DIY Warehouse or snatching the hottie and the bastard. The guys had seemed surprised he hadn't blown up at them like usual for making little changes in their parts on the fly – until they heard where *he* took the melody.

He laid his instrument case flat on the bandstand at the front of the church auditorium and undid the latches.

He would work on the rape track right after church. He had a new idea, and he would compose it in his head during the sermon.

Forty-one

EmmaJane finished the little tub of beef stew and squinched up her face. Eating it at all was gross, and this was all cold and everything, on top of it. But it was all the creeper had left her: two dozen tubs of microwaveable beef stew and a case of Aquafina. It made her feel a little better that there were so many supplies. It must mean that if he planned to kill her, it might be a while from now.

The more she thought about it, though, the more worried she was that this creeper was a total perv and that he was going to rape her.

She couldn't even process how horrible that would be. It would feel like getting beat up and humiliated and embarrassed and pukingly grossed out all at one time, she thought. Sex was weird and mysterious and, well, hot, and EmmaJane liked to think about it a lot, especially before she fell asleep at night, usually one guy or another from school, but sometimes this one teacher, which she knew was wrong and made her ashamed. She thought about a lot of things, as best she could guess they would go.

And two weeks ago in real life, she and a boy named Mario Falcone had taken off their identical lifeguard T-shirts behind the concession stand one night and kissed chest-to-chest until she thought she would faint, and then each gone home in the other's shirt, which had been *so sexy*. But she knew she wasn't close to ready for actual sex with anybody yet. And she knew if the creeper forced himself on her, sex would move from this breathtaking, electrifying place in her life where it belonged – mostly in her control. Sex would become a room of her life where reruns of a nightmare always played.

So as Jacob napped on a soft little mound she'd made on the floor out of her hoodie, EmmaJane went over to Jacob's big box of diapers. She unbuttoned and unzipped her jeans, and she stuffed the diaper partway down her panties, so the end with the cartoon characters stuck out the top.

Like the most godawful maxi pad you ever saw in your life.

She had to leave her jeans button undone because it was so thick. EmmaJane took two more diapers and sat on the floor. She unfolded them, arranging them in front of her. She took the sharp metal lid from the beef stew can. She gritted her teeth and sliced it right across her ankle bone.

Forty-two

Jeff called a taxi to take him back to Ashlyn's apartment to get his car. By the time he got there, all the stuff of his that had been in her apartment was in a pile near the Audi's front bumper. He let out a long breath through his nose. He had thought he might knock on her door to talk some more, to wish her well and apologize for saying everything so suddenly, but clearly it wasn't the time.

He loaded the stuff into his car and realized he might actually never have a conversation with her again. That felt both odd and agreeable. He regretted how hurt she must be feeling, and he realized avoiding that had been the main reason he'd waited so long to break up with her. He had been weak, and he had hurt her more than he should have. Yet he knew she wasn't the right woman to marry, and he felt some sort of deep relief at avoiding that mistake.

He brushed the parking lot dirt off the last item, his blue blazer, and laid it on the passenger seat. As he started the car, he turned on Nickel Creek again and decided to go to the office. No one else would be there. Maybe he'd have some time to think about the case, to make some headway against this burglar who always seemed to be 36 hours ahead of him. One night off was enough. Maybe immersing his mind in the case would get it off of Ashlyn.

Jeff parked under Wachovia Capital Center, slipped the Glock into his briefcase without knowing exactly why, and rode the elevator up. He walked through the dim office bullpen and unlocked his door.

He left his lights turned off and stared at the windows full of cards and marker, now harshly backlit by the sun. He set the briefcase on his desk and pulled out his legal pad. He flipped through it to see what he needed to add to the windows.

He wrote "Corey Hart" next to "Eddie (Eddy) Grant," then, "80's music → age? 35 or older."

This same-sounding guy was popping up at the scene of every crime. They weren't getting descriptions of anyone else. The prints on the forklift matched the prints on the beer bottle from Jeff's place. Yet the crimes seemed so logistically involved – moving truckloads of furniture, and so forth – that a small team of people would be needed to complete them. Maybe the suspect was the leader of the crew, and different helpers came in after he gained entry or set the scene. Jeff wrote: "Number of suspects >1?" in red marker.

Then he added the false address from the vet's below the one from DIY Warehouse. Upsal Street. Germantown Avenue. Interesting that Germantown was an avenue. Not many streets around Raleigh were named "avenue" – there were more "drives," "trails" and "circles."

He sat in his chair and pulled up Mapquest.com to double-check. No Upsal anything in Raleigh. Entering "Germantown" did bring up a Germantown Road west of downtown Raleigh. But the computer told him the street numbers started at 500 and ended at 699. Noblac had listed a street number of 13, which sounded to Jeff like a fake number you might come up with on the fly. He printed the map of Germantown Road so he could drive out there on his way home, but he didn't expect to find anything. The burglar's Germantown Avenue was supposedly up in Rocky Falls.

He stared at the windows and thought until his jaw ached. His mind was traveling down the same dead ends again and again.

Caroline's business card lay next to his phone. He snatched up the receiver. He could consider her an ally at this point, and when you got down to it, he needed to catch the guy who now posed a danger to him. She was looking into the same guy. He punched in her mobile number.

"I was hoping to hear from you before now," she told him.

"Sorry. Things have been a mess. I was wondering whether you'd like to hook up" – he realized it sounded like he was proposing a sexual encounter rather than a merger of investigations – "on this crime spree thing. Help each other out."

She was quiet for a few seconds. "Last time, you got mad at me."

"With pretty good reason."

She was quiet again. "Oh come on," she said.

"I think you got it wrong, anyhow. I don't think this stuff is connected with Mickey Reuss' land deal."

"Oh yeah? First, the guy goes after the two developers. Then he goes after the investigator the developer hires."

"But what about the DIY Warehouse killing?" Jeff probed. "Maybe you've found some connection between sad sack Robert Claypool and Mickey Reuss that I haven't."

She sighed. "No. Although I figured maybe the point of that crime wasn't to kill the guy so much as it was to do that elaborate display of native plants, to protest development."

"Seems like it makes sense, but how many native plants are left on a property that's been a trailer park for a couple of decades? By the way, I got a charity donation e-mail similar to the one you shared with me. If you put the two of them together, I think the guy killed Reuss' dog and the Hegwoods' cat and then stole stuff, sold it and donated the money."

Now she sounded hurt. "You got mad at me for being sneaky with you when you were holding out on me at the very same time!"

"A lot of damn good it did me."

And he could hear her smiling on the other end of the phone. He pressed his advantage: "You ever find out who's behind the Knox Family Trust?"

"You sneaky bastard."

"You could have gotten dressed in front of me, if you wanted to keep me distracted."

"For your information, I like to undress in front of you, but I prefer to dress in private. And you shouldn't go digging through a woman's briefcase."

"The file was lying open on your kitchen table. Anyway, I still think the trailer park angle is bullshit. Not that I have a good idea why else someone would commit all these crimes. Look, the suspect gave two fake addresses on job applications, but they're not around here. Upsal and Germantown. Ever heard of them?"

"Um, no."

Jeff got a sudden idea. He typed "Upsal Germantown" into his favorite Internet search engine. His eyes widened at the results:

> Upper Germantown
> Welcome to Upper Germantown. This area runs south from Upsal to Chelten Avenue ...
>
> Mount Airy / Germantown - Philadelphia Restaurants, Philadelphia
> 7165 Germantown Ave | At E Mt Airy Ave, $$$. Point of Destination Cafe ...
>
> [PDF] 2005 MECHANICAL LEAF COLLECTION and RECYCLING SCHEDULE Lincoln Drive to Germantown .Avenue, from Allens Lane to Upsal Street ...
>
> West Mt. Airy Neighbors - Religious Institutions
> Second Baptist Church of Germantown, Germantown Avenue and Upsal Street ...

He quickly clicked on each link and all the top hits had something to do with Philadelphia – one small section of northern Philadelphia. According to the search result for the Baptist church, the two streets actually intersected. The link led to a listing of places of worship on the website for something called West Mount Airy Neighbors. Jeff's heart beat faster as he browsed around the site and discovered that West Mount Airy was an old streetcar suburb near downtown Philadelphia. Another site told him the neighborhood was unique because when black families started moving there in the'60s and '70s, it had simply made the neighborhood racially diverse rather than causing total white flight. It was full of historic houses and was gentrifying after a period of malaise.

"What is it?" Caroline said through the phone, and he realized he'd left her hanging.

"One second."

Jeff switched back to the Mapquest window and punched "Germantown & Upsal, Philadelphia, PA" into the search box. The site pulled up a new map with a red star on the intersection, smack in the middle of the Mount Airy section of Philly. He was willing to bet the burglar had lived there at some point in his life. It was hard to invent original lies on command, so liars usually just scrambled elements of the truth.

"Sorry – I have to call you back," he told Caroline and hung up.

Jeff clicked back over to the West Mount Airy Neighbors site. He picked up the phone to call Cooperton.

"Hey, beau," Cooperton said. "I was just gonna call you. We got a nice, clear picture of him off that security camera at the vet's office. I owe you a favor."

Jeff checked his e-mail inbox and found a note from Cooperton with the color image attached. Sloppy looking guy with bad fashion sense and a bushy beard, just like the witnesses had described.

"Listen – let me cash in that favor right now and do you another one. I need a handgun purchase permit in my name right away, and I understand your office is the place to get one."

"Stupidest damn law in the world. Didn't the Legislature read the Second Amendment?"

"Look, L-T, anything about these crimes pointing toward Philadelphia?"

"Naw, don't think so."

Jeff told Cooperton about Philadelphia. When he was done, Cooperton kept his mouth shut, for once. When the silence had persisted for half a minute, Cooperton said, "Pretty slick. How much gas you got in that little sports car of yours?"

Jeff grinned. "I need to think about what to pack. Let me get your opinion: Given your constitutional interpretation a minute ago, I take it you wouldn't get upset if a good buddy of the department's had made a pistol purchase somewhat out of order?"

"Not as long as he knows enough about a pistol not to shoot my nuts off with it by accident. What date do you want on the permit?"

"How about last Friday?"

"Sure."

"Perfect." Jeff grinned. "How soon will you be ready to leave for Philly?"

Cooperton huffed into the phone receiver. "I can't, beau. Been getting a couple of questions on why you're always around. I can help you over the phone, but for the in-person stuff, you're on your own."

"Okay. Then I guess I'll go up there by myself."

"Keep me advised."

The voicemail light on his desk phone was flashing, had been ever since he'd arrived at the office. But as Jeff hung up, he decided to blow off the messages until tomorrow. Any important calls would come in on his cell, and it hadn't rung.

He didn't want to go to Philly alone, because it would all be legwork he could use help with, just banging on doors and showing the photo around and asking if anyone knew who it was. He dialed Caroline's number again, and the phone barely rang before she clicked on.

"What was all that a minute ago?"

He explained about the street names. "Come to Philadelphia with me. Let's find out who this guy is."

"Send me that picture, let me write a quick story, and then pick me up at my apartment.

When Jeff picked her up in the Audi, she buckled in, stuck a duffel bag beneath her knees and told him, "I've been getting these e-mails." She pulled several sheets of copy paper out of her briefcase.

Forty-three

Jeff and Caroline stopped in Fredericksburg, Virginia, for a late lunch and bought gas and more cinnamon gum for Caroline. She knew how to drive a five-speed, and Jeff felt wiped out, so he let her take a turn at the wheel. He'd never let anyone else drive the car before, but he liked watching her shift gears in the little miniskirt.

Past Washington, D.C., he took the wheel again, and Caroline fell asleep. At dusk they passed the exits to Center City Philadelphia, and the freeway went through a big park. Jeff exited where Mapquest had told him to and drove through a district that looked like it had been destroyed in a war 30 years before. One brick smokestack actually had the word ASBESTOS spelled out vertically in white bricks, clearly a point of pride at the time it was built. Many of the industrial buildings reminded him of his donut factory, but 30 times bigger and with broken windows. The sites were probably so contaminated that it was too expensive to clean them up and do something else with them. The shells of factories stretched down both sides of the street for a couple of miles, reminding him of the stunning number of identical Southside Chicago housing project towers that had stood along the Dan Ryan expressway while he was at Northwestern. How did a city approach revitalizing this kind of district, so thoroughly desolate for so long? It was hard to believe this was America.

The guys in bandannas and baggy pants made him especially nervous. He felt unsafe even with the pistol in his briefcase.

Finally, Jeff began to see blocks with houses, and judging by street names he recognized from Mapquest, he knew he was drawing near the Mount Airy neighborhood. He touched Caroline's knee to wake her, and she jumped, smiled at him and then sheepishly wiped a trickle of drool that had slipped out of her open mouth.

They stopped for dinner at a storefront deli called Newman's because Caroline said, "We're in Philly, so we have to get a cheese steak," and Jeff thought the place looked local.

The décor was basic and dominated by the white tile floor and a large stainless vent hood over the grill that ran parallel to the lunch counter where Caroline and Jeff sat. They ordered two cheesesteaks and two orders of fries and orange sodas.

"Make mine a chicken cheesesteak," Caroline told the counter man, who turned out to be the owner. He picked up on their non-native accents, and when he heard they were from North Carolina, chatted with Jeff and Caroline as they ate.

Black folks, white folks and Jewish folks all stopped in during their meal to pick up takeout.

The counter man said that New Yorkers who had been priced out of Manhattan and then Brooklyn and then Queens were moving into these North Philly neighborhoods and commuting by train to jobs on Wall Street or in Times Square. But most of the folks in the community still had family connections that stretched back generations.

As Jeff pushed their empty sandwich baskets toward the back edge of the counter, he realized he had no idea where they would sleep. He opened his phone to call the concierge service his credit card company provided to get help finding a room.

"Shit, the battery," he said. The phone was completely dead, and he realized he hadn't been at his factory to charge it in a long time. He would have to find a store and buy another charger.

"Here," Caroline said. "Use my phone."

He took it from her as they passed a hair salon called Nefertiti.

Philadelphia, Mount Airy neighborhood
JULY 1975

Forty-four

The white kid squatted behind the garbage bin after midnight and waited for the knot of black guys down the block to look away. Smoke rose from their mouths in widening cones, as it once had from the dead smokestacks of North Philly a mile south. They laughed and elbowed each other and passed a 40-ounce of malt liquor.

When they turned to holler at a woman leaving the Inside Out Club, the 15-year-old crossed the sidewalk, granite cobbles and No. 23 Trolley tracks of Germantown Avenue and melted into a two-foot alley between stone storefronts.

With the sole of a sneaker on each building, Leonard Noblac climbed the stones until he could rest his feet on a second story windowsill. He pushed up the sash, which was never locked, and hauled himself into the long-vacant shopkeeper's apartment, now a storeroom for the musical instrument store downstairs. The air was moist and stifling, like his mother's breath.

A narrow staircase took him down behind the counter, where the cash register drawer stretched open under a lamp to prove it was empty. Through the windows' iron bars and silver alarm tape, he could see across the street to Nefertiti Beauty Shop and the beautiful black woman in cornrows and beads on its sign. That stood next to a Jewish silversmith. The neighborhood was "going black," and his mom said it wasn't safe any more. But they couldn't afford to move.

Leonard turned the opposite way, toward the rear of the narrow store. He walked past a rack of trumpets and trombones to a raised display platform covered in red shag carpet. He moved a Fender Precision Bass guitar to the floor and climbed into its place. Sweat moistened his hairline.

He picked up the tall double-bass fiddle and embraced her, positioning her neck close to his, feeling the thick veins beneath his fingertips, pressing his pelvis against her curves, imagining she was really his. Gently, he teased each string, reaching above his head to twist the keys and bring her into perfect tune.

For two hours, he played the solos from his favorite jazz records. He imagined the voices of the other instruments, imagined the platform was the stage in a smoky club full of girls in lipstick and heels. There were maybe a couple of record producers at a front table. People shook their heads in wonder, nodded their heads as he grooved.

When he was done, he stepped back to the floor and rearranged the instruments on the platform. He only felt happy when he came here and played – lately, three or four nights a week.

Now, for the first time, he stole something: A set of new strings for his second-hand bass guitar at home. He just stuck them into the back pocket of his Levis. Easy.

Leonard climbed out the second-story window and back down to the alley, the stone rough on digits tender from fingering notes. He stole back across Germantown Avenue and crept unnoticed under the maple and spruce trees, past elegant stone Victorians, to his strip of run-down rowhouses.

From the alley, he climbed to his second-story window on the rope ladder his mother had bought so he wouldn't burn up in a fire.

Leonard undressed to his briefs, stashed the envelope of new strings under his pillow and lay in bed. Mom had taught him it was wrong to steal. A sin. You'd feel guilty and have to pray to the Holy Mother.

But stealing felt fine.

It felt right.

The music store owner wouldn't even let him in to look around while the shop was open.

That guy owed him friggin' strings.

Leonard was so energized that he couldn't fall asleep for two hours. He fantasized about having his own stand-up bass. About the applause when he played her onstage in a real club.

About the lipstick girls introducing themselves instead of the old queers who hit on him on the R8 train to center city.

Forty-five

Leonard walked toward the front door of the Raleigh Statesman Hotel, the portico over which focused brilliant, interlocking circles of light on the dark downtown sidewalk. He had to give VWC credit – their $69 leather briefcase under his arm was better than what department stores charged a couple hundred bucks for. He would gladly have stolen it at twice the price.

Leonard's chin and lip felt odd without his beard. He reminded himself he could grow it back in a week, become himself again, and he felt better. He just didn't want to take any chances. He wore gel in his freshly cut hair for the first time ever, and no hat, also a freaky feeling. Black pants, turtleneck, brown sweater. He looked so friggin' corporate. The Soulless Bitch No. 2 would be so happy to see him like this.

The bellman held the door for him, something that never usually happened, and it felt as good as a round of applause. He smiled and nodded at the dude. Bellman, one of the few jobs he'd never had. The marble tiled lobby made him remember his old steady gig at the Viceroy Hotel in Manhattan, where he'd met TSB-2.

The gig was with a piano player named Patrick, a guy who

was missing a finger from his left hand. But no one could tell from listening to his playing. He was that good. "Cocktail jazz with Leo & Pat," the hotel billed their Saturday night sets. The money was good for New York in those days, $150 apiece, but cocktail lounge gigs were a pain in the ass. Very few people *paid attention* while you played.

Leonard perfectly remembered the night he'd spotted the intelligent-looking redhead at a back table, plainly dressed and not terribly pretty – except when she smiled. And she was not just paying attention but bobbing her long hair as he and Pat jammed out to " 'Round Midnight." She had sat with this old married couple, sipping some kind of clear drink from a double-old-fashioned glass, looking at Leonard – not at Pat like chicks usually did:

When Leonard's solo ended, the girl started clapping. Though the crowd hadn't been applauding solos all night, everyone joined in. Leonard twirled his bass to one side and bowed a little, and when he stole a glance at her, she gave a big smile. Then, right before the end of the set, she and the couple – her parents, he realized – stood and left. Leonard went to the bar to share his disappointment with Johnnie Walker.

He'd heard a woman order a gin and tonic a few minutes later and looked over to find the redhead on the next stool, looking kind of goofy and blushing. But she charmed the pants off him when she sputtered, "That was a really cool number. I mean you were really cool on that number. What a solo!"

She didn't realize that he'd played "Softly as a Morning Sunrise" note for note the way Wilbur Ware had played it behind Sonny Rollins the night of their great live recording together in '57, and Leonard sure as hell didn't tell her. She'd just walked her parents up to bed, she said. They were visiting from Connecticut. And the girl gave him a lip-curling smirk when the bartender set down her drink, and she told him she'd sit in the front row for the second set.

Afterward, she and Leonard ended up at her closet-sized apartment on the Upper West Side, his bass case parked underneath the little loft that held her bed. They spent the whole night up there screwing, her bumping her head on the ceiling when she was on top, sucking the thick calluses that gave his fingertips the shape of lightbulbs and loving that he was a musician.

He'd always heard guys say they found the hottest action behind beige doors. That was true about her. She had a soft but sexy body under those boring clothes, and man, did she put it on him that night.

And that was how TSB-2 had sucked him in; she'd been into him because he was an artist, screwed him like a porn star, then spent the next few years trying to turn him into a zero like her and her folks. His continuing fondness for the memory of that first night made him even more pissed at her now, false friggin' advertising.

A fucking divorce...

Leonard walked straight to the Statesman's front desk. The hotel clerk smiled at him. He gave her a sheepish grin. "I wonder whether you can help me to be a gentleman."

She narrowed an eyelid and looked back at him.

He cleared his throat. "I imagine that sounds strange. Well, Margaret Samuels, the Cincinnati Symphony's associate concertmaster, was supposed to stay with me and my wife this weekend, but we were called out of town unexpectedly. So she had to check in here instead." He was losing her again, and he quickly figured out why. "You have a very nice hotel, of course, but her father is my oldest friend, and we feel terrible for not hosting her as planned. I'd like to take care of her hotel bill to make up for it." He slid a credit card across the strip of black granite between them, just the way a bigshot would do. It felt fantastic.

"Certainly, Mr..." She couldn't read the stamped letters upside down.

"Claypool. Robert Claypool." *Middle initial zero.*

"That's very nice of you, sir."

"Heck! It's the least I can do." He gave a mild smile.

She pulled up the record, hit some keys and swiped the card, and he was relieved when it went through, though he'd brought cash as a backup. Citibank didn't yet know Robert was dead. The laser printer to her right spit out a sheet of paper.

"Please sign here, Mr. Claypool."

Damn, $976. More than two months' rent for his doomed farm. Leonard took her pen and glanced at the top of the page.

He memorized the Cincinnati address and noted the room number, 512. He made a scribble on the line by the X. The clerk thankfully didn't check the card to see if the signature matched. Instead, she rudely answered a phone call while he was standing there. She nodded and mouthed, "thank you" as she handed him a copy of the invoice pressed against the card. That made him smile. He'd sold the part. Maybe he should have been an actor. Jazz guys in New York always told him he should get in with a theater pit orchestra...

Leonard went to the elevators and picked up the house phone, making sure to stand where the front desk clerk could see him. He pantomimed his half of a happy reunion conversation with Margaret Samuels while a dial tone and then an off-the-hook warning siren played in his ear. He grinned ear to ear as he imagined her inviting him up. He replaced the phone and pressed the elevator button.

He watched the green numbers ding down, 3, 2, L, and the doors slid open. He brushed past a guy coming out dressed about how he was. The zero uniform. Leonard turned around and hit 5. The doors closed. He tugged off the sweater, pulled a chef's coat from the briefcase and put it on. He stuffed the sweater into the case. The door slid open, and he stepped out.

Leonard smiled at a room service tray full of dirty dishes on the floor just two doors down from the elevator. He didn't even have to hunt one. This was going so friggin' smooth.

He looked both ways, quietly set the dishes on the floor and took the tray. He went into the little room with the vending machines and pulled from his briefcase a bottle of the Haut-Brión, a white cloth napkin and two wine glasses he'd stolen from the Rocky Falls Brewery and Grille. Ah, and the waiter's corkscrew. Nice touch. He stashed the briefcase next to the candy machine and set up his tray on top of the little ice machine: napkin, bottle, glasses, corkscrew. Man, he friggin' hated being a waiter. But tonight it would be fun.

He smoothed the front of his chef's coat, picked up the tray, and walked down to knock on the door.

The hot brunette opened the door about a foot and peeped out at him with one clear, green eye.

"Wine for you, ma'am, compliments of Mr. J. Davis Swaine."

The eye widened, and she opened the door. She wore a white terry-cloth robe with the gold embroidered emblem of the hotel on it. Leonard's eye automatically went to the vee at her throat where the halves of the robe met, but he moved his gaze quickly to the floor. He wondered if he was starting to blush. She was so damn hot it was making him lose his confidence. Suddenly, he got a rush off of it. He was in control here. Him.

He forced himself to remain professional and stepped into the room, looking not at her but at all of the flat surfaces. Within five seconds, he'd spotted the three things he wanted. One for now, the other two for later tonight. Perfect.

"I wonder why he felt like he had to do this," she was saying. "I should be the one sending something to him." Then her voice went quiet when Leonard lifted the bottle and put the blade of his corkscrew against the foil at its neck. She'd spotted the label, understood what a fine wine had been set before her. He had to give her credit for that.

"Wait," she said. "May I see it?"

He handed her the bottle, looking at his feet again but thinking, holy *crap* was he selling this routine. What a buzz.

"Oh my God," she said, reading the label. "Are you sure you brought the right bottle?"

"I'm positive, ma'am. Mr. Swaine's exact words were, 'a special bottle for a special lady who loves wine.' "

"How much did this cost?"

"Quite a lot, ma'am. It's a selection from our reserve cellar, and we have only three bottles left."

"Eighty-two Haut-Brión ... how could he spend this much on me?" she was saying, smiling through her protest. "I can't drink this tonight. Please don't open it. I'll take it home with me."

She was hugging the bottle to her chest. *So hot.* Leonard folded the corkscrew and looked to her expectantly with his hand extended. "I'll leave this and the glasses in case you change your mind."

When she set down the wine and turned to dig into the purse on the nightstand, he slid the keycard off the table behind him and into his back pocket. He had a spare second to steal a peek at her terry-covered caboose. She gave him twenty bucks – wasn't cheap like those people from Track Five. He'd take that into consideration, too. He turned to leave and then stopped at the door.

"Mr. Swaine also wanted me to give you a message," Leonard said. She waited rapt to hear what it would be, and the moment thrilled him. "He asked that you not try to contact him until tomorrow. He said you would understand why. Good night, ma'am."

* * *

Mount Airy's Crandall Hotel was down to one room, and it had two double beds. Right after the room's door shut behind them, Jeff and Caroline stripped each other's clothes and had urgent, infatuated, noisy sex on one bed, defiling every square foot of the mattress over several hours until Jeff felt a near chemical high from it.

"My God," Caroline breathed. "You know how to rock my world."

Then they kissed wetly for another minute, moved to the clean bed, had sex once more, sweetly, then fell asleep naked, tangled together, each smelling of the other.

* * *

EmmaJane woke when Dylin cried. His little footie sleeper thing was totally grungy now, with drool and spitup and even a little stain from poop on it. But Dylin seemed like he was getting to know her – like her, even. He would settle down a lot faster now whenever she picked him up. He would quiet down and stare into her eyes and sometimes even give her a little grin.

She mixed him up a new bottle of formula and realized the big creeper had been gone all day long. She started to worry that maybe he wouldn't ever come back, just leave them locked in here until all the food and water and stuff ran out.

In case he did come back, and in case her diaper trick didn't work, EmmaJane had a couple of the sharp-edged metal lids in the pockets of her jeans now.

Forty-six

After playing a couple of sets at a steakhouse in Cary with the band, Leonard parked again downtown near the Statesman at five after midnight. This week had been exhausting, but as he thought about what he would do now, artistic energy replaced his fatigue. Yeah, man, Leonard was jammin'. *A jazzman's always ready to play another set.*

He focused on the righteous feeling he'd gotten from killing Robert. The guy had lorded his power over Leonard, and it was only reasonable to expect an oppressed person to lash back if you painted them into a corner like that. It was just natural justice.

He walked through the lobby again, and there was no one at the front desk now. A guy, the night manager or something, peeked out from an office off to the side behind the desk, and Leonard raised his left hand in a magnanimous wave as he pulled the smooth, white keycard from his right pants pocket. The guy turned back into the office.

Leonard zipped up the elevator to 521. There was no light at the crack under the door. Very nice. He put his ear to it just to double check. Just the hum of the vending machines down the hall, the dissonant whine of a fluorescent light a few feet to the right of his head. He shuddered. They were wrong notes, sounds that should never make it into any musical composition.

He pulled a square paper envelope from his hip pocket and gently pulled out the thinnest string from the set of four bass guitar strings – the ones from Landrake's Musical Instruments in the old neighborhood. Finding them in an old cardboard box a few months ago and remembering how he'd obtained them had been the first inspiration for the whole album. That exhilarating feeling… Then, as he'd noodled around with ideas, all of the pieces had fallen into place, making it clear to him that making this album was his destiny.

The yellowed paper crinkled as he pulled out the coiled string. He loosed one end from where it was tucked into the tight circle. The tension in the metal released after all these years, straightened the string in an instant with a sound like a whip slicing air. The string dangled between his knees. Tonight he had options. He had the .380 in his right pants pocket and a capped syringe loaded with phenobarb in his left. He probably wouldn't need to use either of them.

He slid the white card into the slot – yeah, baby, just like *that*. A little green light flashed, and metal scraped, and the lever stiffened under his grip. He pressed down, then paused. In a hotel, you always heard this sound of a door opening during the night, and it always turned out to be next door or across the hall. You stirred and then fell right back asleep. He gave her a few moments to do it. Didn't want any screaming, no matter how on-pitch it was bound to be, coming from her.

He opened the door, stepped into the little hallway that led past the bathroom, onto the nice thick carpet that yielded under his stiff leather shoes. He pushed down the lever on the inside of the door, closed it silently behind him. He was safe now.

His eyes adjusted to the darkness, and then he could see her. He smelled something like bourbon whiskey. He was enchanted.

In the light that seeped between the drapes she looked like a fairytale princess. No wonder J. Davis had fallen in love with her. She lay near the far edge of the king-size bed, face down. She had fallen asleep there under the covers, then cast them off, he guessed. She wore some kind of little tank top. And that perfect, tight little booty, with nothing in his way now but a flimsy pair of low-rider panties over part of it. He raked his gaze across the hemispheres of her ass and down those out-of-this-world legs. He'd never seen a body this perfect in person, only on the Internet. It was inspiring, man.

Here on the desk was the precious violin. She'd left an instrument worth hundreds of thousands just lying in its open case, like maybe she'd played a little before bed. He guessed living with something precious like that made you forget to treat it special, made you forget other people would try to *take it*. He closed the case and latched it quietly, fixed its location in his memory.

He found his way to the overstuffed chair he'd seen earlier.

He sat in it quietly, resting the bass string across his lap. He watched her for several minutes, which had nothing to do with his plan. He savored the feeling that he was again about to fix something, was about to commit another act of justice. He would get J. Davis back for fathering a child with his woman through this girl, who meant the same to J. Davis. His dark-vision grew keener by the minute. He could see her face, see dark hair fanned out like a skydiver's on the pillow above her, hear the smooth breaths through her nose, see her shoulder blades flexing with each one.

He pressed the string between the thumb and forefinger of each hand, stretched it taut across his thighs without meaning to, until the pressure was as painful as his constrained erection.

For some reason, she'd left her toothbrush on the table out here. He leaned over and picked it up. Still damp. He put it in his mouth and sucked, getting a strong spearmint flavor but searching for a taste of her, thinking about being in her mouth like the brush had.

He sat watching, the brush clamped between his right molars, and he fell in love with her, too. She was the girl in the black dress in the club next to the table of record producers, his most reliable fantasy since high school.

She was everything he was always supposed to have but didn't get. She had a perfect life in some country club neighborhood, had been born with all the advantages. She'd used them to live out her dreams.

It would be both fitting and very personal for him to make

her a part of his perfect jazz album, he decided. He scraped a thumb across the string's metal winding, making the faintest harmonic sound, and knew he was truly an artist, and she was his muse.

* * *

Leonard paced the moonlit yard outside his farmhouse. He yanked out a tall weed and beat the roots against the ground until the earth fell away from them. He was so friggin' pissed at himself. He had run away! Total stagefright. It hadn't happened to him in years.

He'd had one knee on the mattress next to her pretty ass, was ready to throw his other leg over, press his crotch against that butt and lean his weight against her, be close to her, commune with his muse. Sitting in the chair in her room, he had imagined that, though she would be surprised at first to find him in her bed, she might simply throw her head back in ecstasy and welcome the embrace of a fellow musical prodigy...

But as he had leaned down to smell her neck, somehow that woke her up.

And just like all the other others, she had turned from a perfect princess to a fucking castrating bitch in one instant. She had rolled him off of her and kicked him hard in the ribs before he could press his weight against her – he felt the sore spot now each time he breathed in.

Instead of calmly coming back in at the next measure like a good musician – jumping back on top of her to pick up the part as if he hadn't been ready to play a waltz when a hot jam was next on the set list, he had just grabbed the violin and run out of the room. What a friggin' wuss. Damn, he hated himself for that.

At least he'd grabbed the violin.

What had happened in the hotel room was why he hadn't been much of an improviser before now. What if you fucked up? What if you played wrong notes? With that possibility out there every time you strayed from the score, who could let himself go, be creative enough to make up something awesome in an instant? It didn't always come as naturally as at the home center. You we-

weren't always in the zone. Things didn't work out the way they were supposed to every time.

As Leonard had driven away in the Lexus borrowed from another body shop, he'd seen the police coming to the hotel, lights and sirens. That had freaked him out. Everywhere he went these days, some cop car was on his tail...

Now he had the violin over there on the seat of his station wagon. It was evidence. He wondered whether he should maybe ditch it. He walked to the car and looked through the open passenger window at it. Next to it was the still-unplayed bass guitar string that served to mock him.

Then he'd gotten back here, and the babysitter girl was on some kind of monster period, bleeding on everything, so she was too disgusting to even consider, and anyhow, she looked like a skinny, scared little kid now, nothing like the confident little thing he'd first spotted or the sophisticated musician he'd BLOWN IT with. He had already broken her spirit. So he'd find another way to write her into his composition.

He pulled another weed and just threw this one as far as he could. Disappointingly, it wasn't very far.

He hated doubting himself like this. Hating himself like this. He couldn't stand it. He had to do something. He was angry enough to go ahead and lay down the final track, but that wasn't what he needed right now. He was lonely. He needed the love of a good woman, someone to understand and be sweet to him. And suddenly he knew *exactly* how to make the feeling go away. Marinna. Nothing could make her anything but sweet.

Forty-seven

Leonard downed two mouthfuls of sanitizer and drove the station wagon to Centurion Apartments and looked for the Honda Civic Hybrid he knew Marinna drove. He found the notepad where he had written down the address from Marinna's personnel file, and he clutched the picture from the vet office birthday party that showed her smiling with Dr. Nagra and her coworkers he'd stolen off the bulletin board. He gave her picture face a big kiss, put it into his front pocket. He splashed on some Old Spice from a bottle in the glovebox, then put it back.

He needed to be with her *now*. His pride in the album had vanished again when he had put on the CD in the car and listened to the track he'd FUCKED UP, heard how the burglary he had performed last night now wasn't true to the musical score at all. His blood pressure still felt sky high. He started thinking the whole album was worthless.

He bounded up the concrete stairs, pounded on her door and shouted, "Ma'am, wake up! Please, wake up! Maintenance man! Come to the door, please!"

She opened the door just a crack, and he could see that as sleepy as she was, and with his new hairdo and clean shave and zero duds, she didn't recognize him. "There's an emergency," he told her.

She opened the door wider, and Leonard stepped across the threshold, nudging her backward, feeling in control of this situation and determined not to let that change this time.

He closed the door behind himself and grinned. "Hey. It's me."

She yanked the chain to turn on the lamp on the end table behind her.

"Corey." Her eyes widened, and fear crept into them. "You took the phenobarbital from work."

"My real name's Leonard. Sorry to play a trick on you just now," Leonard told her. "And to introduce myself using a BS name. I just came here because I really need another one of those great hugs of yours. I need to talk to you."

She was backing away from him. Fear widened her eyes, and even though she knew he was in control, she hadn't turned into a bitch. She'd stayed a princess, just like he knew she would. In a way, she had subconsciously been his muse for this track all along.

"I love you, Marinna."

Her back was flat against the living room wall now because she'd run out of space.

"Corey – Leonard, I do NOT want to kiss you," she was saying. "NO. I want you to leave. Please, leave. LEAVE RIGHT NOW."

She loved him. He clutched her right hand – felt a sudden wave of nausea. He doubled over, gagged. The bitch had kneed him in the balls! They were all the same!

"Corey, you get away from me!" she screamed, and ran for the door. He chased her, fishing in his pocket for the bass guitar string. He caught up to her next to a bookcase, pressed her to the wall, made sure she didn't get another shot at his nads, still expecting to puke any second from the first one. He wrapped the string around her throat; the color of her face changed to scarlet. She cracked him on the head with a crystal paperweight, which rolled down his back and clonked onto the floor behind him. That friggin' hurt! Sticky wetness was pooling underneath his hair... He slackened the pressure without meaning to.

Something sharp made him yelp.

He looked down. She had jabbed a friggin' No. 2 pencil into his armpit. "Oh, Marinna." He felt so betrayed. He pulled her to the middle of the floor where she couldn't reach anything else. She pulled out the pencil and stuck it into him again. This time, it broke and half stayed inside him. Now she was whacking at him with her hands, really hurting him, staring at him with terrified blue eyes.

Not sweet eyes. Animal eyes.

But she was losing her strength.

Leonard still felt like puking from the shots between his legs and under his arm, and now blood from his scalp was running down the left side of his face. He was really upset, starting to weep, feeling bad for her, wanting her to be okay, wanting to be nice to her, for her to like him again.

But she had disappointed him. He remembered the desperate, helpless, weak feeling in the car. Though grief and sadness and love had flowed back in to replace his rage, he sniffed in the tears and pulled the wire tighter.

"Marinna? Why? I love you."

She couldn't speak any more, but it was several minutes before she was still, and her eyes never closed. Leonard curled up close to her body and wept for a long time.

Forty-eight

When Jeff woke at 7 a.m., Caroline was still naked but now had a towel wrapped around her hair and was sitting at the room's small desk, listening to her cell phone voicemails. She playfully slapped him away, protesting that she'd just showered.

Jeff looked at Caroline's phone and remembered his own. It was made by the same company, and he realized that her charger fit it.

He plugged the cord in and held down the power button until the phone played its little song. It beeped to indicate that it had retrieved voice mails from the cellular network. Five missed calls. He wondered how long it had been dead. He put his finger on the button to check messages,

"Hey beau, the crew is bugging me about when can they get that furniture out of your loft," Cooperton said in the first message. "Nobody's got a key but you. Is it all right if they cut off the padlock and put a new one on there?"

The next one made him sit down on the edge of the bed: Sarah, his boss, sounding stunned and frantic: "Jeff, my ex-husband has broken into my house during the night and taken Jacob. Um, taken Jacob. He's just gone." A noisy pause. "I know it's the midit's the middle of the night, but I'm hoping you'll get this and come over right away…"

The voicemail system said the message had been left very early Sunday morning, well over 24 hours ago. How long had Jeff's phone been dead, and why hadn't he noticed sooner?

The next message was from Sarah, too, and it didn't make very much sense besides reiterating that she wanted him to come and help her. "… just took him right out of his crib, and called me on the phone while they were leaving, and I think Leonard might – kill, um, the baby, and there wasn't anything to do … Deputies aren't *doing* anything to get him …" She was a mother leveled by the grief of not knowing that her son was safe. Concern tickled Jeff's shoulders and tensed his abdomen.

Caroline read Jeff's face as Jeff ended the call and dialed Sarah's mobile number, and he told her, "My boss' ex showed up in the middle of the night and stole their son out of his crib," and Caroline sucked her lower lip into her mouth.

Now when Sarah answered the line, she was calm and driven. It was clear Jeff hadn't wakened her.

"Haven't found him yet," she told Jeff. "Where are you? Where've you been?"

"My investigation of the Reuss thing led me to Philadelphia," he said, remembering how his boss had arrived at his loft the other night when he'd needed her. "I had some problems with my phone. I'm so sorry I just now got the message.

"Damn it. Philadelphia?"

"Yeah, the fake addresses on the suspect from both the home improvement store and the food delivery business are both streets in the Mount Airy neighborhood of Philly."

Sarah said nothing for a moment. Then: "That's where Leonard's from."

And they both made the connection at the same moment. Sarah's ex-husband was doing all this.

"He's doing all this to get back at you?" Jeff said. "Let me send a picture to your phone to make sure. Call me back."

He used the phone's camera to snap an image from the printout of Cooperton's e-mail and explained to Caroline at the same time. He sent the picture to Sarah, and within a minute, she called

called back.

"Yeah," she said. "That's Leonard. He's been in bad shape lately."

She explained that her husband had been despondent since she'd asked him to move out, that he'd never gotten attached to the baby the way a father ought to, that he'd sounded wild and manic when he'd called this week. "He wanted to settle the divorce in my favor. I tried to make it to where he wanted to meet, the mall, where he was playing with his band. He wanted me to sit and listen to the set, but I didn't get there in time, and he just flipped out, was the opposite of how he'd been on the phone."

"Well look," Jeff said, "I was here to identify a suspect, but if we know who it is, I'll just head back right now. Do you think flying would be faster?"

"It will be faster," Sarah told him. "And I'll have Annie charter you a plane. But as long as you're already there, there's one thing I want you to do."

* * *

A door slammed, waking Leonard. He sat up, turned on the lamp. It was 7:30 in the morning.

Probably Marinna's downstairs neighbor. He wiped his eyes with her stylish blue-and-brown bedsheet.

He reached for the plastic bottle on the nightstand to swallow five more ibuprofen tablets with a double mouthful of Waterless Hand Sanitizer. He smacked his lips.

He had plucked out the pencil fragment and then squeezed half a tube of Neosporin into the puncture wounds under his arm before bed. He'd mended his scalp with butterfly closures, also from the first-aid kit he'd found in Marinna's kitchen. That would do fine. He knew this persistent ache in his nuts wouldn't let him sleep any more, even though the blinds were still dark. He hoped the ibuprofen would dilute the pain.

He'd been afraid there would be an odor, but there was none he could detect so far. He stood and walked to the living room, peeked around the corner. It all felt so much like a dream that he half didn't expect her still to be there.

But the blanket-wrapped bundle was on the floor in front of the couch. He knelt by her shoulders and sobbed until his stomach hurt from the heaving breaths he was drawing.

Get it together and finish the composition, Leonard. He slapped himself on the right cheek, focusing on the cool, muted sting. *What have you let happen these past few days?*

He sniffed again, wiped his nose with a tissue, stood and turned away from the girl.

He had lost his artistic focus. He had gotten caught up thinking about girls, an obsession that had threatened his art – threatened anything of potential value to him – for most of his life.

He had hurt Marinna.

Quickly, Leonard gathered the few things he had brought inside – and the bottle of ibuprofen and first aid kit. He took her keys from the mahogany box on top of her dresser. He stepped outside, not making a sound.

As he gently closed the door to her apartment for the last time, he didn't lock it. He took a silent vow to remain celibate and disciplined and focused until the album was finished. He would make a pilgrimage this morning, have a cleansing experience.

Refocus.

Forty-nine

Jeff and Caroline turned left at a corner where a store's window advertised "water ice," the local name for Italian ice, and showed a drawing of a paper cup containing a brightly colored, frozen sphere.

The address on a street called Tulpehocken was only about 12 blocks from the hotel, an old, two-story white clapboard house that had been divided into three apartments. Nora Noblac had lived here for 20 years. Sarah said Leonard had just been up here visiting her. Mrs. Noblac hated Sarah, but Sarah thought Leonard might have called her in recent days – or even dropped by again – and Sarah wanted Jeff to check.

Nora Noblac's apartment had its own little stoop halfway up the steep driveway. Jeff and Caroline climbed the grade and then the single concrete step, and Jeff found the doorbell button, encrusted with white paint. An old buzzer sounded harshly, heralding footfalls inside the house.

Soon, an inner wooden door opened, and a dour face peered suspiciously through the aluminum storm door.

"Hi, Mrs. Noblac," Jeff said, with a winning smile. "Is your son around?"

The woman frowned. "What's he done?"

Jeff worked to hide his astonishment. "We're in town from North Carolina, and we hope you can help us with an investigation we're working on down there."

Now she looked at Caroline, who was smiling. The woman opened the door, which swung out over the step, forcing them back down to the driveway. "What'd he do, kill his ex-wife?"

Fortunately, Caroline hung a winning reporter grin on her face and made the right move. "Oh, no ma'am, nothing like that. Could we step in and talk to you? Then we can explain everything."

The old lady didn't reply. She just pushed the storm door open another two inches. They had to open it the rest of the way for themselves.

The doorway led directly into a stairwell. The old steps creaked as Jeff and Caroline climbed slowly behind the older lady, and Jeff noticed the smell of some kind of polishing oil mixed with the chemical tang of mothballs. The stairs were wide, as if this must once have been the house's grand staircase, accessible from the first floor before the house had been cut into apartments. At the top of the stairs, Mrs. Noblac took out an antique key and opened a French door with a glass knob and led them across an anteroom to a living area with gold, short-pile carpet.

She glared at Jeff and dropped her weight into a threadbare burgundy recliner. "Well, you gonna answer me? What'd he do? Did he kill her?"

"No, he didn't," Jeff answered carefully.

They hadn't been invited to, but Jeff took a seat on a Victorian sofa with worn, teal upholstery, and Caroline took a rocker off to the side. "When's the last time you talked to him?" Jeff asked.

Nora Noblac dropped her bulk into a chair and took a sip from a tall glass that waited on a table next to it. "He was up about two weeks ago, but I don't like to talk about it. He was dreadful to be around, moreso than usual. Could barely talk to him, he was so upset about the divorce. Very angry. I finally made him leave. I guess he went back down there, huh? I don't know why he did that after she kicked him out. All he wanted to talk about was some album he was about to record, and how that would show me and everybody else what a musical talent he was. That he should never have been stupid enough to give up his music. Seemed to me like he was completely losing his marbles. I thought he might finally go ahead and kill himself, but other than that, I've been kind of afraid of what he might do. So, like I say, what'd he do?"

Other than that? Jeff thought, and wondered if his distaste showed on his face. Caroline looked at him for a cue, and Jeff drew in a breath and said it: "He broke into his ex-wife's house yesterday night and took the baby."

The woman shook her head scornfully and displayed no evidence that the news surprised her. Jeff thought she didn't know about it before he told her, though.

"Lennie always was a screwup," she said. "All he ever wanted to do was play that colored music. His teachers in high school thought that was just the end-all and be-all, and so did he. So he was always goofing around on that big bass fiddle, thump thump thump, all the time in the house. But you see where it got him. I always told him musicians were fruits and what he ought to do was learn a trade. You see the kind of rathole he lets his mother live in."

Jeff leaned forward to urge her on, and she kept going.

"He never should have moved to Raleigh. That snooty woman he married in New York dragged him down there. He knew he'd be miserable in the suburbs, but he was too much of a pansy to stand up to her about it, so down he went. Then she was pregnant. Sure enough, she left him not six months after it was born."

There were five seconds of awkward silence. This was how the woman referred to her own grandson? *It?* Jeff looked around the apartment. There were no photos or other mementos to indicate the woman had a family.

Mrs. Noblac let out a nasty laugh. "I would have divorced him, too. Couldn't get him to grow up and keep a real job. All he wanted to do was lie around the house and play that marijuana music, mess around with bands that were never going to make anything. The girl was right about one thing – if he couldn't make it as a bass player after 20 years of trying in New York, it was never going to happen."

"What kind of music?"

She gave a bitter chuckle. "Jazz."

She stood to indicate that she wanted them to leave.

"But whatever else he did, whatever else he does, that's not my son. I didn't raise him to be like that."

* * *

Halfway down the staircase to the driveway, Jeff's phone rang, and the display said it was Margaret's cell number, so he answered. The phone hadn't been plugged in very long this morning, so the battery gauge already read low.

She sounded like she had been crying, something he had never known her to do.

"Jeff, I'm so sorry to bother you, especially after you specifically asked me not to, but something happened last night, and I don't know anyone else around here, and I'm feeling really upset and afraid, and I'm not used to dealing with the police ..."

He interrupted and asked her to calm down as gently as he could. "What's wrong?"

She sucked in a breath, then begin again, irritated.

"I was sleeping, last night, in my room, and I felt somebody's breath on my cheek," Margaret said. "That woke me up, and my cheek brushed against this wet piece of plastic. Jeff, I think he had my toothbrush in his mouth, and his spit was all over the handle. I bit his hand, then sort of rolled to the other side of the bed and kicked him. He made this little squealing sound and grabbed the Marquis de Savigny and ran into the hallway. I double locked my room door and called the front desk on my room phone while I dialed 9-1-1 on my cellphone."

Jeff's pulse was racing now. He was sure this was Leonard Noblac, too. The guy had targeted Margaret. And he realized the only reason he would have done that was because of her connection to Jeff. A blood vessel at Jeff's temple felt like it might burst. Why hadn't Cooperton told him about this? Then Jeff realized he hadn't known, because city PD would have handled it, and they would have had no reason to believe it was connected to the string of Rocky Falls burglaries.

Jeff's fury returned, and he squeezed the phone so tightly it hurt his hand.

"I think it's the guy I've been hunting. My boss' husband, actually," Jeff said. "I'm up here in Philly looking for him. And shit, he's down there, coming after you. How did he get into your room?"

"Well, either I didn't close the door completely, or he had a key. Nobody forced the door."

"Maggie, are you all right?"

"Yes."

"Did you hurt him?"

"I hope so. It felt like I landed a pretty good one. It hurt my heel, anyway, and he groaned like it hurt, and then he scurried away. Thank God."

"He climbed into your bed? Was he trying to rape you?"

"I don't know. He had this piece of wire in his hand," Margaret went on. "I think he was planning to choke me with it – but I woke up. Jeff, what if I hadn't woken up?"

"You did wake up," Jeff said, on the driveway now, and leading Caroline down the precipitous driveway to the curb. "You made him run away. Where are you?"

The Raleigh Police had taken her to their station to get her statement, she said.

"And he stole your violin?" Jeff couldn't believe it. He tried to center his swirling thoughts. The burglar must have planned all along to take the instrument, because grabbing it wasn't the sort of thing you'd think of while you were running away from someone who'd just kicked the shit out of you. "Did they catch him?"

"No. It was dark, so I didn't really see him, other than he moved like a man. And that he seemed kind of short. And he's another string player."

Definitely Leonard Noblac. "How do you know?"

"Calluses. I bit one of his fingers, and the end was just like leather. He didn't even feel it. You have to play for years to get calluses that big and lose the sensation in your fingertips. I'd say he's a cellist or something. Makes sense – he would know what the Marquis was worth, then, maybe –"

"He's a jazz bassist," Jeff interrupted. "Upright bass. Do the police have anything?

"No. There hadn't been anybody strange in the lobby all night, the hotel managers said. The police searched all the streets and alleys by the hotel. There wasn't anybody. They said there haven't been any similar crimes recently. But he could have driven right past them."

Caroline was staring at Jeff and taking in the end of the conversation that she could hear, concern lining her face.

Jeff knew Margaret could take care of herself, but he had some caveman instinct to protect her. "What are you going to do now?"

"They said they'd send an officer to the hotel with me to get my stuff. We have today off, and then tomorrow the bus takes us to D.C., which is the next tour stop. But I don't have a violin. I'll have to see if anyone else brought an extra that I can play. If so, I'll need to practice my ass off. The Marquis has a different feel than most violins, so I might sound like crap playing something else unless I work."

"You should think about taking a concert off."

"Can't do that. Don't want to."

"Well, call and tell me where you check in."

"Okay."

"I'm coming back down there today, Maggie."

"I wish you were here now. You could be my bodyguard." She said it with an affectionate smile in her voice.

"Like you need one."

By now, Jeff and Caroline were climbing back into the Audi. He glanced behind the seat at the briefcase that held the Glock. He realized that he was feeling so angry and worried now that he would have to be extra careful with the gun, be sure not to jump to any conclusions. Just focus on making the next right decision, then the next.

Margaret gave an ironic laugh. "Ashlyn would pitch a fit, anyway."

"Ashlyn and I broke up." Her end of the line went silent. "It wasn't your fault. It hadn't been working for a while, and my slee-

sleepover with you just forced the issue. It's the right thing."

Jeff sensed something and looked to his right. *Shit.* Caroline was still listening, now boring into him with angry eyes.

"I guess that explains the wine," Margaret said. "By the way, thank you for that. It was very sweet and generous of you to send it. It touched the softest part of me, just like spending the evening with you again touched me."

In trying to do the math on Caroline's reaction and what he would say to her after the call, Jeff's mind reacted too slowly to what Margaret had said. What the hell wine was she talking about?

She was still talking: "It's why I knew I could call you this morning. But, like I was telling you, I have my own knots to untangle right now, even as I realize how totally in love with you I still am. I need you to give me a little time."

"*What wine?*"

"The wine you sent to my room."

"I didn't send you wine."

"What? 1982 Haut-Brión. From the reserve list? You spent more on a bottle of wine than my boyfriend spends on jewelry for our anniversary of dating. I couldn't believe that the robber didn't steal it. But in the dark, it could have been a $10 merlot."

Jeff was shaking his head and squeezing his fist in the air now. "A man delivered the wine to your room, last night?"

"Yeah, a waiter from room service."

"Older guy. Salt-and-pepper hair."

"How'd you know?"

"I think that's the same guy who attacked you. What can you remember? You have to see this picture. Check your phone for a picture message after we hang up."

Jeff held the phone in front of him, bracing it on the steering wheel as he called up the picture and punched the keys to send it to Margaret.

"Who is Ashlyn?" Carolyn was asking, "And was she your girlfriend when you were screwing my brains out last week?"

"Like I said," Jeff told her. "We broke up." He hit send.

"So I'm a rebound thing? And who is Maggie? Is she your rebound too? Just in case I ever have to track the origin of a sexually transmitted disease, how many current sexual partners do you have?"

"Look," Jeff said, "none of it has anything to do –" Jeff's phone rang, and he shrugged to extract himself from the conversation with Caroline and pressed the TALK button.

"It's him, but with a beard." Margaret was strident. "The guy who brought up the wine. Now that you say your guy is a bassist, with the beard, I think it's the guy from that jazz band we saw at the brew pub. The bassist who knew how to play. I'm pretty sure. Yeah, double-bass fiddle calluses."

Caroline was staring out her window, fuming, and Jeff started the car, pulled away from the curb with a yelp of the tires and tried to remember how to get to the airport.

Fifty

Leonard had a copy of the *Independent Weekly* newspaper open on the passenger seat of Marinna's ice-blue Honda Civic Hybrid. Since he wasn't hauling anything heavy, this eco-friendly car was a socially conscious choice for the 25-mile trip to Durham. There wasn't a commuter train.

He'd stopped at a filling station, called 911 and said he'd heard a struggle. He'd told them how to find Marinna's apartment. He'd said he wanted to remain anonymous.

He swallowed past a thick lump as he merged from Interstate 40 onto the Durham Freeway. They had probably found her by now. He focused his thoughts on the newspaper critic's review of the new exhibit at Duke University's Nasher Museum of Art.

Leonard exited at Duke Street, and just when he could glimpse the old tobacco factory buildings in Durham's downtown, turned left on Chapel Hill Street. That soon turned into Duke University Road and took him onto the elite campus.

He pulled into the museum parking lot, got out and used Robert Claypool's credit card at the kiosk to buy a parking receipt to leave on his dashboard. They would be watching the card now, probably, but he was willing to bet he'd be gone from here before the Raleigh cops could show up or send someone. Maybe a Leonard sighting here would divert attention from Raleigh for tonight. That would be good.

The museum building itself was a sculpture by a world-famous architect, an elegant jumble of white steel beams holding up a glass roof over a plaza among three huge galleries set amid a forest. It was a place that meant something. Getting this built had taken focus. Leonard took note.

He paid his seven dollars at the desk in the center of the plaza and ducked into an exhibit called, "Memorials of Identity: New Media from the Rubbell Family Collection."

The gallery was dark, and in each chamber, a DVD projection by a different video artist played on a wall. Leonard walked briskly through the pale blue glow from the screen in the first chamber, rounded a partition and caught a chill. This was what he was looking for: "Sprawlville" by Sven Påhlsson.

A projector played Påhlsson's computer animations across the wall, a series of 3-D scenes – architectural renderings, really, viewed from crazy camera angles over and over:

A vast, near-empty parking lot as viewed from above, its light standards and stripes like the hairs of a freakishly regular beard, the only detail of interest a couple of curbstones askew in an otherwise monotonous grid of angled parking spaces. The camera dived on the empty scene again and again, crashing the viewer's nose into the asphalt over and over, the angle changing slightly each time, dizzying you with new perspectives yet revealing nothing new. There were a dozen pans and zooms of a blank billboard in the parking lot, a relentless search for meaning in an object that held none.

Leonard sat on a bench. Now the camera moved down the street of a generic tract subdivision as if the camera were pointed from the window of a moving station wagon. Identical houses scrolled through the frame, house after house after house, the only differences being whether it was a motorcycle, a car or a boat in the driveway, whether there was a barbecue grill or a lawnchair or not. Påhlsson showed random lumber and cinder blocks strewn in the yards, telling the viewer that the houses were just bland piles of these same prefabricated elements.

Påhlsson got it. Påhlsson hadn't bothered to depict any people in this emotional desert landscape. Like the houses, the people were all so similar to each other in the suburbs that they weren't worth drawing. The people were just the tiny white rocks in the suburbs' endless sheet of sun-bleached asphalt.

A new scene: Påhlsson's virtual camera panned again and again around a shopping mall showing the buildings for what they truly were: a pile of empty boxes with air conditioning units on their roofs.

Leonard was humming softly to himself. He wanted to work on a project with Påhlsson, compose some music to go with his projections.

Leonard nodded to himself, felt the energy of communing with another artist, admired the Scandinavian for being so singular in his purpose – indicting American suburbia. The more Leonard thought about it, the more sure he was that this album was his life's entire purpose.

On the gallery wall, a plain white garage door closed again and again and again. Leonard wiped his eyes on his sleeve, stood and walked from the gallery.

As he stepped outdoors, the trees that surrounded the museum yielded to gusts strong enough to flex their sturdy trunks.

Now all the fragments lined up in his mind; he saw how it would all work.

The pain in his side tugged at him harder now.

The people Leonard had chosen to make him famous had to be at least as smart as he thought they were, and they must be close to figuring out who he was.

He had to finish. It was time for the final track. Today.

Fifty-one

Jeff called Cooperton on the way to the airport and told him about Noblac, told him to fill in Raleigh PD about the connection to the attack on Margaret, to put out Noblac's picture to all the TV stations.

Cooperton ordered his lead investigator to do a criminal background check.

"Hey," Jeff said to Caroline, touching her arm gently. "I know you're mad, but wait to hear what I have to say. When we get on the plane, I'll explain. I'll tell you right now, I'm not toying with you. But right now, we have to get to the airport, because we have to get back to Raleigh and help catch this guy. Let me tell you what he did last night to Margaret."

They picked their way through neighborhood streets as Jeff recounted the attack.

"All of this is stressing me out," she said, turning her gaze back inside the car. "There's the freeway, and the airport is south."

When Jeff checked in again with Cooperton from the airport, Cooperton said the check on Noblac had come back completely clean, no arrest history or warrants.

"His last known driver's license was out of New York in the 1970s. We ain't got a local address on him. Not listed in the phone book, neither."

"Shit."

Jeff hung up, found the airport road to the general aviation terminal, and within 15 minutes, he had given the key to his Audi to a dubious looking stranger, and they had shaken hands with their pilot – a trim, crewcut guy in his early 30s who was probably ex-military – and climbed into the cabin of a Beechcraft KingAir C90 B, a small turboprop plane.

Jeff had to duck when he wasn't sitting and could easily touch both sides of the little cabin. With seats for seven, all done in creamy white leather and burlwood, it looked like the most luxurious minivan interior Jeff could imagine, with a lavatory in the back.

The pilot started to taxi and turned around and told them, "Tower just radioed that we're second for takeoff, so I'll have you there in a little under two hours. Once we level out, help yourselves to a cocktail." He pointed out the bar.

Alcohol was the last thing Jeff wanted, but 10 minutes after takeoff, he reached into a refrigerated compartment and pulled out Diet Cokes for him and Caroline.

Jeff's seat faced Caroline's across a narrow, pull-out table. It was surprisingly quiet in here. As they passed over D.C., Jeff told her everything about Ashlyn, how he'd known the relationship was ending and failed to handle it soon enough, how he had spent the evening with Margaret but not shared a bed with her, how he had thought Caroline was just playing around with him at first. And how it *was* over with Ashlyn, now.

She listened to all of it glassy-eyed, looked as if she might start to cry. She said, "I didn't know I had to take a fucking number," and then just shook her head. She turned to peer out of one of the circular windows at the freeways and streets and parking lots of the Eastern Seaboard that were flowing beneath the plane.

Jeff decided to leave her alone. He'd felt a strong bond forming with Caroline, and he wanted to say something to let her know that he hadn't intended to offend or hurt her, but he was sure he couldn't come up with it right now. His personal life seemed an insoluble mess. So he pushed his woman troubles aside; catching Noblac was more pressing, anyway.

He looked out his own window, and his thoughts kept coming back to what Mrs. Noblac had said about her son being obsessed with making an album. He visualized his office windows, considered the stylized nature of the all the burglaries, remembered each carefully crafted bit of graffiti.

He thought about laying out his theory for Cooperton, then realized it was Margaret he needed to talk to.

He leaned around the partition, and the pilot pulled his headset away from his ear, and Jeff asked, "Any way to make a phone call from up here?"

"You got a cell with you?"

"Yeah. Is it okay to use it?"

"Sure. The only reason they don't let you on commercial flights is they want you to pay for their expensive seatback phone service. Best to keep calls short, though. The network has to swap you from tower to tower a lot, so it's easy to get dropped."

Jeff went to a seat farther from Caroline and placed the call.

"What do you think about the idea that the guy is composing a jazz album of crimes?"

"God, Jeff, of course," Margaret said. "That has to be it."

"Listen, that apartment that the guy filled with furniture? It was my place."

"Why didn't you tell me?"

Jeff had a momentary thought that having told her might have kept her safe from being attacked, but that didn't make any real sense. "I didn't want to ruin the fun we were having together the other night."

She made a little squeaking, incredulous noise, and he could see what a huge mistake it had been to keep it from her. But he pushed ahead in the conversation.

"Listen, though, the note he left at my place had some weird acronym or word and said, '5. Emptiness and Fullness.' Maybe the five meant 'Part 5,'" Jeff said. " 'Emptiness and Fullness' sounds like it could be a composition title. He capitalized the nouns in it — at the house where the furniture that turned up at my loft was stolen, there were these two shapes painted on the wall. One was an empty glass, and the other one must have been full. He took their master suite, full of furniture, emptied it and then filled up my place. The other graffiti at the house said, 'One bedroom apartment, fully furnished.' Like what he stole from them was enough to furnish a whole apartment. It also said, 'You won't really miss it.'"

"You and your loft were the end of the fifth movement of the composition," Margaret said.

"At the bar, the guy said they were recording an album," she said. "I remember the name of one of the songs because it was so bizarre: Everything Comes Due at Once."

"Yeah," Jeff said. Caroline was pulling out her own phone to make a call.

"Oh my God. So this guy probably felt like I upstaged him," Margaret said. "So last night, he came to attack me. I thought about it after we talked, and I think that wire he had was some kind of an instrument string. It was thicker than a violin string, though."

"Well, probably from a bass fiddle."

"Not that thick. The other thing, was, when he woke me up, he was humming. I don't think I told you that. But I think back, and it had a jazz swing feel to it."

She hummed a few notes, but Jeff only caught a few of them over the erratic phone connection. "That melody will always be stuck in my head."

Then a pause. "I can't *believe* you didn't tell me it was your apartment."

* * *

First, Leonard had to scoot from the farmhouse.

He drove the little Civic back to Raleigh and got there well before noon.

He was risking everything he was and had for this album, including his recent contented life in that little doomed farmhouse. Through the whole project, he had wondered how he would feel when he got to this point, when he would leave this place. He decided he felt perfectly true to himself about it. The album was brilliant so far; he loved every note of it, and it wasn't yet finished. He had to finish it. That was what artists did, poured themselves into their art without worrying about the consequences. He would move on to a mansion after the album was done, as long as he didn't get arrested.

Leonard stopped at a U-Haul store, which was also a Texaco gas station, and rented a 14-foot panel truck. He bought a load of cardboard boxes and rolls of packing tape. He made the freaking storekeeper's day. This time, he wouldn't need a furniture dolly. His arms and legs were still sore from moving everything by himself, but that was nothing compared to the wounds from the last 12 hours.

He took the truck back to the farmhouse and spent the rest of the morning packing his things, loading the boxes onto the truck one at a time.

He panicked mid-morning, worrying he had waited too long to make this move and that the fancy legal investigator and nineteen cop cars would roll into the yard at any minute. How many security cameras had captured his photo?

After he rolled closed the door of the U-Haul and locked it, he checked inside the farmhouse one last time. He looked at what he'd left and tried to see it through the eyes of J. Davis Swaine, legal investigator, imagined him finding it.

He decided to paint the title to the album's final track on the gray, glossy tongue-and-groove boards of the house's comfortable old front porch:

LIBERTY AND JUSTICE FOR ME

Leonard drove the rental truck to the shopping center parking lot where he had stashed the Nissan Pathfinder in plain sight. It was still here. He used the key remote from his pocket to unlock it, then opened the rear hatch. He pulled out two magnetic signs: Two big diamonds that said "Raleigh Alarm Security." He'd peeled them off a wrecked van at the junkyard. He stuck one onto each of the Pathfinder's rear doors without anyone noticing – or at least, if anyone did notice, no one seemed to care.

* * *

The creeper came into the stinky little room late in the morning and stared again at the diaper sticking out of EmmaJane's jeans – not at her face or her boobs like when he had first grabbed her. Her little plan seemed like it was working.

"Get the kid and the stuff you'll need for the next day or two," the creeper said. "We're going somewhere else."

The next day or two. EmmaJane felt like someone had dropped ice cubes down her back. She put two cans of formula, several bottles of water and a few cups of stew into her hoodie and tied the arms together to make a bag. She looked at the creeper's feet and said, "You need to carry the rest of the diapers, or we'll have a mess."

And she couldn't believe it, but the guy just bent down and picked up the diapers, just did like she said. EmmaJane put Dylin on her left hip, slung the bundle of supplies over her right shoulder and followed the creeper out of the room and out the front door.

It was overwhelmingly fantastic to be outdoors, and suddenly she realized she could run. Just then, the creeper pointed his little pistol at them, and she felt like crying.

He loaded them into some kind of SUV thing, and she was concerned about Dylin riding in it without a baby seat. She sat in the back seat, on the right, and set the bundle of supplies on the seat to the left of her. When the creeper sat the handgun on the seat between his legs, she switched Dylin to her right knee and stuck her left hand into her pocket, pushing her index finger through the pull ring of a beef stew lid.

Fifty-two

Just a few minutes after the Pathfinder turned onto Rocky Falls Boulevard, EmmaJane saw a bunch of police cars heading the other direction, and the creeper sighed and told her "We were just in time, sweetheart. They almost caught us."

Why hadn't they gotten there four minutes sooner?

The creeper was smart, EmmaJane had to admit. He had left just in time, somehow. And he had turned on the child locks in the back seat of the car, so she couldn't open the door and jump out with the baby at a stop sign. In fact, he laughed when she tried the door handle.

When the car was moving, she knew that attacking the creeper would make them wreck, and Dylin would get hurt, maybe her too. She wasn't quite sure she could hurt the man enough with the sharp lid to get away, and, like, now she didn't even want to try it.

And as soon as the car pulled into a neighborhood, he took Dylin in the front seat with him.

"I will snap this baby's neck if you do anything cute," he said. "So you just follow me into the house."

EmmaJane didn't recognize this neighborhood. It was a lot

like the one she lived in, but with townhouses. Judging by the short distances the creeper had driven her, it couldn't be far away from her house. Still in Rocky Falls, for sure. She was trying to decide whether she should run and when, but the creeper pressed a button on a big, honkin' remote control, which opened the garage door, and then drove the car inside this townhouse's garage.

Then he put the door down behind them, got out and opened her car door.

It was a townhouse with no furniture that seemed brand new, like nobody had ever lived here. But for some reason, there were a bunch of big jugs of Purell lying on the floor right inside the door. The creeper led EmmaJane into a downstairs restroom with no windows, handed the baby back to her and told her, "His name is Jacob. He's not my son."

Duh, EmmaJane thought. The creeper threw the bundle of supplies into the bathtub behind her with a clunk.

Then he shut the door, not slamming it, just pulling it gently until it clicked. A whining noise repeated over and over. He was using a cordless drill to screw the door shut. She and Dylin were trapped again.

* * *

As the Beechcraft landed at RDU, Jeff was thinking about how to get a line on Noblac, trying to think whether there was any predicting what "song" a flipped-out jazz musician would perform on them next.

Sarah'd said she didn't know where Leonard was living. He had refused to tell her. He could be renting a place under some sort of alias.

The plane taxied to the private terminal, and Jeff and Caroline climbed out.

"I guess we have to rent a car," Jeff said.

"Someone's picking me up." She ducked underneath the strap of her overnight bag.

"Can we please talk later?"

Caroline shrugged, turned, and walked the short distance through the terminal to the sidewalk.

Jeff ran a hand across the top of his head and decided to let her go for now. Either she would calm down, or she wouldn't. There was a little car counter. He stopped by and got a rental in the works.

Next he went into a pilots lounge with a computer for checking weather reports and e-mail. Jeff used it to sign onto the website for the skip-trace service CB Allison subscribed to. It was a database compiled from mostly private records, such as data filed to the three major credit reporting agencies, and he was willing to bet Cooperton's guys either didn't have a subscription or hadn't thought to try it. He ran a trace on Leonard Noblac, sipping burnt-tasting complimentary coffee as he punched the search parameters.

The first result was bingo. The electronic dossier, a compilation of information from dozens of public records databases and several private ones, started with a history of all known addresses for the suspect. The Philly address matched Mrs. Noblac's house, and there was an Upsal address from the '70s. A North Raleigh address showed that "associated persons," Sarah Rosen and Jacob Noblac had shared the address until a few months ago.

And there was a current address on Rocky Falls Boulevard, updated to the credit bureau just a week before, in the northern reaches of Rocky Falls. Jeff snatched up the phone and called Cooperton. "I got the address."

"All right." Cooperton sounded edgy. He scribbled. "You back home?"

"I'm at the airport, and I'm about to rent a car."

"I'll send a few uniforms out there to keep an eye on it while we gather up the SWAT team. Meet me behind the Kroger on Rocky Falls Boulevard up the road from his house in half an hour." Jeff grabbed his rental car folder and key and jogged toward the parking lot.

Fifty-three

Leonard Noblac rented a motel room just to have a private place to get ready for the show.

He was having a big lunch. He sat at the foot of the too-firm bed and popped the lid of a Styrofoam container. He stared at a 16-ounce T-bone steak, so rare that it was barely warm. He fixed up his baked potato with butter and sour cream, a little black pepper and lots of salt. He swallowed five more ibuprofen tablets and poured the rest of the last bottle of the H-B into the plastic cup from the bathroom and started to eat.

The game show on TV ended, and the news theme music played. They led with a helicopter shot of his farmhouse surrounded by cop cars.

"New today at noon: Wake County deputies have surrounded a North Raleigh farmhouse, and now we understand the SWAT team is ready to storm it," a grandfatherly anchor said. "This may be related to the terrifying string of bizarre burglaries and killings recently in the Rocky Falls community. Also at this hour: Another murder, possibly related: a young woman found strangled this morning in her Rocky Falls home. We're live on both scenes with team coverage."

Leonard dropped the forkful of meat. He grinned and grabbed the remote to change the channel. "… been here all morning, at this white house you see behind me, David, but so far they aren't telling us why. Armed officers are making us wait here, a good distance away, and we hear that they may be preparing to storm the house …"

Leonard flipped to the third station, the CBS affiliate, the most respected news operation in the Triangle. They were rolling the videotape of a report that said nothing that Leonard hadn't already heard on the other stations. Afterward, the anchor asked the reporter, "Do police think this house could be somehow linked with the recent string of burglaries in the Rocky Falls community?"

The answer, "Patricia, that's an excellent question, and one we're all asking, but one police just aren't willing to answer right now. We'll stay on the scene all day and have more this evening at 6."

"Thank you –"

Leonard wanted to shout, "Plug the album, man!"

Pride filled his belly like a meal he'd been hungry for all his life.

He flipped back to the other channels in time to hear both reports ending. He leapt to his feet and cheered that his name hadn't been mentioned, that no composite sketch of his face had been broadcast. His show today was extremely important, and with any luck, he'd have just enough time to play it before they got too close.

Leonard had his laptop plugged into the room's Ethernet cable. He'd been uploading some final updates to the album.

And now, even though the newspaper reporter had never written him back, he signed onto America Online and composed a note to her: "Dear Ms. Kramden: I'm playing a show this afternoon. You should come. You'll know it when you see it. Here is a link to my new album, which I've just released for free online. I think you will find it very interesting." He hit send.

He turned off the computer, snapped it shut and left it on the motel room's little table, stood up, and left.

Fifty-four

Jeff found the SWAT team members sweating under a high afternoon sun as they staged behind the grocery store.

They had a converted half-length school bus, painted blue, which contained the SWAT guys' gear. Team members arrived one by one, eyes screaming with adrenaline. In the cloud of diesel exhaust from their bus, they strapped on body armor, radio headsets, goggles and helmets. Each man took and checked a fully automatic machine gun pistol with a foldable stock: a Heckler and Koch MP-5.

Jeff realized the bus was armored with plate steel.

"Our sniper says there's been no movement in the house since he set up on it more than two hours ago," the SWAT commander told Cooperton. "Noblac's car's there, a ratty old Brady Bunch station wagon. No house lights on. Suspect might be there, but if he is, he's probably asleep. We should probably move soon."

When the warrant arrived, the SWAT team huddled for some instructions Jeff couldn't hear. Then they boarded their bus.

"What about us?" Jeff asked Cooperton.

Cooperton walked toward the Crown Victoria, pulled his walkie talkie from his belt, turned up the volume, and handed it to Jeff. "Get in. Listen and pray. Get ready to go in there with me when they say, 'Clear.'"

Jeff sidled into the passenger seat and realized with sudden alarm that he'd left his briefcase and the Glock in the rented Toyota. Cooperton might not want him armed, anyway.

"Hey, L-T, should I have brought my Glock?"

"You mean you didn't?"

"I'm not used to having it yet."

Cooperton just shook his head solemnly. "Glovebox. You can borrow my throwdown. Anyhow, keep it in your pocket if you can."

"Your throwdown?" Jeff unlatched the compartment and found a little silver .38 with fake mother-of-pearl grips on top of the Crown's owner's manual. He turned over the pistol, cool against his fingertips. The gun was the unreliable, shiny brand the woman at Protection Armaments had first showed him.

"Yeah. In case of a police emergency, it's the gun you throw down." Cooperton retrieved a Coke bottle that was waiting in the cup holder and spat. "I think that one shoots. The drunk I got it off of had just popped off a couple rounds in his back yard before I took it away. See how many rounds are in there."

"What's a police emergency?"

"Like in case you shoot a guy in self defense and he doesn't have a gun, after all."

Jeff felt as if he'd taken another bite of the apple from the tree of the knowledge of good and evil. The world's institutions worked a lot more messily than anyone wanted to believe, and the firm's deal with Cooperton was recorded in the same shady section of the moral ledger. So was Jeff's romantic life.

Yet if all went as planned, they were about to stop a crazy guy who was violating the sanctity of people's homes and murdering them and their pets.

Jeff checked the pistol's magazine and counted eight rounds. He slapped it back into the handle and chambered one with a click. Someone on the radio said, "Keep this channel clear. The bus is going in. As soon as it stops, send Perkins and Jeffries around back. Everybody else wait a ten-count and take the front door."

* * *

"Empty. Nobody here. All units stand down."

When Cooperton heard the words over the radio, he gassed the Crown Victoria and the car lurched into the yard of the run-down farmhouse, making Jeff grab the door handle to steady himself.

He and Jeff both piled out of the car and jogged to the front porch, where two SWAT guys were sitting on the steps. Someone had painted the words "LIBERTY AND JUSTICE FOR ME" on the tongue-and-groove floorboards behind them in black spray paint. It smelled like the paint could be fresh, and a couple of the letters were smudged as if someone had walked across them while they were wet.

"Nothing, L-T," one of the cops told Cooperton. "All the furniture's gone. It looks like he just moved out. There's packaging from moving supplies lying in the kitchen. Power's still on."

"Do me a favor, son," Cooperton replied. "Go check the mailbox. Maybe we can tell how many days' worth has come since he left."

The guy walked to the road and hollered back, "Ain't no mail in here."

"Might've just missed him." Cooperton keyed his radio and ordered everyone out of the house. Then he switched channels and called for his forensics team.

A young deputy in SWAT gear came out the front door and grabbed the lieutenant's arm. "There's a plastic what-you-call — instrument case — in one of the bedrooms, in the middle of the floor. It's the only thing in the room. I'm worried it might be a bomb."

Cooperton covered his whole face with his hand. "I guess we're gonna play with all our toys today, then. Call out the bomb squad."

As the guy described the case, Jeff realized it sounded like the one for Margaret's violin. "Y'all can't blow that up just to see whether it's a bomb like you usually do," he cautioned Cooperton. "That's a half-million dollar violin."

* * *

"My day keeps getting worse," Cooperton said, spitting with special force when a cell phone call notified him that there'd been an apparent homicide, a strangulation by ligature at Laurel Lake Apartments, just outside his own patrol district.

"Any graffiti?" he asked the patrol sergeant on the other end of the phone. After a couple of seconds, Cooperton added, "Then y'all just work it like always and call me if somethin' weird comes up."

It was 1:19 p.m. when the bomb squad arrived at the farmhouse. The squad had its own panel truck full of gear. It turned out that two of the guys from the SWAT team were also on the bomb squad – though not its commander, who took his time arriving.

Once that guy had been briefed, he decided to use the bomb retrieval robot, a remote-control vehicle the size of a toy dump truck that ran on miniature tank treads. Two men set it inside the front door, then hurried away from the house.

Jeff, Cooperton and the commander sat in the back of the panel truck, where the video monitor for the robot's camera and its control joysticks were located. They watched the monitor as the squad commander drove the vehicle down a dingy hallway, consulting a rough layout of the house one of the deputies had drawn.

"You'll use the robot to bring it out?" Jeff asked.

"You crazy? We're going to open it right there where it sits."

On the monitor, the violin case came into the frame, looking as big as a bus from the low camera angle. It sat near the center of a filthy rug.

"Watch this," another bomb squad member said. "Sarge's good with this thing."

The violin case was resting flat, and when the robot got close enough, there was Margaret's name on the leather-framed tag. "That's hers."

The sergeant grabbed two new joysticks, anda robotic arm came into view. The joysticks clicked slightly as the cop manipulated the robot's arm to lift the tab of one brass-plated latch. When it flipped open, the hasp naturally fell away from the case. The sergeant grinned.

He backed the robot, drove it up to the other latch, then repeated the procedure. But this latch held firm while the whole case lifted off the ground. He cursed, backed the robot out and made the approach again. "The thing must be pretty light. I reckon that's a good sign."

"Be careful; maybe the violin's still in there," Jeff said. "They weigh nothing. Half-million bucks, maybe more. Seriously."

On the next try, the latch popped right open. "Now we just have to lift the lid," the sergeant said.

"Remember," Jeff said. "Half a million bucks."

"Shit, My kid's cost $179." The sergeant looked at Jeff. "I'll just flip it open. Cover your ears in case it's full of C4."

He finessed a blade from the robotic arm between the halves of the case, then jerked the joystick.

On the monitor, the whole case flipped over and landed face down, its black plastic blocking the camera lens.

"Nothing blew up," the sergeant said.

Jeff cringed for the Marquis de Savigny, but when the guy backed the robot away and re-oriented the camera, they could see that the case had been empty.

"Shit," the sergeant said. "Why don't y'all ask me for something tough, next time. Y'all can go on in."

* * *

Cooperton stood in the middle of one of the farmhouse's bedrooms, the violin case at his feet, and plucked the note from the case using a pair of forceps too tiny for his sausage fingers. "Recognize the handwriting?"

"Yeah," Jeff said.

The note from inside the violin case matched the one that the burglar – that Leonard Noblac – had left at Jeff's loft.

"The answer you've been looking for is so cool," the note

said, "that I left it in the fridge."

Cooperton opened the bedroom window and hollered for the bomb squad captain again.

"Quit loading that robot. We need y'all to send it back in here to open up the fridge."

* * *

The refrigerator didn't explode either, though the possibility of a bomb cleared the house again.

When the bomb squad leader gave the okay, Jeff and Cooperton rushed into the kitchen.

The old, avocado-colored fridge held a few food crumbs, an empty bottle of fancy Bordeaux and an orange vinyl binder labeled, "Libretto: ~~Stolen Inspiration~~ In the First Degree."

An evidence tech gingerly pulled it out with two latex-gloved fingers.

"Go on and open it," Cooperton instructed.

The tech used the tweezers, and Jeff looked at the first page with bleary-eyed fascination.

> Track 1. Everything Comes Due at Once
> Track 2. Rich Pets / Poor Kids
> Track 3. Choke Point
> Track 4. The Natives are Priceless/Murder
> Track 5. Emptiness and Fullness/Aggravated Assault
> Track 6. Babe Watching/Aggravated Stalking
> Track 7. No Son of Mine/Kidnapping
> Track 8. She's Your ~~Margaret~~ Marinna But She's My Muse/Rape

and written in pencil next to that, "Homicide." Last on the list:

> Track 9. AND JUSTICE FOR ME / *Come and see*

The tech gingerly turned to the next page using the forceps. Sheet music drawn in by hand on paper printed with blank staves, intricate-looking compositions with parts for several instruments, ran pages apiece. Words underneath the lines, like lyrics. The first one said, "The dog is gone before she begins to feel the drug coming into her system…"

The other pages were similar, with music and words that seemed like stage direction, describing the series of crimes Jeff and Cooperton had been investigating over the past week or more.

"Can you go back to the first page, please?" Jeff asked the tech, his voice trembling.

He looked down the song titles. Jeff knew he and the Ellises had been Track 5. He didn't think he knew what crime Track 6 was – Jeff worried that there was another body to be found. Jacob was Track 7. He realized with dread that Margaret was supposed to have been Track 8.

"Call your homicide guy," Jeff told Cooperton. "See if that dead female this morning was named Marinna." Then, "Shit, that's the receptionist from the veterinarian's."

Cooperton made the call, asked the question, and shut the phone with a grim nod.

Jeff called Margaret to make sure she was still okay.

Fifty-five

Back in the Pathfinder driver's seat now, Leonard pulled on the shades and a ball cap with the same diamond logo and company name as the door signs. He'd snagged the hat through another van's open window in the alarm company parking lot two weeks ago. He grinned as he thought of the same diamond-shaped logo on a stick in most of American Estates' postage-stamp lawns.

The neighborhood's 40 homes were packed into 10 buildings, two of which were still under construction.

He pulled into the main road, then drove past the townhome building right in the center of the development, the one where Jacob and the babysitter were penned up in the downstairs bathroom of the end unit. People had moved into all the units in the building but that one, and Leonard had been able to steal one of the keys out of the real estate lockbox when an agent had met him there a week earlier to show him the property.

Next door to that building on one side was a fully occupied building. On the other, the still-naked bones of an even newer one had been framed, and roofers were hammering plywood onto the rafters.

Feeling the ache in his side twist into a live current of pain,

Leonard swiped the heel of his hand across his forehead and did another mouthful of sanitizer. That would be the last one.

He parked the Nissan at the curb of the occupied building. He allowed himself a couple of deep breaths to suck the pain back into his belly. Then he got out and ploomped down orange safety cones near the front and rear bumpers and clicked together the plastic buckle of his tool belt. The pleasant bulk of the pistol weighed in a cargo pocket of his jeans.

He walked down the sidewalk looking for indications that anyone was home; he found none. Three o'clock on a Monday, and everybody was at work 30 miles away earning the money to pay the mortgage that gave them this place to sleep before they got up and went to work to earn the money to pay the car payments, insurance and gas that let them drive to work and earn the money to pay the mortgage. Leonard smirked and shook his head. And all day long, nobody was enjoying or even watching all the stuff these cats were working so hard to have! It was inspiring, man.

He walked around the end of the building, where he spotted the plastic conduit that carried a bundle of telephone cables into the row of townhomes.

He took a battery-powered reciprocating saw and cut through it in about nine seconds. And that was all it took to keep five expensive alarm systems from calling the police on him, not that the police took alarm calls seriously.

Back around front, he pulled out his black-market garage door opener and hit the button while standing at the garage door to the end unit. Soon, the motor cranked the door open, and Leonard walked inside, and, as usual, found the door from the garage into the house unlocked.

When he opened it, a siren blared – a lot like the trumpet part for this track – but the alarm system computer wasn't even getting a dial tone. A little dog of some kind started yipping it up next door. Leonard pulled the flimsy door shut but didn't let it latch. He calmly walked back to the garage opening and looked up and down the street, then pretended to make some notes on his clipboard, the siren wailing the whole time. One old lady poked her head out her front door across the street. He waved at her, stifling a wince as he raised the arm, and pointed at the Nissan, complimenting himself for turning the hazard flashers on.

"Sorry about that," he yelled. "Testing."

She glared at him and went back inside. Everyone in the suburbs knew an alarm siren was just annoying evidence of a malfunction, yet everyone still had alarms. Leonard shook his head again, went inside and pressed the button to lower the garage door. He found the circuit breaker for the alarm and shut off the siren, which was making him crazy.

* * *

Sarah Rosen's desk phone rang. She caught a chill when she recognized her ex-husband's voice in the earpiece.

"I'm calling to tell you where to find Jacob."

Sarah tried to measure her tone, not to say anything that would make him change his mind. Sarah's heart throbbed dangerously fast. She settled on a flat, "Okay. Is he all right?"

"He's, uh, living the American dream." The phone clicked off.

It was Leonard's joke about the house of Jacob's babysitter, a modest, three-bedroom townhome in an ever-expanding neighborhood called "American Estates." Whenever they'd gone there to drop Jacob at Lauren's house, Leonard had always said, "If this is the American dream, I hope I wake up soon."

Sarah cleared the line and punched in the number for Lauren's house. It rang three times and went to voicemail. Damn. She called Lauren's cell.

"He's not with me," Lauren said. "I wish he was. I'm at the mall right now putting up posters with his picture."

Sarah grabbed her keys, tugged on her purse strap and strode toward the elevator. She opened her phone and asked Jeff Swaine to meet her at Lauren's house.

* * *

Leonard looked down the block and was pleased that no one had come outside from the row of buildings where he would be working. He'd be able to finish the album without interruption. He was humming the bass riff now. He set a plain cardboard carton onto his handtrucks, ignoring the ripping feeling under his arm when he lifted it. This album was going to be a classic, just like he'd planned. He'd rehearsed it a hundred times in his mind.

Inside the townhouse, he opened the carton, reached in and unscrewed the top of one of the jugs of sanitizer. He pulled out the plastic pump spout and threw it onto the floor. He doused the sage green living room sofa with the alcohol gel. He soaked the carpet leading all the way up the staircase with a second jug. He connected the two locations with a line of goo across the floor from a third jug. And upstairs, he pulled down the attic stairs and poured gel on them, too. That way, the fire would spread into the attic and all the way down the building.

Leonard stood there reveling in the alcohol vapor. What was an artist supposed to do with a godawful place like Rocky Falls when it had a store that sold napalm by the shipping pallet?

The little blondie and the bastard were eight units away, in the next building, Leonard realized. There was a 15-foot space between the buildings. Leonard would not set their building on fire. But if it caught on fire naturally, it was the way things were supposed to be.

"Relax," Leonard remembered Reverend Ted saying on Sunday, "Everything will turn out just as it's supposed to."

Back downstairs – this part was crucial to the composition – Leonard searched the people's kitchen for a book of matches. He found a silver bowl filled with matchbooks from local establishments. Rocky Falls Brewery and Grille. Perfect.

He tore out a match, struck it. He used it to ignite the rest of the pack. They flamed up with an angry shush. Leonard threw that onto the line of gel across the living room, and the gel ignited with a such a magnificent whoosh that Leonard was inspired to rewrite the score of the final track to include it. But there was no time now.

* * *

After an hour, sweat was running down EmmaJane's back.

Dylin – she wouldn't let the creeper re-name the wittle guy – was asleep in the tub on most of her hoodie. She had sheared off one corner of the fleece fabric with the stew lid, and now she used the little scrap to protect the palm of her hand from the metal as she used the stew lid to cut through the wall. The wall wasn't made out of wood; it was that kind-of chalky stuff sandwiched between two layers of paper.

The tub was surrounded by tiles, so she hadn't tried cutting through there. And the wall with the sink and toilet or the one with the door didn't give her enough room to work. So she was kneeling just past the end of the toilet, cutting in the middle of the wall beside it, just cutting a little slot, and suddenly, she the lid sank an inch into the wall. She'd broken through.

As she rested a minute and looked at the little cut, she thought about the time Katie's dad had gone all mental and punched the wall. It was made out of the same stuff, and he had punched right through it. It was, like, hollow.

EmmaJane stood raised her foot, and kicked like hell. She made a little dent along one edge of the slot. She kicked again, and this time the chalky stuff gave way.

"Yeah!" she shouted, and that woke Dylin up, but she kept kicking until a one-foot square of the stuff had caved in.

"I'm getting us out, sweetie," she told Dylin, and she knelt by the hole and started digging the junk out with her fingernails, making the hole grow.

EmmaJane ripped the wall material away in bigger and bigger chunks. She'd uncovered a shallow space, but behind that was another layer. Some kind of plywood stuff. She ripped more wall stuff out until she found the seam between two pieces of the plywood. She slipped the stew lid between them. Something scraped.

This was the outside wall on the front of the house. And that wall had a layer of brick, at least the first story did. She wanted to sit down and cry. But somehow, she knew that wasn't good enough. She had to get her and Dylin out. The creeper would come back. Something really bad would happen.

She turned around and checked out the door. It was made out of some kind of fake wood, cuz when she knocked on it, it sounded hollow. She took the stew lid and started sawing a little slot right in the middle of it.

* * *

Back in the driver's seat, Leonard grabbed a pack of Marlboros from the Pathfinder's passenger seat. He stripped off the cellophane, flipped open the top and plucked a cigarette from the front row. He put it between his lips, lit it with the dashboard lighter and tried not to cough or breathe in too deeply.

He slid off the seat, walked around behind the Pathfinder and stuck his head into the hatch and took two more gallons of the gel. He had a craving to swallow some more of it now, but he disciplined himself not to.

An electricity consumed his whole body, the rush of a man fulfilling his life's dream. He grabbed the jugs by their handles and walked to the townhouse building under construction, right through one of the gaping front doorways into what had been destined to become a center unit. That destiny was changing.

As he looked through the forest of two-by-four studs with no drywall on them yet, a dozen shirtless, stubble-bearded guys sawed and marked lumber and wandered all over the place. But Leonard had a tool belt and a ball cap with a company logo, probably from some other subcontractor, they'd figure, so he looked like he belonged on the jobsite. And he kept the cap's bill pointed toward the floor, so none of these framers or roofers, or whatever they were, said a damn thing to him.

He looked for an area downstairs away from where they were all working. He settled on the niche under a middle unit's staircase. He carefully opened one jug and poured a big puddle of gel onto the floor there. Then he climbed the stairs, opened the second jug, and walked slowly down, trailing the cleansing goo behind him.

His cellphone was ringing now. He smiled at the display. His wife, again. *Just keep driving honey. Come see me.* He pocketed the phone.

He inhaled the alcohol vapor, took two more steps backward toward the front doorway. He tossed the cigarette into the puddle of gel.

Whoosh.

And the workers were all looking at the fire and yelling to each other to get the fuck out of there.

Fifty-six

Jeff smelled smoke like a house fire – burning wood and plastic – as he pulled up to the address Sarah had given him, a cheaply built townhouse in a new neighborhood that might be in a working-class family's price range for a starter home. Maybe the construction guys down on the next block were burning their trash or something.

Sarah's Lexus sedan squealed in behind the Toyota Corolla he'd rented at the airport. Jeff got out. He tried to tell her about finding the libretto, but she was fixated on finding her son, and she believed he might be inside this house. Together, they went to the front door and banged on it.

When Sarah finally explained that Leonard had called and told her Jacob was here, Jeff said, "Shit, you should have told me that on the phone. Did you call the cops?" And when she shook her head no, he speed-dialed Cooperton.

No one answered the door. Jeff stood on tiptoe and peered through the semicircular glass window at the top of the door. It seemed pretty obvious that no one was home.

"Huh," Cooperton said through the phone. "I'll get some deputies out there."

* * *

EmmaJane's tennis shoe stretched the little cut in the inner skin of the door upward and downward. "Yeah!" she shouted, and kept kicking, excited about maybe escaping, but still feeling bad that the noise was making Dylin cry.

Once she got a big hole, she was able to peel away the door's skin in big pieces. There were some squiggly pieces of, like, cardboard honeycomb stuff in the middle, and she just kicked at them, and they flaked away, and pretty soon, the outer surface of the door peeled outward from a bottom corner. With three more kicks, enough of the outer surface of the door was loose so that she could bend it out to make a little flap they could fit through.

"Dylin, honey, we're outta here!" EmmaJane picked him up, pushed the flap out, being careful to hold it so it wouldn't spring back and hit him, and set the baby on the tan carpet on the other side, where he suddenly started bawling louder. Then she burrowed her own way through, laughing and whooping a little as the flimsy material dragged across her back. She stood up.

The creeper was sitting cross legged on the floor, five feet away. He set down his cordless drill and picked up a violin he had sitting there.

"You're slick."

EmmaJane squealed. The creeper stood and stuck his hand into his front pants pocket.

She grabbed Dylin and balled herself up in the corner, curling her body across the baby to protect him.

EmmaJane knew from watching TV that the clicks meant the man was getting a gun ready to shoot. She peeked up at the silver pistol pointing toward them again. She tried to think what to do.

The gun fired.

EmmaJane's mind leapt. A warning shot, she realized, off to the side of them a couple of feet, but enough to let her see he was serious. She didn't want to, but she stood up, totally shaking, and Dylin was screaming his head off, still, on the carpet.

"Come here."

She walked as slow as she could toward him, and he was holding out his hand with a hundred-dollar bill.

"Thank you for babysitting. I'm sorry if you were uncomfortable. You can go now."

EmmaJane just stared at him. Was he like, planning to shoot her in the back as she left? But he looked serious. Now she looked down at Dylin, and she stepped over and knelt to pick him up.

Bam! The pistol fired again, and EmmaJane was crying and her ears were ringing even worse, but she didn't think he shot her or anything, but maybe he was about to.

Now the creeper said, totally calm, "Just *you* leave. I'll take care of *him*."

He had her by the collar now, half dragging her toward the door that led to the little hallway and the front door where they had come in. She was sniffling; Dylin was still crying, and now the guy was prying open her fist and sticking something into it. Through her blurry tears, EmmaJane saw she was holding the violin now, which looked real old. He stuffed the money into her front jeans pocket real slow, and she thought she would vomit.

"Be careful with this," the creeper said, almost, like, flirting with the violin the way he ran his finger across the strings of it. "It's the only thing of true value I've come across while working on this album."

Now his gross hand was finally out of her pocket, and he was pushing her toward the open front door and onto the steps and still talking:

"About the album – I friended you on MySpace, so if you click Accept, you can listen and hear what you've been a part of."

Now EmmaJane was standing on the townhouse's little brick stoop, and the sun was so bright that she was squinting back against it, and all she could think about was how *Dylin was still in there.*

"Two more things," the creeper said. "Be careful. The neighborhood's on fire. And could you try to find my wife? She should be here in a minute or two. She's a redheaded bitch named Sarah. An asshole named J. Davis Swaine will probably be with her. Tell them where to find their son. Tell them I'll be here waiting to talk to them.

EmmaJane ran down the steps and up the sidewalk, thinking the guy was mental and that there was no wife or David Swaine around here, but determined to find somebody who could help before he had time to hurt Dylin.

* * *

Jeff stuck the phone back into his pocket. A loud crack sounded like a gunshot.

"Oh dear God," Sarah said, and grabbed his sleeve.

"Where'd that sound come from?" Jeff asked.

"I don't know!"

"Well, it wasn't inside this house. It was somewhere else. Behind us, sounded like." Jeff noticed the smoke smell again, and as he scanned the buildings across the street. Smoke in two places: Leaking from under the eves of an end townhouse a block over, and erupting out of the construction site two buildings from there.

Another shot. Jeff and Sarah hastened down the steps to the sidewalk and took a few steps toward their cars.

An SUV sped past as they were looking around trying to figure out what to do. Then a teenage girl ran up to them, unkempt, upset, wildly waving her arms. Holding a violin.

"Are you Sarah?" and when Sarah nodded, went on, "There's a creepy man. He has your baby in a house back there." She pointed to the next block. "He, like, kidnapped me from my house and made me take care of the baby for the last few days," and the girl pushed back a couple of sobs and said, "He wants me to take you where he is. He says he wants to talk to you."

Jeff grabbed the violin. It was definitely Margaret's, and a shot of adrenaline poured into his blood. "Wait one second." Jeff jogged back and opened the door of the Corolla and set the violin on the passenger floorboard. He grabbed the briefcase with the Glock. He was about to see the man who had done all this.

Meanwhile, Sarah had gone the other direction after the girl, inexorably pulled toward her child, and Jeff sprinted to catch them and told them both, "We have to be really careful. He might want to kill all of us." He turned to the girl: "Stay here, by the cars."

She nodded and backed away, looking lost.

Jeff handed Sarah his phone and said, "Call 9-1-1," and she did it as they jogged down the block, beseeching the dispatcher for the police and the fire department, trying to describe where they were. Now her own phone rang, too. She told the dispatcher to hold on. She stopped running, and Jeff stopped too, and she opened her phone and told it, "Leonard, damn you, where are you? ... He says put him on speaker."

She pressed the button. A man's voice whispered, "Hi there, Mr. Swaine. I have your son here, the little bastard you put in my wife's belly, and I can either shoot him now, or I can give him a little shot with this needle. But either way, I'd sure like to talk to you."

"Sarah's my boss. I didn't give her a baby!"

"I see you met the babysitter," Leonard's electronic voice continued, as if he hadn't heard. "I already paid her. She did an excellent job. I'm right across the street from where you are. You can see me standing by the window with the baby."

Jeff found the silhouette in a window. Flames chewed a hole through the roof of the building next door. And the unfinished building on the other end roiled with flames now, which licked at the end of the building where Leonard was.

"Sarah, honey, drop your phone onto the sidewalk," Leonard whispered. "The girl can stay where she is. She's done with her job. But I'd like to speak with the two of you. It's number 318. Hurry. Not much time now." Then he shouted, "Come on up. He's ready for his shot."

Sarah dropped the phone, and they ran around the block to the front of the building, found the right door, which led into an end unit and was standing open a crack. The vinyl siding was melting off the end of the structure from the intense heat from the fire next door. The heat made it difficult to stand there.

They dashed into the house, and the place was empty, never lived in. They stumbled up the stairs toward the second story, the main living area where the baby was crying, hearing the fire roaring next door, Jeff certain the building they were in was catching on fire by now, too. He stuck his right hand into the briefcase and drew the gun. Just as Sarah registered the gun, Jeff spotted a second pistol lying on the landing, a little chrome automatic that

Leonard must have dropped.

Sarah reached down and picked it up, so Jeff beat her up the stairs and was the first to spot Leonard Noblac in the dining nook, his back to them, facing out the window. Jeff trained the sights of the Glock on him. A small, portable CD player spouted jazz, and he was holding the crying, writhing baby down on his lap, and Jeff's vision was a tiny circle, as if he were looking at the son of a bitch through a drinking straw. The man seemed oblivious to Jeff's presence behind him, was squeezing an air bubble out of the syringe, and when Jeff told him to stop, the man said, "He needs this," and Jeff was within five feet now; the point of the syringe stuck in the child's chubby thigh with the plunger extended and the son of a bitch's thumb reaching for it.

And Jeff was kneeling with Leonard's neck and back framed in the sights, and the split second seemed to last a minute, and he told himself, *Careful of the baby; just one shot.* And he squeezed it off, concentrating on not letting his trigger finger's movement spoil his aim.

And blood soaked his strawhole of vision.

Before Jeff could lower the pistol, Sarah appeared in the sights, taking the baby in her hands, wailing and wiping away blood and trying to see whether he was wounded, and what was left of Leonard Noblac was lying crookedly against the baseboard, gurgling. Lumber creaked in the structure above them, and he screamed at Sarah that they had to get out before the fire trapped them.

They sprinted downstairs and across the street, away from the fires, and knelt on a tiny, green front lawn to tend to the baby, and the syringe still dangled from the thigh by its needle. Jeff snatched it out and saw liquid still inside the barrel, the plunger depressed about halfway. How much sodium phenobarbital did it take to kill a baby? Or worse, damage his brain?

The child screamed shrilly and Sarah was saying something about baby CPR, and Jeff stripped off his dress shirt and began wiping the child down to try to see whether he was hurt any other way. He couldn't find any wounds, and he cracked open the phone with slippery fingers and called 911 for an ambulance and screamed that you didn't do CPR while someone was breathing.

How long did they have before the drug started shutting down the baby's body?

And now the teenager was here again, clutching Sarah's phone, kneeling next to them and bawling and for some reason screaming over and over, "Dylin!"

All the help seemed to arrive at once, an ambulance, more fire engines than Jeff could count, police cars. Jeff quickly explained and pointed to the townhouse where they'd been, but it was totally engulfed in flame now and no one was going in there, especially when Jeff told them he was pretty sure the only person in there was dead. Paramedics listened to the baby's chest and said something about good vitals, and Jeff gave them the syringe and explained what he thought was in it, and then their relief turned to full professional alert, and he and Sarah and the child were in an ambulance headed to Wake Med, and a paramedic was on the radio demand4ing to talk to a doc to find out what dose of the stuff was fatal and what countermeasures they should take.

AFTERMATH

Fifty-seven

Jacob was fine.

The syringe contained no sodium phenobarbital. There was a trace of insulin that probably meant it was a used syringe, but Noblac had filled it with a harmless liquid, injectable sterile saline. The son of a bitch had made Jeff the instrument of his suicide.

It was a brilliant misdirection to give him or Sarah absolute justification for shooting Noblac dead on the spot. He had even left his pistol – which had been stolen in the Hegwood burglary – on the landing in case Jeff or Sarah hadn't thought to bring one.

Trinity turned out to be right about the Glock's knockdown power. Jeff's single shot had entered the base of Noblac's skull and pureed the lower half of his face on the way out. A clean shot.

Because the fire had instantly cremated the body, the medical examiner was pissed that he couldn't use dental records to confirm the ID. Instead, he had Jeff and Sarah swear out affidavits that the deceased was "personally known to them."

* * *

Jeff could have saved the child and put Leonard Noblac in

jail for the rest of his life simply by pocketing the gun, walking over and taking the kid out of Noblac's hands.

Jeff had killed a man. That changed him somehow, made him someone he'd never wanted or expected to be.

Cooperton sat with Jeff in the hospital waiting room as Jeff doubled over with the realization of it, Cooperton telling him, "You didn't know, beau. You had to figure he was fixing to kill that baby. Me and every other cop in the state of North Carolina would have pulled that trigger. You did right. We needed to be rid of him."

That was true, Jeff knew. It was good that Noblac was gone.

Yet even killing for a noble cause infected Jeff with a heart-sickness he knew would always stay with him. He would have liked to discuss it with his grandfather, who had never talked to Jeff about the horrors he had seen and inflicted in the South Pacific. Pa-Paw, a jovial, good-looking storekeeper from a tiny town, had military discharge papers that read, "MACHINE GUNNER." He had come back to Albany, Georgia, with that experience weighing on his shoulders heavier than the ammunition belts that had draped them in combat.

And the man had found a way to delight in the next 60-some years, singing in the church choir and teasing with his children, grandchildren and then great-grandchildren. He never drank. He never abused his family. But even in the few years before the funeral, asking any question about The War stretched away the smile, silenced the baritone, glassed over the eyes.

Lots of fellows in Pa-paw's generation, the ones who made it back to America, shared that heaviness, understood it with him, Jeff knew. And Jeff thought maybe his grandfather would have discussed this with him now.

* * *

Jacob was so young that he would never remember his abduction, of being in his father's arms when his father died.

But people would tell him.

* * *

No one besides Leonard Noblac died in the fire at American Estates. A chocolate Labrador broke a window of his unit to escape, then barked at the door of the neighbor's unit, a night-shift cop, waking him so he could get out, too.

The blaze destroyed 16 townhouses – four buildings with four townhomes each. That configuration had been chosen to avoid building code requirements for firewalls and sprinklers when more than four units shared a building. Six fire departments needed 10 hours to control the blaze, and afterward, all that was left of three of the buildings was brick veneer and naked concrete slabs. Firefighters counted it a miracle that they contained damage to four additional townhouse buildings to melted vinyl siding.

Public officials made noises about changing the fire code, but with the money that developers contributed to campaigns, Jeff knew it would ultimately go nowhere.

Families had been living in seven of the destroyed homes. Six didn't want to move back, but neighborhood covenants required them to use their insurance proceeds to rebuild on the spot. If they wanted to sell after that, they could.

The same company that built the townhomes the first time said it would be happy to rebuild them.

* * *

Trinity called the day after the fire to remind Jeff he'd never turned in his handgun permit. He picked it up at Cooperton's office and took it to Protection Armaments.

Trinity gave Jeff his grandfather's watch back and told him the sheriff's investigator had already come by that morning to do his pro-forma investigation of Jeff's shooting of Noblac. She'd told the guy she had taken home some documents to file and that the permit was among them. She'd told the guy to check with Cooperton that it had been issued.

"I asked him if you was in trouble," Trinity told Jeff. "He told me, 'Naw, we don't prosecute the good guys.'"

Trinity said she was off work in half an hour and would love to hear the story of what had happened over a drink at a bar she knew.

Jeff told her no thanks.

* * *

Caroline's series, "Inside story of the Rocky Falls Jazz Murderer," with an icon superimposing a bass fiddle, a forklift and a musical note, led the front page of the *Triangle Progress Leader* for a week. It started with "E-mails from 'reader' were actually messages from killer," and worked up to a climax on Friday with a vividly drawn scene of her "exclusive interview" with Noblac's mother and "the moment all the pieces suddenly came together during a quicksilver private-plane flight from Philadelphia back to Raleigh."

Though many of the trailer park residents had complained about being displaced, they certainly hadn't killed Mickey's dog in protest, it was now obvious. Yet *The Triangle Progress-Leader* dropped that thread of the story without explanation.

Jeff no longer worried about how to apologize or explain to her. The way she'd handled the story, he didn't feel he owed her any more. He wasn't sure she hadn't been using him all along for access and inside information anyway. Plus, she wouldn't be living in Raleigh much longer, he figured. She could pretty much write her own ticket.

* * *

Jeff drove the Marquis de Savigny to Margaret's new hotel in downtown Raleigh, and when he knocked on the door of her room, her boyfriend from Cincinnati answered it.

"This is Jeff," Margaret said. "My old buddy from college." And the boyfriend regarded Jeff with suspicion, especially after the long, emotionally freighted hug that he and Margaret exchanged.

She thanked Jeff for retrieving the violin and put it into a brand new case, and Jeff gave all the credit for getting it back to EmmaJane, whom Margaret said she would have to be sure and meet someday. Jeff said he was sorry about what had happened to

Margaret, and she said what could you do about wackos – at least she was safe now.

And as Jeff stood to leave the room, she squeezed his hand and told him, "Thank you for being such a great friend."

* * *

Two weeks before the pet killings, Leonard had stolen the credit card bills from the truck that drove mail from RDU to the local Raleigh post office, the Sheriff's Office concluded. In the middle of the night, the driver always stopped at the same diner for coffee, and Leonard had apparently gotten inside the trailer and stolen the big burlap bags on three separate nights.

* * *

EmmaJane's parents had gone to the Sheriff's Office about her disappearance, and because there was no evidence of a crime, they'd put her down as a likely runaway, never thinking she was connected to the Rocky Falls burglaries.

After being reunited with her parents, EmmaJane went into counseling for post-traumatic stress, and the woman was actually kind of cool. Plus her life was better after that, because her parents *paid attention* to her again. When they asked how she was doing, they really wanted to hear her answer.

* * *

Now Sarah Rosen remembered introducing Mickey Reuss' new wife to her husband a few months earlier when he was on the lookout for new piano tuning clients. And New Wife remembered making small talk during the tuning appointment about how her husband had spent more than ten grand to cure the dog of cancer. In fact, she'd told Leonard, they had taken the dog to the same vet who had cured the cat two doors down. Indian lady at the pet hospital out on Rocky Falls Boulevard. It was amazing what science could do these days.

And Leonard had told her, "You know, I should write a

song about that."

Fifty-eight

EmmaJane had told the police what Leonard had said about the album and about friending her. When she'd signed onto her account at the police station and accepted the Myspace friend request, they'd all gained access to Noblac's page, where he had posted tracks that matched the titles in the libretto that Jeff and the deputies had found in the farmhouse refrigerator, plus the demented explanation for the "album." The last track, added the afternoon of his death, was called, "Liberty and Justice For Me," with the note: "If my wife and her adulterous lover are going to wreck my life, I can't let them do it halfway. They have to WRECK MY LIFE."

A notation said, "Download now – major promotional effort underway will make this highly collectible."

In real life, Leonard Noblac may not have had a single friend, but online, he had 1,200, and hundreds of them had already downloaded every track on the album and passed it along to their own friends who had sent it along to theirs. There were thousands of messages complimenting Leonard on "Felonious Jazz," the project that inspired his crime spree, including praise from jazz scholars at famous universities.

Myspace took Leonard's page down right away, but the damn album was on the Internet now, reproducing in the wild. And when the media realized the burglaries and the music were connected, they played the songs on the air, and more sick minds around the world began to copy and share the music. It was achieving the cult status of Charles Manson's drawings. Leonard had been right to post at the top of the page, "This is the project that will make me a famous jazzman."

* * *

So Jeff had become the executioner of a jazz antichrist. Of what Noblac had posted on the page, what most troubled Jeff was how right he thought the disturbed man was about suburban sprawl, meaningless existences, shallow social connections, demeaning jobs.

But it wasn't like being trapped in poverty, Jeff finally decided. People in the suburbs had choices, and if living a comfortable, bland, safe existence was all they wanted from their historically unprecedented freedom as Americans, they were entitled to that without a Leonard Noblac bursting in and fucking it up for his own reasons.

Leonard Noblac had had a choice, too, Jeff knew. He could have taken his divorce settlement and moved wherever he wanted and lived the kind of life he wanted. But he was too crazy or crazed to do that.

Instead, he'd stubbed out his life on the mechanically reproduced landscape of Rocky Falls.

Jeff took two weeks off from work. He spent the first few days trying to work through the tangle of negative emotions on his own while getting the loft ready to live in. Cooperton offered to return the Glock, but Jeff asked him to hold onto it. Jeff wasn't going to do anything. But still. He also decided not to drink for a couple of weeks.

And four days into his time off, the morning after the third time he found himself yelling in the middle of his loft to vent the toxic emotions balling into something like a tumor at the back of his throat, he found the number for a counseling center, called and explained his situation and got an appointment before lunch the same day.

The therapist was a woman about 15 years older than him named Riley who reminded him how his mom had looked when he was 10. She gave him a seat in the middle of a comfortable blue sofa in her dim office, sat in an office chair and faced him holding a yellow notepad. It took most of the 50-minute session for him to tell her the whole story that had led to the shooting. She listened carefully, making a few empathetic noises and extensive notes.

"My God, what you've been through!" she said when he finished, and he knew she'd been listening to him, deeply. That felt good. She was looking right into his eyes now. "What's bothering you the most?"

"Why would a guy do all of that? It doesn't make any sense. I want you to tell me exactly what was wrong with him."

Riley pushed her shoulders toward her ears. "I don't know, of course, but it sounds like pretty classic narcissistic personality disorder slash antisocial personality disorder. Patterns of thinking that gave him a lust for fame, a disregard of other people in favor of himself. But who knows."

Jeff shot back: "And how does a guy with serious problems like that live a normal life for decades and then one day start killing dogs and kidnapping teenagers?" He checked his tone; he was behaving as if he were angry at Riley over it.

Riley cocked her head to one side, intrigued, not taking it personally at all. "Psychologists might say he 'decompensated.' Lots of people live decades with serious mental health issues by creating coping structures that keep the problem in check just enough to get by. Some of those habits are positive, like exercising to burn stress. Lots are destructive, like alcoholism. But if you put enough weight on those psychological braces, sooner or later, they break."

She shifted position in the chair again as he thought about that. "But I'm asking how *you've* been feeling since the shooting, Jeff."

Jeff blinked twice. "I've been wondering how in the hell does the guy get the idea that I'm the father of his wife's baby?

Sarah is just my boss. I can't imagine that she slept with anyone else, either."

One corner of Riley's lip turned upward. "Well, surveys show about half of all men have at least fleeting doubts that they're really the father of their newborn. But 98 percent really are. It's poor self-esteem, men not believing they're worthy to help create new life. This might explain why he didn't actually kill the baby. Because on some level, he knew ..."

Jeff was failing to hold the train of what she was saying. He kept thinking about Leonard, marveling that as near as anyone could tell, the guy had committed the elaborate series of crimes by himself, through meticulous planning and the use of tools. Using handtrucks to move heavy pieces of furniture. Parking his ingeniously stolen vehicles inside garages so that he'd have plenty of time to load stuff undetected. Identifying gaping security weaknesses and exploiting them.

Now he noticed Riley had stopped talking again. She was looking at him. He met her eyes, and only then did she resume speaking.

"Jeff, that's my best-guess explanation for Leonard's suspicion of you, but the bigger point is, again you're telling me what you've been *thinking* since the shooting. What have you been *feeling?*"

"Pissed off."

"At who?"

"At Leonard Noblac."

And Riley stared at him in the most curious way. "You must be kidding."

"No, I'm not kidding."

"Pissed off at him? Really? You seem absolutely fascinated with him. Honestly, you seem a little in awe of him."

And in that startled moment, Jeff realized two things: A part of him did admire the man he'd killed. And the reason he was angry was that the guy had been completely in control of the whole string of burglaries, and he'd led Jeff down a breadcrumb path like a chump. If Leonard hadn't wanted it, Jeff doubted he would ever have found him.

"I'm pissed off because he set me up to shoot him, set me

up to look like a hero, be called a hero, when I know it's not true. He made me his tool. It all ended exactly how he wanted – *exactly* the way he wanted, and he loaded me down with a horrible experience of killing a man."

"But according to the news, you solved the mystery. You tracked him down. You stopped him."

"No. He was in control. I just walked along at the right moment. I just played the part he scripted for me. That's what I always seem to do, drift along until something happens to me. Or I just do what I think someone else expects."

And Jeff thought of drifting so long with Ashlyn. He realized how he blamed himself for failing to find a way to stay with Margaret after college. He'd let the last woman he was sure he loved float away because of – because of logistics.

"Well," Riley said, beaming. "That's interesting."

He looked at her. "Yeah?"

"Yeah. We're learning a lot about you here. You admire Leonard Noblac because no matter how antisocial and destructive, he seized control of his life. You feel you're too passive. Leonard Noblac, over the last few weeks at least, is the least passive person I can imagine. And on some level, you envy that."

Jeff was shaking his head no, and then he stopped. He nodded instead. "Maybe that's true. But what I was thinking before you said that is, if I'm not careful, I could snap like that one day myself.

"That frightens you."

Jeff nodded. "What do you think was the last thing that pushed him to that point?"

Instead of answering, Riley softly said, "I think that's a real breakthrough you've just made, Jeff," compassion thick in her voice. "But that's enough of analyzing of that guy. We might talk about him some more, but only as it relates to helping you. We're going to spend our sessions together talking about *you*."

LATE MONDAY

Fifty-nine

Leonard Noblac turned around too quickly in the narrow aisle, and he knocked five bottles of pills off the shallow shelves with a crash like a handful of baby rattles. The alarm – this one an old-fashioned boxing bell – hammered away, hurting his ears. Yet he bet he easily had five minutes before the first deputy arrived.

He scanned the alphabetized labels behind the pharmacy counter until he found the Cipro. Pharmacists locked up the narcotics in a safe overnight, and that was okay, because he still had some Vicodin he'd stolen from the vet for the pain. But they didn't bother to secure this great drug, the antibiotic that could kill just about anything that infected you.

The wounds under his arm complained louder every minute, but still Leonard had driven the U-Haul truck hundreds of miles, waiting for nightfall, before stopping here to treat the infection. The closed Walgreen's stood not far off the interstate in a strip shopping center. Leonard pocketed two brown bottles of the 750 mg capsules and then felt his way to the small storeroom in the back.

He'd thrown a brick through the glass front door from the parking lot. The cops would definitely come in that way. So he left through the metal back door, which opened onto a paved area where the store received deliveries. He closed the door carefully, took 15 steps, ducked between some hedges and was behind the U-Haul, parked across five spaces in a McDonald's parking lot. The truck nicely shielded the back door of the pharmacy from people inside.

He opened the truck's passenger door, climbed in and slid across the bench seat, opened the driver's door and stepped down to the ground. Inside, he bought a Big Mac combo – super sized – and swallowed one of the antibiotic pills with a mouthful of Diet Coke.

He'd eaten half his sandwich before the deputy cars streamed into the pharmacy parking lot. Fast food; slow cops. The night shift was usually staffed thinly, and some deputies didn't hurry because they didn't honestly want to face down an intruder inside a dark store.

Leonard wondered how long it would take Wake County deputies to agree with Noah Jakes' wife that the pediatrician was missing, not at a strip club or taking in a movie or away on vacation somewhere with a mistress.

Jakes had been almost exactly Leonard's age and looked superficially like the clean-shaven version of Leonard wearing the zero uniform. The doc's office was just down Rocky Falls Boulevard from the townhouses that had burned. Leonard staged the finale there just to be near Jakes, a complete zero who had humiliated Leonard over dinner months before by joking that no one made a decent living playing jazz.

Careful who you insult, Leonard thought, smiled and bit a fry in half.

Leonard had called Jakes at his office, pretending to be frantic. He said he'd stolen Jacob and brought him to the empty townhouse. Then he told Jakes a series of lies: He regretted kidnapping the child, who had Type I diabetes because his pancreas didn't produce insulin. Jacob was past due for an insulin injection and was acting very sick. He felt bad now for snatching Jacob. He cried and told Jakes he knew if he tried to get insulin, the police would find him and arrest him.

And Jakes, with that ego of his, had suggested coming to the townhouse to give the baby his shot. Then Jakes would take the child and see that he got back to Sarah. Leonard could leave. Jakes wouldn't look. He wouldn't call anyone. He'd just take care of the baby.

"Give me a few minutes," Jakes had said. "I don't keep any infant insulin here. I'll have to make a dilution. Don't hurt him. I'll be there soon."

And Leonard said, "Don't stall to call the cops. If you aren't here in exactly five minutes, he's dead."

Jakes had arrived seconds after the babysitter left. Leonard made him wait downstairs for a minute, yelling that he had to make a quick call. When TSB and her buddy answered, he gave them the address, then called the doc upstairs. Saying he was making a show of good faith, Leonard tossed the .380 down to the landing when he handed the zero the baby. The doc was messing with a syringe and two little bottles when the front door banged open.

Leonard stepped inside a closet where he had a hole cut through the wall into the next unit's stairwell. From the sidewalk outside, he heard the single shot.

Presto-change-o: And Justice For Me. Leonard had composed alternate endings in case something went wrong, but he'd seen on TV that it had played out ideally. Zeros were so predictable.

Leonard was a genius, so Leonard got to live.

Maybe they would yet figure it out. But when a community's string of crimes appeared to be solved; when there was a young, good-looking investigator to celebrate as a hero, no one asked too many questions. Besides, the simplest solution was usually the correct one. Usually.

Leonard wadded the rest of the terrible sandwich in its paper and left the tray sitting there on the table. He took the soda. A deputy was pushing into the restaurant now, and Leonard waved to get the guy's attention: "Hey, officer, I think there's some kind of burglar alarm going off over there at the drugstore."

"Uh, yeah," the young cop said, irritated. "Why do you think I'm here? Did you see anything?"

"No," Leonard said, acting chastened. "I was in the bathroom taking my antibiotic, and when I came back out here, that bell was ringing."

The cop pushed past Leonard and strode toward a woman sitting at a booth ignoring the bell.

Leonard took a pull of Diet Coke and ambled into the parking lot. He climbed behind the wheel of the rental truck and turned the key. He had to find a new place to live. He wasn't sure now that he was tired of the suburbs.

As the truck's wheels rolled, he hummed to himself.

He was getting a new idea for a jazz tune.

THE END

ABOUT THE AUTHOR

Bryan Gilmer has made his living as a writer for more than 15 years, working first as a night-shift crime reporter in Greenville, South Carolina, before moving on to Florida's largest newspaper, the St. Petersburg Times. Now he teaches newswriting at the University of North Carolina at Chapel Hill and writes for institutional and corporate clients in addition to his fiction. He lives with his wife, Kelly, and their son, Quinn, in Durham, North Carolina.

E-mail him at bryan@bryangilmer.com, or visit his website at BryanGilmer.com.

GEOGRAPHICAL NOTE

Though it bears some resemblance to the emerging suburbs north of Raleigh, North Carolina, Rocky Falls is a fictitious place, a composite of Southern suburbs around Raleigh-Durham, Atlanta and Tampa Bay. Really, it could be anywhere in the New South. Let's not build more.